A Mountain Man for the Sweet Bride

STAND-ALONE NOVEL

A Western Historical Romance Book

by

Nora J. Callaway

Copyright© 2022 by Nora J. Callaway

All Rights Reserved.

This book may not be reproduced or transmitted in any form without the written permission of the publisher.

In no way is it legal to reproduce, duplicate, or transmit any part of this document in either electronic means or in printed format. Recording of this publication is strictly prohibited and any storage of this document is not allowed unless with written permission from the publisher

Table of Contents

A Mountain Man for the Sweet Bride 1
   Table of Contents 3
   Letter from Nora J. Callaway 5
Prologue 6
Chapter One 12
Chapter Two 19
Chapter Three 25
Chapter Four 33
Chapter Five 41
Chapter Six 49
Chapter Seven 55
Chapter Eight 64
Chapter Nine 73
Chapter Ten 81
Chapter Eleven 88
Chapter Twelve 94
Chapter Thirteen 103
Chapter Fourteen 113
Chapter Fifteen 121
Chapter Sixteen 127
Chapter Seventeen 135
Chapter Eighteen 142
Chapter Nineteen 149
Chapter Twenty 158

Chapter Twenty-One..164
Chapter Twenty-Two...170
Chapter Twenty-Three 184
Chapter Twenty-Four 194
Chapter Twenty-Five..200
Chapter Twenty-Six..208
Chapter Twenty-Seven...214
Chapter Twenty-Eight..218
Chapter Twenty-Nine..226
Chapter Thirty..236
Chapter Thirty-One 245
Chapter Thirty-Two 252
Chapter Thirty-Three...258
Chapter Thirty-Four 265
Chapter Thirty-Five 274
Chapter Thirty-Five 283
Chapter Thirty-Six..297
Epilogue 314
   Also by Nora J. Callaway 335

Letter from Nora J. Callaway

"How vain it is to sit down to write when you have not stood up to live."
-Henry David Thoreau

I'm a lover of nature in the mornings and a writing soul at nights. My name is Nora J. Callaway and I come from Nevada, the beautiful Silver State.

I hold a BA in English Literature and an MA in Creative Writing. For years, I've wanted to get my stories out there, my own 'babies' as I like to call them, as inspired by my own experience leaving out West and my research of 19th-century American history.

All my life I have been breeding horses, cows and sheep and I've been tending to the land. It's time to tend now to my inner need to grow my stories, my heart-warming Western romance stories, and share them with the rest of you!

I'm here to learn and connect with others who enjoy a cup of black coffee, a humble sunset and a ride with a horse! Bless your hearts, as my nana used to say! Come on, hope in!

Until next time,
Nora J. Callaway

Prologue

Clinton, Missouri

July 20th, 1887

Louise lifted her skirts, the wind tickling her ankles as she walked home through the Missouri cornfields. The afternoon sun highlighted the lush green farmland and she looked over acres of field as far as the eye could see. She was grateful for how at home she felt in the gentle rolling hills.

She wasn't in a hurry to get back to the family farmhouse. She knew her adopted parents would be waiting for her with more chores than she could shake a stick at. She allowed her mind to drift back to the events from church that morning.

***

Her friend, Allie May, had been so excited to talk about the new *Clinton Gazette* that had just come out, with fresh requests for mail-order brides out west.

"Can't you just see us now?" Allie May asked. "Imagine us on a grand adventure out west with handsome cowboys ready to whisk us away…"

Allie May's fiery red curls swirled around her face as she danced around the inside of the small, single-room church. Louise's heart was just aching for a grand adventure, a fairytale romance, or anything like that to whisk her away from this lonely place.

"I wouldn't mind being whisked away by a cowboy," Louise admitted with a giggle. "But I couldn't go out west. It's too dangerous!"

"Well, I'm gonna give you this newspaper clipping anyway," said Allie Mae. "It's worth a thought."

***

As the warm breeze blew pale blonde hair over Louise's eyes, she wondered if Allie May was right. Was there a princely cowboy waiting out west to whisk her away?

Ever since she'd been dropped on Edward and Annie Canker's doorstep as a baby, her life had been filled with misery. Louise always had double her fair share of the chores and rarely received a kind word. She knew they resented having taken her in when they found her on their small porch.

At least she had Minnie the cat, her best friend and confidante. Walking in nature was one of her favorite past times and she was grateful for the opportunity to take in the fresh air and the small bit of freedom. She took her time as she ambled toward the Canker family farmhouse.

The plain house was covered in whitewashed planks. Every time Louise saw it, she remembered all the times she was forced to scrub or repaint it. What looked like a lovely home was a constant reminder that she was treated as more farmhand than daughter. She knew she wouldn't receive a warm welcome at home, but she had no idea what lay in store.

"Hello dear!" Maw said with an unusually gentle hug when Louise walked through the door. Louise knew right away something was off.

"Hello... Maw," Louie echoed back nervously.

Her adoptive mother, which was a strong word to use for the bitter woman who had raised her, had a short, stocky stature that made her appear deceivingly maternal. Louise knew she was never that happy in her tone and never that sweet unless it was set to impress somebody else.

Louise knew almost immediately who that somebody was. Mr. Johnson, the curmudgeonly old banker, sat across the narrow room. His portly frame wobbled as he walked, and his heavy breathing was proof of his struggle to get enough air into his ample frame. Paw poured him a fresh glass of brandy, his slight figure comical in contrast to the plump banker.

They were preparing to marry her off, she realized. She'd heard them whisper about it, but she didn't think it would happen so soon.

Old Mr. Johnson, at least thirty years her senior, was looking at her like a wild hog who had spotted a fawn in the woods. The only thing to do with a wild hog, she thought to herself, was to either stay clear of it or put it down. From the smiles on the faces of everyone in the room, Louise gathered that Mr. Johnson had not been invited to be put down. She knew the only one about to be slaughtered for the common good was her.

Louise felt panic start to build up in her chest as Ella, Maw and Paw's birth daughter, poked her head into the narrow sitting room. The walls of the cramped, windowless room seemed to close in on Louise as old boards creaked under Ella's feet.

Her presence was a reminder, as always, that Louise wasn't the favored daughter, and her heart sank at the contrast in how they were treated. She was the only one allowed to call Paw *Daddy,* and she did so whenever they were cruel to Louise.

"Hiya, Daddy!" she said with a kiss on Paw's cheek. The ample-waisted girl with flowing raven locks looked like a younger caricature of Maw with the ruby red lips of youth.

Ella smirked wickedly at Louise, clearly enjoying her "sister's" torture, and then left as quickly as she appeared.

Maw's hand on Louise's back, once friendly, became more forceful as she smiled tightly and pushed her to the center of the room.

"Come on now, dear!" she said. "Mr. Johnson's come a right long way from town to discuss your future."

Louise froze in fear, and she didn't think she could move. An awkward silence hung in the air until her adoptive father broke it with a forced laugh. Paw, as he preferred to be called, had a deeply gruff voice that always sounded funny coming out of such a skinny frame.

"Oh Louise, you don't need to be shy around Mr. Johnson. We know how deeply you admire him."

"Oh my, but how she does," Maw chimed in. Her voice was coated with a slick sweetness, but Louise knew it covered up a deep pit of misery.

"She's always saying how she looks up to you and how impressed she is with all you've done for the town by bringing in the bank."

Louise couldn't speak. All she could feel was fear and a fierce, white heat flowing throughout her body. Her eyes darted around the narrow room, looking for an escape. Then, the wild hog stepped up to have his say.

"Well now, Louise, I've gotten to see you grow from a young rosebud to a right lovely rose in full bloom, clearly ready to be plucked, and well, I'm here to pluck you before you wither. What do ya say?"

Heat flashed through her again, this time in Louise's face. It crept all the way down to her toes. Her breath sped up and the air around her suddenly felt thick. Before she knew it, she was gasping for air and running to her room, just to find somewhere to breathe.

She heard the portly hog gasp in offense while Maw and Paw tried to reassure him in desperate tones, but Louise's only thought was figuring out how to breathe again.

***

"What are they thinking, Minnie!" she exclaimed to her cat, once safely tucked inside her little room. The tears she'd been holding back fell freely as she collapsed to her bed.

"I can't marry that miserable old man! What do I do, God?" she pleaded desperately.

Her heart wrenched in two as she realized finally that she meant nothing to Maw and Paw. A lifetime of little parental love hit its breaking point and she wept like a small child who just realized they were an orphan.

When the tears finally stopped flowing, Louise grabbed her Bible to search out some comfort. As it opened, the newspaper clipping Allie May had given her fell onto her lap, still wet with her tears.

Was Allie May right? Should Louise tempt fate and travel out west as a mail-order bride? Would she even reach the Wild West with the desert wasteland in between?

Louise stared at the newspaper clipping. It read: *"Loving Christian wife wanted for rancher in Austin, Nevada."* The name at the bottom said *Jacob Montgomery*.

"Who are you, Jacob Montgomery?" she asked.

When she said his name, a sudden warmth rushed through her, and she imagined what her future might be. She envisioned a handsome man, tall and strong—someone with charm to spare and love to give. Could it be true?

"Well, Minnie," she said to her furry friend curled up in her lap. "Let's find out."

Louise picked up a pen and started scratching away. With every stroke, she felt Missouri drift away and the wide, blue skies of Nevada open before her.

Chapter One

Clinton, Missouri

September 30th, 1887

"Hush, Minnie!" Louise urged as she hurried around her little room, packing her bags. "If they hear us and wake up, we are done for!"

Louise looked down at the little tabby cat who continued to meow and rub up against her skirts, begging to be picked up.

"Sure, it's fine for *you* if we don't escape tonight," Louise continued. "But if they catch us tryin' to run away, I'm liable to catch a beating."

Louise sighed and reached down to lift the persistent kitty. Her gentle purring and soft, tickly fur were a welcome comfort.

Louise walked over to her tiny window, eager for a breath of cool air. Her escape was coming along as planned, but she was nervous thinking about what the night might hold. The gentle breeze soothed her and reminded her of her favorite verse in Psalms, chapter forty-six: *"Be still and know that I am God."*

Louise repeated the verse out loud as she took a long, deep breath in, and then slowly let it out again.

"I know You have a plan, Lord," she prayed. "Please help me to trust You and not fear."

Putting off her marriage to the wild hog of a banker, or as he preferred to be called, *Mr. Johnson,* had been no easy task. She'd managed to convince him that waiting a month to marry would allow her time to prepare her heart for the ceremony of it all. He'd conceded but reminded her daily that come October, he would have himself a bride.

Only the thought of Jacob's letters filled her with hope. With each passing day, she became more certain that her prince was waiting on the other side of the Wild West. When she first replied to his ad for a mail-order bride, she didn't yet know what to expect or say, so she was simply honest. Her first letter had read:

Dear Jacob,

I'm writing you regarding the ad you placed for a wife. While there were plenty of ads to choose from, I was taken by your request for a loving wife. It struck me that you were hoping to find love and not just someone to raise children.

More importantly, I was encouraged by your search for a Christian woman, because that's what I am. It matters deeply to me that whoever I wed must be someone who knows the love of God, for I'm fully convinced that's necessary for him to love me.

For the sake of full transparency, I am additionally in need of a plan soon, lest I be married off to an old man very much against my will. If all this seems like something you'd be interested in, I would very much like to hear from you.

Sincerely,

Louise Parker

It had felt like an age waiting to hear back from Jacob. She'd checked the mail every day, eager to find any letters before Maw set eyes on them, as she would've had questions. Each day, when a letter didn't arrive, Louise wondered if it was perhaps Maw taking and destroying them instead.

***

It was a full month later when, to her shock, she received his reply at last. She was even more surprised that she was able to get to the letter before Maw saw it, and she took that as a sign that perhaps it was meant to be.

Dear Louise,

I must confess I am a bit taken aback by your honesty. I find it refreshing and full of the warmth that having a wife would bring, for indeed I do hope to find love with my wife.

I'm glad to hear you are a Christian, as I am, too, and I can think of no better way to raise children but in the love and fear of the Lord.

I feel the need to confess to you that placing the ad was not my idea, but rather, the advice of a trusted friend. In truth, I was wary of placing the ad, but when I received your letter, I knew I had done the right thing.

As to the matter of the unwanted older gentleman, please take this letter as a means of betrothal on my part, if proof is needed, that you are already promised to another. I have enclosed twenty dollars for anything you might need on your journey, and I invite you to come at your earliest convenience.

Yours Truly,

Jacob Montgomery

Louise held the letter to her heart and took another deep breath. Her prince did exist! Not only was he a Godly man looking for a true love match, but he knew how to smoothly use words with the simple stroke of a pen.

Just a few days after his first letter, another letter arrived—this letter more unexpected than the first.

Dearest Louise,

It has been nearly three weeks since I sent my first letter. I am not sure if the absence of your reply is due to your previously pending nuptials or simply the fault of the pony express. There is a third option of course—that perhaps I was too forward in my previous letter and scared you away.

If that is the case, please accept my sincere apologies for being an uncouth mountain man. I know that love takes time, and I want to assure you that getting on a train to come to Nevada will not indebt you to me, nor any man.

Should you arrive and no longer desire to marry me, I promise to give you a safe home while you find another husband or a suitable position in town. But I must admit, I look forward to courting you. I look forward to earning the right to take vows with you. I look forward to calling you mine, but the choice is yours.

Yours Truly,

Jacob Montgomery

While she was flattered that Jacob had penned a second letter, it was his gentleness and humility that touched her the most. She wrote back to him as fast as her excited fingers could move.

Dear Jacob,

What is there to say except that the slowness of the mail must have been a blessing from above because it allowed me to receive your second letter just days after your first. While your first letter assured me of your passion and purpose, your second letter assured me of your character.

I plan to leave on a west-bound train next Thursday, on the first of October. My train is due to arrive in two days' time from then, on Saturday the third. Look for me at the train station in a yellow dress. I'll be holding a blue carpet bag and the hopes of a future bride.

Truly,

Louise Parker

***

The old grandfather clock in the sitting room struck midnight, and Louise snapped back to her senses.

"It's time to go, Minnie," she whispered. "It's now or never."

She tucked her precious friend into the top of her carpet bag. She laughed softly when Minnie poked her head up and snuck a paw out through the opening.

"You're as stubbornly determined as I am, aren't you? That's okay because we're gonna need some determination where we're going. I've probably lost my mind bringing a cat with me, but you're my only true friend. Come on, Minnie. It's time to head west."

***

With courage she didn't know she possessed, Louise walked five miles to the train station in the dark of night. The streets felt ominously quiet, with everyone in town home in bed. It frightened her, but not near as much as marrying Mr. Johnson did.

She used all the money Jacob had sent her to secure her ticket and tried her best to keep her ornery cat quiet while they waited to board. It wasn't until she stepped onto the train that she stopped a moment to doubt her decision. She turned to look back at Clinton, Missouri, and the only life she had ever known.

Have I been too hard on Maw and Paw?

Louise thought back on her childhood and doubted herself for a moment. Didn't she always have shelter from the summer heat and the winter storms?

"No!" she choked out loud. No storm was harder to weather than the verbal beatings she received from Maw, and the painful reminders every day that she wasn't wanted.

She remembered being a young girl and crawling into Maw's lap for a cuddle. "Get down, you filthy little thing! You're so pale that every grain of dirt shows on that grubby little face. Ugh! Go take a bath in the river and take our clothes to wash as well! If you're gonna need another bath, you might as well be useful."

Paw was no better, constantly commenting on the extra mouth he didn't ask to feed, and always reminding her to be grateful for the measly portions she got. Louise wondered often why they even bothered to take her in as a baby on their doorstep if they were just going to spend the next eighteen years hating her. She knew the answer, of course, though it was painful to admit. The Cankers cared about nothing but raising their standing in the eyes of their pious town. After they'd taken her in, everyone wanted to do business with the sainted couple.

The most painful part of it all was watching how much they adored Ella, their birth daughter. It was obvious that Ella cherished her parents and the attention that was lavished upon her, too.

For every time Louise was rejected, Ella was embraced. For every time Louise was insulted, Ella was praised. While Louise knew it wasn't Ella's fault her parents treated them differently, Ella seemed to bask in it and constantly reminded her she was just the doorstep baby.

"Enough is enough, Minnie!"

Louise let out a deep sigh, built up by years of holding in her pain. She gave her furry friend a pat on the head and tucked her back into her carpet bag.

"So long, Missouri. We've been miserable together long enough."

With one last look over the cornfields that she'd called home for so long, Louise whipped around and marched up the train steps. Something better was waiting for her in Nevada, and she wasn't going to keep him waiting a moment longer.

Chapter Two

Austin, Nevada

October 2nd, 1887

Jacob Montgomery laid sunflowers on his father's grave and set a hand on his gravestone. Sunflowers had been his mother's favorite flower. Although Jacob had never met her, as she died in childbirth, his father had made sure they were always growing near the house as a tribute to his late wife. When Jacob brought fresh sunflowers each week, he felt like he honored both of his parents and kept their tradition alive.

"I really wish you were gonna be here tomorrow, Pop," Jacob said. "How am I supposed to woo a woman I've never met?"

Jacob sighed and breathed in the fresh mountain air. The mountain top views filled his heart with wonder. He always felt closer to God in the mountains. As he admired the handiwork of the Lord, he was humbled by the beauty and grace of God.

He could see everything from his hilltop. As he looked over Austin, he could even see the small town's train station. It would arrive tomorrow with his blushing bride aboard.

Jacob wondered what he'd say to someone he'd never met. He'd never been a man of many words, his talks with his father and the Lord on the mountain notwithstanding. He'd put more words into his two letters to Louise than he had said to any other person in the last year.

He had been touched by the honesty and sincerity of her letters. She was so forthcoming, and it made him feel like he could be as well. Even then, however, it took him nearly a week to pen the first letter. The only other person he'd spoken to recently was his ranch hand and beloved friend, George.

While Jacob knew little of love or fancy words, he knew how to provide, and provide he would. He had carved a new pair of rocking chairs that sat by the fireplace. He mused that he and Louise might sit there quietly together on cool winter evenings.

Jacob knew it was just about time to meet up with George. He took one more breath of unsullied mountain air and started the trek down the hill.

***

When Jacob strolled up to the large log cabin, his friend was already there. George was a bit shorter than Jacob and about ten years older. His hands were rough, and his pockets were empty, but he always had a gentle smile and a kind word. After Jacob's father passed away, George was one of the few people he really trusted.

"Well, howdy neighbor," George called. "Ready to head out to the cattle?"

"I need you to go without me today," Jacob said shortly as he kept walking toward the house.

"What's the matter, Jacob?"

"Mind your business," Jacob said with a grunt. "I just got some work to do."

Not easily dissuaded, George followed his friend up the steps to the grand cabin. They stopped for a moment on the porch.

"If you're coming in, at least take off your boots," Jacob said as his tall Stetson hat barely made it under the doorframe.

When the two friends walked inside, they beheld a mess in the large, single room cabin. Wooden furniture appeared strewn about the room, along with a handsaw, sliced up logs, and sawdust on the floor. The scent of pine permeated the air.

"It's a good thing I talked you into placing an ad for a wife," George said with a chuckle. "This place is gonna need a woman's touch, I reckon."

"She'll be here tomorrow, George," Jacob conceded with a sigh, "and nothin's ready."

Jacob motioned to the right of the door at the pair of new rocking chairs he'd made just that morning. His eyes drifted past the chairs to the far side of the room. There sat the four-post bed that'd been there longer than Jacob had been alive. Next to the bed lay a pile of sawdust and a misshapen baby cradle.

"Well," said George as he turned about the room, "I know you aimed to fix the place up for Miss Parker when she came, but I had no idea you were making a baby cradle."

"I'm sure having kids is a long way off but... I just want everything to be ready for her... in case it all works out. I've made almost every piece of furniture in this house, George, but I can't for the life of me figure out how to get that cradle right."

Jacob was used to being in control of his surroundings but preparing for Miss Parker's arrival made him feel unsteady. He was convinced if he accounted for everything, it would go smoothly, so he was going to get that cradle right if it was the last thing he did.

George breathed a deep, knowing sigh and put his hand on his friend's shoulder.

"I can show you how to straighten out that curve on the cradle. Nothin' that can't be fixed, friend."

While George worked on the cradle, Jacob used the horsehair broom he'd made as a boy to sweep the sawdust out of the house.

A few months ago, I wouldn't be having to sweep up this sawdust, Jacob thought. *Jessie was always better at cleaning up.*

As he swept up the mess, he remembered Jessie's full figure rustling about as she cleaned up his house.

She had lived on the farm since they were both children. Her parents worked on the ranch, and when they passed away, she'd stayed on as a maid.

It was always quietly assumed that Jacob would marry Jessie one day. He'd fallen in love with the raven-haired beauty when he was still a young man but never found the words to tell her just what she meant to him. Jacob hadn't done anything to pursue Jessie and took for granted that everything was settled. They were never officially betrothed, and he regretted deeply that he hadn't courted her properly.

She took off a few weeks after Pop passed. When Jacob asked why, she'd said she was bored. Bored of living with the quiet mountain man.

Jacob had been crushed, though he never admitted it. Her abandonment deepened the wound left by his father's death and served to solidify in Jacob that he was meant to be a recluse. That's how he remained until George convinced him to place an ad for a wife.

As he sat there, holding the broom and thinking of the girl who'd left, he couldn't help but wonder. *If I couldn't keep a girl I knew my whole life, how can I keep girl who hasn't known me a day?*

Suddenly, the thought struck him like a bolt of lightning. If he wanted Miss Parker to feel at home, he'd need to make it a home fit for a woman... fit for a *wife!* Jacob ran inside and grabbed his hat.

"George, if I take the carriage into town, can you finish up here?"

"Why, Jacob Montgomery," a surprised George said. "Did you just say you're going into *town?* I haven't seen you go to town since... well, I don't rightly know when!"

"Never mind that," Jacob said in a rush. "The sun's sittin' high in the sky, and I'll be home by supper."

***

When Jacob strolled into town, the townsfolk stared at the mythical mountain man. The shop owners were thrilled, if not a little taken aback, as the wealthy rancher strutted through the square, read to buy anything. For the first time in his life, Jacob had a real reason to go to town. It was nearly time to fetch himself a wife.

First, he bought a hand-knitted blanket for the bed with a little bit of lace around the edges. He bought two fine baskets for fresh fruit, some yarn and needles. He even bought a right fancy parasol for Miss Parker to use outside so that she wouldn't be consumed by the hot Nevada sun. He packed everything into the wagon, grateful that the ranch afforded him the ability to prepare for what was needed.

Finally, Jacob bought a simple, delicate, and lovely looking wedding ring. The gold band gleamed in the sun and forced hope into Jacob's heart. Maybe if he played his cards right, just maybe, he'd be able to offer this ring to *Louise* one day soon. And then, she would be Mrs. Montgomery. This time, he would do things right!

He loaded up the wagon with gifts for his betrothed and then hopped into the wagon with a fresh kick of confidence. But as he drove the wagon uphill toward the ranch, he couldn't help but notice dark clouds roll in over the horizon.

"I hope those clouds don't stay here too long," Jacob thought aloud. "Her first impression of Nevada better not be the one day it gets wet."

Chapter Three

Austin Nevada

October 3rd, 1887

Louise stepped off the train straight into a muddy puddle.

"Oh! Just what we needed. Rain!" exclaimed Louise. "Minnie, what have we gotten ourselves into?"

She looked around in disbelief at the muddy land before her and the rain that pattered the ground.

Minnie's curious head poked up from inside the bag and an icy raindrop fell on her nose, causing her to let out a cry. Louise lifted her friend out of the carpet bag and cuddled her close, wiping off the raindrops with her shawl.

She looked around, wondering where Jacob was. Her heart danced in anticipation. Somewhere there should be her prince—the romantic gentleman from the letters—her soon-to-be husband. With a determined breath, Louise lifted her skirts and stepped out of the puddle into her new life.

Louise found a patch of roof covering the outside of the train station where she and Minnie could stay dry while she scanned the area for Jacob.

"He must be around here somewhere, Minnie. He's just *got* to be!"

***

Long after the last traveler left the train station, Jacob was still nowhere to be seen. She looked at the large grandfather clock standing at the front of the small wooden building.

"It's been two hours! Where on earth could he be, Minnie?" Louise was becoming more and more anxious when the thought hit her that perhaps he wasn't coming.

Louise spent the last of the money on her train ticket. The only food they had was what Louise had packed, and they'd run out of that the night before. Louise picked up the cat who mewed hungrily, pacing back-and-forth.

"Please God," Louise said quietly, "show me what to do."

"Be still and know that I am God. I will be exalted among the nations! I will be exalted in the earth."

Her favorite verse filled her heart. The rain had softened to a sprinkle, and she could see in the distance where the clouds ended, and blue sky began.

Surely, You can take care of me, Lord, if You created all of this.

She allowed herself to look off at the sky and take deep breaths, as she wondered what on earth they were going to do.

***

"Hello, dear," a warm voice called out behind her. Louise turned to see a kind face, fit with the deep smile lines of a life well lived. The warmth in the woman's eyes assured Louise that she could be trusted. The kind woman introduced herself as Alice.

"My husband Jethro and I were just headed out of town when we saw you looking wetter than the rain itself with that there cat on your shoulder. Whatcha' doin' all by your lonesome, anyhow?"

"I'm here to meet my husband," Louise said. "Well, *future* husband. He was supposed to meet me here at one-thirty when the train arrived."

"To be fair, we had a storm all night so it's possible he got stuck on account of the rain. Who might your betrothed be?"

"Jacob Montgomery," Louise said with a smile wider than the Nevada sky. She was relieved to know he might have a good reason for having not shown up after all.

"You're marrying the mountain man?" the woman asked in a high-pitched voice that nearly made Louise jump.

At first, Louise thought she was making fun, but she could see in the woman's kind but serious face that it was not a joke.

"That man has lived alone for a very long time. We don't see neither hide nor hair of him in town. But he did make an odd appearance yesterday. You must be the reason he was buying out all the baskets in town!"

Louise's heart warmed, and she felt bad for having been angry with him. Perhaps he had a good reason after all.

"Your future husband lives up in them there hills. Jethro and I live on the other side of the mountain. We can take you up there in our wagon if you like."

"Thank you ever so much," Louise said as she stood up and fell into Alice's welcoming arms.

Louise felt grateful to have found a kind soul in an unknown land. She took it as a reminder that the Lord would provide for her, just as He always had. As Louise lifted Minnie into Alice's wagon, she was filled with hope that everything might turn out okay—

as long as Jacob had a good excuse, that is.

***

As the little wagon headed toward the edge of town, it trudged and sloshed its way through the mud. Minnie meowed discontentedly with every bump, and Louise held the cat close to her chest.

Louise was relieved it had finally stopped raining, and she turned her attention to the little town. She looked at all the shops spread across the street. The muddied streets were lined with narrow beige buildings. While run down and a bit drab, it still brought the hope of civilization.

Could be worse, she thought. It was nothing fancy, but she was glad to see a general store, a blacksmith, and a saloon that doubled as an inn. She was encouraged when she saw a little church at the end of the soggy road.

Most of the people had cleared out because of the rain, but she was glad to see people start to poke their heads out of doorways as the sun came out again. Things were starting to look up.

The hills rolled gently in the background. As they started up the hill, Louise looked behind her, eager for her first big view. The further they climbed up the hill and away from the drab and dirty town, the more glorious and colorful her view became.

"Oh my, but it's lovely," she said quietly into the wind.

Excitement surged through her as she felt the cool breeze blow through her hair, and she felt suddenly eager for the journey forward. Perhaps she was made for the Wild West after all!

She soaked up her surroundings as they traveled higher into the mountains. There was more sand and rock than anything green, but small patches of sagebrush and cacti fought courageously to survive and push a pop of green into the hills. Most lovely of all were the wildflowers. She was fascinated with the bright patches of yellow, blue, and orange.

While Jethro drove the wagon, Alice asked Louise what had brought her to this place and what made her want to be a mail-order bride. Louise was surprised by how easy it was to talk to Alice. Perhaps it was the warmth in her face or the simple fact that she'd rescued her, but she felt safe with the sweet woman. She opened up about her childhood with the Cankers, the forced nuptials from which she'd escaped, and the kind words in Jacob's letters that had given her hope.

"It's hard to explain," Louise said, "but I think he may be what I've been looking for all along. It sounds silly, but I get the feeling everything will be okay now."

"I don't think it's silly at all," Alice said gently. "Every girl wants to find her prince, but I would be remiss if I didn't tell you what I have learned from years of experience. No man can fill the hole you've got in that there heart. Only the Lord can do that."

Louise smiled and then looked away. She knew that Alice meant well and was just trying to help, but she didn't know Jacob the way that Louise did. She was sure Jacob wasn't like Jethro. His letters promised something different.

Jethro was short and stocky with a hole in his hat, and he smelled of the land that he worked on. Louise could tell that he was kind, but a handsome man he was not. Perhaps if he was as handsome and romantic as she was sure Jacob would be, Alice would've been happier with him.

Louise turned her attention back to the beautiful land around her and the hungry cat in her lap. She petted her friend and felt hopeful as they traveled further up the mountain.

They traveled for what felt like days until Jethro announced they were pulling up to the Montgomery Ranch. Louise sat up a little taller to see her new home. Minnie perked up as well and meowed in hungry frustration.

"Don't worry, Minnie! We're almost there now."

She was amazed to see green grass filling parts of the wide valley. She saw a creek off in the distance that fed water to the ranch, allowing for this small oasis in such a dry place.

At the far end of the valley was a hill rolling up gently toward some pine trees. At the top of the pass sat a large log cabin. It was grander than she'd imagined, though she could tell it was old and weathered from a generation of ranchers coming and going. Still, it was lovely.

Suddenly, two men came barreling out of the house with one of them hollering rudely. She could not tell what they were clamoring about, but something was amiss. As the wagon pulled up, the men were startled and whirled around to face them.

The man who had been yelling was short and looked well over forty. Certainly, this wasn't the writer of her letters. He'd hollered something about not being stuck at home with a baby. The second man was large and hairy. With dark, wavy hair touching his shoulders and a scraggly beard around his face, he looked more like a common ranch hand than a head rancher.

He looked wild and unkempt and reminded her of what she always thought John the Baptist might've looked like. He appeared as if he'd been living in nature without a bed to sleep on. Louise chuckled at the thought of him living off locusts and honey, just like the old saint.

He was holding a baby, so she knew he could not be Jacob. She thought he must be in trouble for bringing his baby to the ranch.

"Shouldn't that baby be with its mother?" asked a confused Louise. "Where is that man's wife?"

Jethro gasped and Alice laid a gentle hand on her shoulder.

"Well, dear, that would be you."

Louise's heart sank in disbelief. An unwelcomed heat filled her body as she realized that this terrifying, dirty mountain man was Jacob. He looked more like a beast than the gentle poet she'd envisioned. Certainly, he wasn't the man who'd written to her. While his letters were full of warmth, hope, and promise, the man before her was full of dirt, grime, and silence.

Jacob looked flustered, if not a bit in shock, and stood there with a serious look on his face.

"Hello. You must be Miss Louise Parker," he stammered. "I can explain."

Louise was speechless. Minnie meowed angrily for them both, demanding to be fed. Louise's hands clenched into fists. Her head started to spin. What was she going to do? Fresh fear rushed through her and turned to anger as she wondered if she had been duped by this man.

Not only had he not bothered to pick her up at the train station, but he'd lured her here under the pretense of a love match. In reality, he had a baby and was looking for a mother for the young thing. Then, she noticed the baby's head drooping off the side of his arm.

Why, he doesn't even know how to hold his own baby!

Louise was in a state of shock and reached for something that made sense. Identifying with the tiny creature, her urge to rescue it took over. She hopped out of the wagon and walked over to the man.

"Why are you holding the child like that? Hand him over right now! Come on, give him to me before the poor thing's head falls off."

With a look of downright confusion, Jacob handed the baby over to Louise. She felt bad for being uncouth, but she feared the babe would catch his death of cold.

She felt the baby shiver and knew she needed to get it inside and out of the cold, damp weather. She pulled the baby quickly to her chest and covered it with her shawl as she hurried toward the house.

"Perhaps we could talk privately?" she said with all the courage she could muster up inside of her. Mountain Man or not, she needed an explanation, and she and Minnie needed something to eat.

Chapter Four

Jacob stood in shock at the little lady standing before him. While her stature was short and she looked frail, she was all guts when she stormed into the house. He couldn't believe what he'd seen. What kind of woman was this?

He took a moment to compose himself before going in. He'd already had the hardest day of his life, and he needed to take a moment to think upon it before he went in to properly meet this wild desert rose.

***

He'd taken his coffee out to the porch that morning but found a surprise on his doorstep.

There was a baby wrapped in a blanket, laying in a picnic basket.

"Hello?" Jacob had called out. "Is anyone there?!"

He'd finally picked up the basket and set it in the rocking chair next to him. He noticed a small handwritten note tucked into the side of the blanket, and he picked it up to read it. *"Please take care of my sweet boy, as I truly cannot,"* was all it said.

Questions filled his mind like rainwater overflowing a lake and it made him feel dizzy under the weight of it. He couldn't leave this baby there by itself, and the nearest neighbor was too far away to fetch.

He knew that George would swing by around noon, as always. As soon as he arrived, he would hand the baby off to George, and be off to fetch his bride.

***

He explained the situation to George when he arrived, but to his disappointment, George was not willing to take the baby off his hands.

"What are you doing with a baby anyhow?" George had asked. "You have no idea what to do with that thing!"

"You're probably right," Jacob said gruffly. "But right now, I just need to figure out how to get Miss Parker from the station. She's been waiting for hours, George! I gotta pick her up!"

"Well," George replied, "I'll go to town to fetch her for you, but I'm not taking that there baby!"

As the two barreled outside to hitch up the wagon, they continued to argue over who would stay at the cabin with the babe. The pair turned with a jump as the wagon approached, eyes wider than a deer stumbling upon a hunter.

**

As Jacob stood in front of the log cabin with its thick pine logs, he was taken aback by all that had transpired.

He looked at his ranch house and knew Louise was inside, waiting for him. George put a hand on his shoulder.

"You better get in there. The stew you made can't be quite that bad," he said with a chuckle. "I'll do you a favor and stay for dinner, but why don't you go in and talk to the girl by yourself first?"

Jacob groaned. *Oh no! The stew! It must all be mush by now.*

He had set some fresh venison and vegetables to boil earlier that day, but he'd forgotten all about it amid the day's events. He knew that the stew was likely ruined, but there was nothing to be done about it now.

Jacob let out a deep sigh as he walked up the front steps. The logs creaked under his heavy feet, as if the house also dreaded what was to come.

When he entered the house, he saw Louise sitting in the rocking chair he'd made as she talked to the baby. The huge chair engulfed her slight frame. How would this fragile creature survive out here, much less be any help on the ranch?

"My, what pretty blue eyes you have, little one," she said. "I'm sorry your daddy doesn't know how to hold you quite right."

"I'm not his daddy," Jacob said. Louise nearly jumped out of the chair when she heard him behind her. She whirled around, appearing surprised.

"How dare you, Jacob Montgomery?" she demanded with a crack in her voice. Her heart-shaped face came to a point at her dainty chin, which began to quiver, and Jacob was taken aback by her beauty.

"Why would you lure me out here under the pretense of a love match, when you know full well that you're just looking for a mama for this here baby?"

The hair raised on the back of Jacob's neck as he realized what she was implying. He may not be a man of many words, but he was certainly a man of honor. His pride was pricked, and his chest swelled in frustration.

"It's not my baby," he insisted urgently, in a hushed tone. "He was on the doorstep this mornin'. Honest!"

"Do you really expect me to believe that a baby was dropped on your doorstep the very morning I was coming to town to be your bride? That's the craziest, most hair-brain story I've ever heard."

Jacob couldn't believe she thought he was lying. Sure, this was a hard reality to swallow, but had his letters meant nothing to her? He wanted to say that, but just couldn't bring himself to speak the words. Instead, he stormed back out of the house and slammed the door behind him.

Outside, Jethro and Alice were holding an orange cat and a carpet bag as they stood next to their wagon.

"I believe these things now belong to you," Jethro said with a half-cocked smile.

"You must be wanting to get back," Jacob said as he took the bags and watched the small orange cat rub up against his leg. "Thanks for everything."

Jacob turned to go back inside, hoping the cat would wander away along with the unwanted guests. He was almost halfway back to the porch when George spoke up.

"Y'all should stay for supper," George said as he slapped his friend on the back. "Come on in and sit a spell before you travel back."

"Well, I suppose we could, if you insist." Jethro said.

Jacob cringed at the thought of guests staying for supper. His whole life had been turned upside down in the span of a few hours, and the last thing he wanted was more company.

***

Jacob brought his bland disaster of a stew to the table. The group talked happily, undeterred. Jacob sat reservedly at the head of the table while the townsfolk chattered around him. Although he wasn't eager to have guests, he felt relieved that their conversation kept them all busy and allowed him the chance to sit quietly and think for a moment.

He couldn't help but watch Louise as she talked to Alice and held the baby close.

For someone so upset at finding a baby here, she sure hasn't put the thing down.

He couldn't believe the situation he found himself in, or the frail, pretty girl sitting opposite him on the other side of the long wooden table. Her tiny frame stood in contrast to her brave and outspoken disposition.

How would she be any help on the ranch at all? he wondered. She was more liable to be broken by a horse than she was to do the breaking.

As he gazed at her face, he caught his breath. Her blonde locks fell softly around her face like an ornate frame showcasing a painting. She was a pale creature with soft freckles speckled across her nose, and her cheeks had a soft rose-like blush. Blonde eyebrows and eyelashes set atop light blue eyes the color of the sky. She had a gentle, heart-shaped face, and he admitted to himself that she looked like an angel. Wondering if he looked as embarrassed as he felt, he looked away.

Suddenly, there was a tickle on his ankle, and he looked down to see the bright orange cat rubbing against his leg. He stood up, surprised.

"How did this varmint get in the house?" he exclaimed.

"That's not a varmint! That's my precious Minnie!"

"But… why is she in the house?" Jacob asked, confused.

"I'd never make a family friend sleep outside," Louise said, looking embarrassed at Jacob.

Jacob wondered in awe at Louise's strange fondness for the animal. It certainly wasn't a practical companion. What was so special about it?

He wondered how his whole life could be turned upside down so quickly. Just that morning he had been the undisputed king of his domain. Now, he sat around a table with unwanted guests, a mystery babe he didn't ask for, a woman who kept disagreeing with him, and a cat that wouldn't leave him alone.

He stood up, frustrated, and went to fetch some milk for the babe. If it was going to be here, it would have to be fed. He grabbed a jug of milk out of the ice box and a metal spoon from the countertop before returning to the long farm-style table.

He set down the milk and the metal spoon with a thud and reached over the table to take the baby. Louise almost jumped out of her seat.

"You can't feed the baby like that!" she said in obvious shock. "He's got to have warm milk."

"This milk is fine," Jacob said gruffly. "If I can drink it, why can't he?"

The two stared at each other awkwardly across the table, tension hanging in the air.

Jacob despised how unnerved he felt. He wasn't used to being so easily affected by other people and much preferred his time on the ranch to his interactions with the townsfolk.

What he detested most of all was that people rarely said what they meant. Animals weren't like that. When they were hungry, they told you. When there was danger, they let you know that, too.

He had thought, based on how forthcoming and honest Louise had been in her letters, that she would be an easy person to talk to. The sincerity and warmth in which she spoke had been refreshing and had made him feel hopeful.

Horses and cows were easy to figure out, but this woman sitting across the table was a complete mystery.

Tension hung in the air over how to feed the baby and the two continued to glare at each other until Alice spoke up.

"Why don't you let *me* help with the baby?" she asked with a gentle laugh. "I've raised enough of my own, after all."

Jacob was relieved that Alice was there to help. She clearly knew what she was doing as she warmed the milk and fed him in the rocking chair with Louise sitting beside her. Inside, the men talked at the table.

***

"Well, we best be headin' out," Jethro said a few minutes later.

Jacob looked around nervously as he realized he was going to be left alone with this new woman. That is, if she was going to stay.

When the slew of guests finally left, Jacob sat at the table a moment longer and watched Louise rock the baby to sleep. Why was she so attached to the babe when she'd been so upset about finding it there?

"How do you know so much about babies?" he asked at last.

"I was a governess for a while," Louise said. "I wasn't expecting a baby, but I know how to care for one." She raised her dainty chin high in the air as if daring him to disagree.

My, but she's a spitfire. She might be tiny, but she certainly had the spine and bravery to make it out west. She infuriated him, but he was also curiously drawn to her.

"You must be wantin' to get some sleep. You can have the bed. There's a cradle for the babe… not that I knew it would be here." Jacob paused, aware of how crazy that sounded. "I'm not a liar, Louise—I mean—Miss Parker. I'm a man of my word. You'll be safe here." He sighed before conceding, "…and that goes for the cat, too."

Louise didn't say anything, but Jacob noticed her frown softened into a slight smile.

"Thank you," she said slowly. "I think I'd rather sleep in the rocking chair tonight, though. The baby is asleep, and I don't wanna wake him."

"Well, at least take this," Jacob said as he lay the pretty, store-bought blanket across her lap.

He said good night and went to sleep on the pallet he had made, just in case Louise decided to move to the bed later. As he lay there with his eyes closed, he heard Louise singing softly and sweetly to the baby. He couldn't help but notice once more that, for someone so mad to have found a baby, she sure hadn't stopped holding him since.

Jacob was surprised to hear her voice singing and speaking so gently. Why was she so disrespectful to *him?* Maybe it was his fault or maybe this desert rose didn't want to be in the desert at all.

Chapter Five

Louise put on the white cotton dress, alone in the log cabin at last. Today was the day she'd be wed. She admired the lace Alice had sewn into the hem for her. She used a hair pin with pearls across the top to pull back the sides of her long blonde hair. It might not be fancy, but she looked ready to get married.

George had taken the baby to his wife just for the day, as it might have looked a bit strange for a bride to walk up to the altar with a baby. This was her first time alone in the big ranch-style log cabin, and her first time to properly think uninterrupted.

"What am I doing, Minnie?" she asked her furry friend. Minnie danced around the log cabin and pawed at the edges of Louise's dress. Louise picked her up for a cuddle and giggled as her cat licked her cheek.

The two friends stepped out onto the porch for a breath of fresh air. Louise settled in the rocking chair and picked up her pen, opened her journal, and thought back on the last few days.

***

Aside from their first meeting, which had been a catastrophe by any standard, her interactions with Jacob had been mild, if not perhaps a bit dull. She was a bit ashamed of her behavior her first day there. She had been so taken aback upon finding a baby, and had been so certain she was lied to, she cringed to think of how spitefully she'd behaved.

Despite all that, Jacob had been kind and respectful, if not altogether quiet. He rarely spoke and kept to himself most of the time. Whenever she attempted to engage him in conversation about their relationship and upcoming marriage, he gave short, one-word answers, barely looking at her.

He'd spent most of the last few days working on the ranch, and she'd spent that time caring for the young baby.

Taking care of the babe was one of the relatively easy parts of her day, as she was used to being a governess and a nursemaid back in Missouri. Caring for children was one of the few things she truly enjoyed, so of course the Cankers had taken that away from her as well. Perhaps she'd been too cocky when she came home from work each day, or maybe they were just irritated they didn't have a whipping girl while she was gone.

At any rate, they made her quit the job after she'd been there just a couple of months. They might've taken away something she enjoyed, but they weren't able to take away the valuable skills she learned about taking care of children.

She'd come to believe Jacob's story about the baby being left on the doorstep, after George confirmed the tale.

Truth be told, this endeared the baby to her far more than she cared to admit. She saw herself in him. Whenever she looked into the blue eyes of the tiny babe, she saw herself abandoned as a baby. She was overwhelmed with feelings of love and devotion. She had no idea she could become attached to a child that wasn't hers in such a short period of time, but she felt as if she were already this baby's mother.

She thought of how different her own life might've been if she'd had warm and loving parents who had wanted her—instead of the resentful and punishing Cankers. If she could do anything to protect that baby and give him a better life, she would.

She'd also spent time reading through the book of Esther, as it inspired her. Esther hadn't chosen her marriage to the king, and yet, the Lord had brought her there, "for such a time as this." While Louise did not hold any far-fetched delusions of grandeur, she wondered if God had brought her here specifically to care for this baby. Perhaps she could give it the loving home she'd never had. Marrying Jacob Montgomery would be a small price to pay if that was the case.

She could see why he was known in the town as the mountain man, from his rough, rugged appearance and reserved disposition. However, there was also a warmth in his eyes that she had noticed when he sat by the fire. While his outward appearance was hard and off-putting, his eyes told a different story. While he said "yes" or "no," or sometimes even answered with just a grunt, his eyes were wistful and begged to say what his words could not.

She was surprised to find that she felt safe with him. She felt respected even—

which was something she had certainly never felt in her family growing up.

It may not be a love match, she wrote in her journal, *but at least he's a decent man.*

"I know You have brought me here, Lord," she prayed in the rocking chair on the wide wooden porch. "You rescued me out of deep and troubled waters and set me firmly on this mountain. It's not what I thought it would be, but I know you brought me here. Please give me strength, Lord. I'm gonna need it."

With a fresh determination that this was the right path forward, Louise closed her little journal, and went inside to finish getting ready for her wedding.

***

A few minutes later, she heard horse hooves trotting across the rocky terrain.

"Wish me luck, Minnie," she said as she picked up her furry friend and hugged her close. Minnie mewed and tickled Louise's nose with her whiskers.

"I wish you could come with me, girl, but I don't think you would like a trip down the mountain much more than the trip up."

She set out a cool metal bowl of water, scratched her furry friend behind the ears, and with a deep breath, opened the door to see what lay in store.

She came outside to see George leading the rig, with Jacob sitting beside him. He wore his best Sunday suit and it brought out his firm muscles the way his overalls did not. He wore a wide brimmed Stetson that highlighted his large stature. It even kept his hair out of his eyes.

She could tell he was nervous by the way his right knee kept bouncing. His whole body looked rigid, as if he was bracing for a punch in a saloon brawl.

They rode the whole way into town in silence. It was a sunny day and Louise delighted herself in seeing the beauty of God's creation. She noticed a mother deer grooming her new fawn on a rare patch of green grass. The sky laid open above them, and her eyes traced the outline of clouds until she saw an eagle hovering on the breeze. The warmth of God's design felt like a warm hug and nod of reassurance from her creator.

If God made all this, and cares for all of it, he can certainly take care of me.

At long last, they began down a steep hill into the bustling little town below. The small mining town was mostly filled with men, but Louise noticed a few families gathered at the small church for Sunday service. There was not a regular preacher, but the whole town turned out for the traveling one. Jacob had gone down to speak to him just the day before, and the preacher agreed to wed the young couple after the Sunday service—or so he'd told her.

The wagon came to a stop in front of the church, and Louise's stomach became a pit of nerves. Her mind swirled with anxiety.

She looked down to see Jacob offering her his hand and her heart stilled a little. She placed her hand in his strong one, and she marveled at how tiny her hand looked in his. As she jumped down onto the rough dirt road, she started to trip, and Jacob stretched out his arm to catch her.

As she felt his strong arm around her waist, she looked up slowly into his deep, brown eyes. She wondered what was going through his head. She opened her mouth to speak but was stopped by a lump in her throat.

"Shall we?" Jacob asked, as he pulled his left arm from her waist and offered out his arm.

Oh, so I get two words today, Louise thought with a chuckle.

"Why yes, I think we shall," she said as she looped her small arm nervously through his and they walked into the old, white church together.

She was surprised to see that it looked much larger inside. The arches loomed above them like a colorless rainbow, but equally grand. The complex work of the arches and the immensity of their design gave her the impression that what would happen today was equally immense, and she felt light-headed in response.

**

The sermon seemed to go on forever. While Louise normally enjoyed hearing someone deliver the word of God, on this particular day, she was eager for the sermon to end. Her palms started to sweat, and her head began to race when she realized what was about to take place.

Louise looked up when she heard a stir and realized that people were exiting the small assembly.

"Are you ready?" Jacob asked, extending his hand. "If you're not, I will understand."

There was something about his gentle acquiescence to her consent that reminded her he was a safe person. Marriage might be a coin toss in the west, but it was certainly a far better risk than what waited for her back in Missouri.

"I'm ready," Louise said, as she placed her hand in his tightly, and felt as if all her anxiety flew into her grip. She must've squeezed harder than she realized, because he winced, which made her let out a giggle. She was relieved that the giant mountain man was human after all.

They walked together to the front of the church, where the preacher was ready to perform their vows.

"I reckon you're prepared?" the preacher asked. Jacob didn't respond, and she could feel the preacher and Jacob's eyes fixed on her, awaiting her response. She was shocked to realize that it was her approval they were waiting on. She was amazed at the respect the wild men in the west had for women.

She took a deep breath and looked behind her at the small church. The room was mostly empty pews, aside from a few friendly townsfolk. George and his family sat in the first row with smiles of encouragement. George had brought his wife, who was holding the sleeping baby, as well as his daughter, and Louise was glad to see another young woman in town. Perhaps they would be friends. Farther back in the church sat Alice and Jethro. Alice smiled encouragingly and the warm wrinkles in her face comforted Louise.

"Yes," Louise said softly, turning back to the traveling preacher.

"All right, then," said the preacher. "Let's get started."

The wedding was short and to the point. Once they both said they were willing to wed, the preacher asked if they had anything to give each other. Jacob produced a small golden band and slid it smoothly onto Louise's finger.

She looked up, surprised, and met his warm brown eyes with a small twinkle in them. He could be handsome if he bothered to trim his beard. She felt flustered and her stomach flipped. *When did he have time to get a ring?* Before she could process it, the preacher turned to the townsfolk and said simply, "I hereby present you Mr. and Mrs. Jacob Montgomery. Jacob, you may now kiss your bride... if'n she'll let ya."

The small crowd chuckled and cheered in approval, and Louise's eyes grew larger than a Missouri cornfield. Was he about to kiss her? It sure seemed like he was supposed to. She closed her eyes and puckered up. If she was lucky, she figured, it would be over and done with soon.

When she felt his kiss, she opened her eyes suddenly, surprised at how warm it was. He smelled like pine and leather, and while his outward appearance was hard, his lips were pillowy soft. She had the sudden urge to melt into his arms, but then, he pulled away, and she was left standing there—a married woman.

Just like that, it was over. The newly married couple turned to face the pews, and everyone came up to congratulate them.

Last was George's daughter, Sarah. Louise had never met her before, but as George introduced the two young women, she felt as if she had met her before. Her long brown hair was as thick as a log and as wild as the Nevada territory. Her waves bounced on her shoulders and flowed freely with the confidence of a single young girl. She wasn't sure why, but Louise felt a kinship with Sarah.

"Congratulations, Louise," Sarah said warmly. "I've heard all about you, and I'm so glad we finally get to meet. I'm sure we're gonna be fast friends!" Sarah threw her small, tanned arms around Louise's neck and almost knocked her over. Louise laughed out loud for the first time that week.

Jacob insisted that George and Jethro bring their families over for Sunday dinner, which was very unlike him.

Since when did he want to have anyone over to the ranch who wasn't working on it?

Alice chuckled and insisted she be the one to bring the stew this time. It struck Louise, as they walked out to their wagons, that she felt more welcome with these people she barely knew than with the family she'd known her whole life.

In a matter of days, she'd gone from a neglected single child in the deep south to a married woman in the wild and uncertain mountains of Nevada. Things had changed so fast—too fast—truly. As the friends traveled out of town and back up the mountain, Louise realized she didn't know what

to expect. She h
But she was su

NORA J. CALLAWAY

Chapte

A light kiss tickled Jacob's
jump. Minnie the cat pu
again.

Not quite the way
wedding night.

He rolled over
cheek.

The mornin
know the ti
the brigh
sun, refl

I'm
on

...r Six

...cheek and woke him up with a ...red undaunted and licked him

...*imagined I might wake up after my*

...with a begrudging chuckle and wiped his

...g sun shined through the window, letting him ...e to sleep was over. He lifted a hand up to block ... morning rays and his eyes caught the gleam of ...ecting off the thin metal band around his finger.

...*married,* he thought to himself, *and somehow, I'm still* ...*he floor.*

He thought it felt too quiet in the large, single-room cabin and went to check on the new inhabitants of his home. The tiny babe was still fast asleep, tucked inside the arm of his new wife.

"My wife," he said out loud, accidentally.

She stirred after he spoke, and he covered his mouth and backed away slowly. He wasn't sure who he was more afraid of waking up—the baby or the woman.

What was he supposed to do with her when she woke up? Sure, they had been existing in the same space for several days and he'd treated her respectfully as a stranger in his home... But now, she was his *wife.* There was that word again. It felt strange to think and even stranger to say.

Jacob busied himself and found something to do. Perhaps if there was food when she woke up, Louise would be less likely to talk to him too much.

He lit a fire in the hearth. The fall mornings in the mountains flipped between cool and warm, but this was a crisper morning than usual. If he didn't know what to say to Louise, at least he could make sure she was warm and well-fed.

He put a pot of coffee on the stove and warmed some biscuits in the skillet. George's wife had been kind enough to bring them and fresh strawberries from her garden so that the couple would have food when they awoke in the morning.

Jacob was grateful he didn't have to cook since he wasn't very good at it, as he was reminded every time he had to eat what he made. He was relieved to finally have someone who could cook and hoped that she knew how to flip a good flapjack. He figured he'd find out soon enough.

The smell of the coffee and the gentle crackling of the fire filled the log cabin. Before long, Jacob heard a yawn coming from his young bride. He panicked when he realized she was waking up, and he turned to the stove to look busy.

That's when he grabbed the biscuits without thinking. A searing hot pain shot through his hand as he touched the burning pan. He dropped the biscuits—and their breakfast—onto the wooden floor.

"Is everything okay?" Louise asked as she sat up in bed. "I heard a loud noise."

Jacob felt like a fool. He had mucked it up again. He had to think quick. "Oh, good morning," he said unceremoniously. "That silly 'ole cat of yours knocked over the hot biscuits. No matter. I'll scoot over to George's place and see if Martha has any more."

Minnie meowed from the other side of the room, vying for her innocence.

"That's so strange," Louise said with another yawn and a stretch. "She's never grabbed food off the counter before. No mind. I can whip us up something right quick. Let me just change the baby." Louise bent over and picked up the still sleeping babe out of its cradle.

"You cook?" asked Jacob with renewed hope. Perhaps breakfast wouldn't be a total loss after all.

"Of course, I cook! I cooked for the Cankers every day of my life for the past ten years."

Jacob watched Louise tuck in the baby and make her way over to the little kitchen. The long white cotton nightgown that Alice had given her as a gift dragged across the floor. Jacob chuckled at her short frame, not quite long enough for the dress. But he caught his breath when he saw the way her hips moved in it. Embarrassed, he looked away to the coffee that he'd managed not to spill.

"Are you laughing at me, Jacob Montgomery?" Louise asked with a hint of frustration in her voice.

"Oh, no. I, um..." His voice caught in his throat. "I'm gonna take my coffee on the porch." With that, he made his escape out of the cabin.

Once outside, Jacob realized he hadn't bothered to bring a cup of coffee with him.

I'm gonna have to go back in, he realized with a grunt. He took a couple of deep breaths and devised a plan to get away and think.

He straightened his shoulders and poked his head through the door.

"I'm gonna step out for a bit. I'll be back before supper."

"But..." Louise said, looking confused. The girl's soft round eyes looked up at him. "I am making fresh biscuits for us. I thought we might sit and talk a spell while we have breakfast. Where are you going in such a hurry?"

Jacob wondered why the woman was being so friendly. Part of him was intrigued but mostly he felt the need to escape and be alone with his thoughts. *Darn woman's confusing me.*

"I just gotta take care of something on the ranch," he said gruffly.

"Is there something I can do to help?" Louise replied as soon as he'd finished his sentence.

The woman was maddening. She was more persistent than a fox in a henhouse and had the potential to be twice as deadly.

"No!" Jacob said, louder than he had intended. "You just take your time settling in and I'll see you 'round supper time."

Jacob grabbed his hat and hurried out the door before the wily woman could force a conversation out of him again.

Normally, Jacob would walk up to his father's grave, but this time, he decided to take his horse. He had to get out of there fast, and he couldn't risk the chance that she might open the door and call out to him as he walked up the hill. No, now was the time to make haste and escape. Heat flashed through his bones as he remembered the disappointment of the past, and he couldn't get to his horse fast enough.

He threw a saddle over his favorite gray stallion, Gus.

"Giddy up," Jacob said as he threw his leg over the saddle and mounted him.

True to his name, Gus took off up the hill, galloping hard. Jacob urged the stallion onward, as if he could outrun the pain of his parents' deaths, the aching rejection of the maid who had left him, the fear of the unknown, and the trouble in which he now found himself. The mix of brown and green plastered into the side of the mountain comforted Jacob as he climbed farther upward, and he hoped the blue sky ahead might offer peace.

When he got to his parents' graveside, Jacob slowed Gus to a halt and hopped down off him with a deep sigh of relief. Finally, he could get alone to think. The loneliness built up from the absence of his father and best friend hit hard—even here on the mountaintop.

Poor Louise. What have I gotten her into?

"Well, Pop," Jacob began. "I married the girl like I said I would. I was a man of my word and now the whole thing is a mess. There's a baby in the mix and everything."

Jacob laughed aloud, knowing what his dad would say if he had a baby outside of wedlock.

"Before you ask, Pop, it's not mine. I've been nothing if not honorable."

Jacob felt deeply frustrated. He had done what his dad taught him how to do. He had kept his word. He had been honorable, just like he had been with the maid. Then again, that hadn't worked out too well, either.

His heart seared with pain—much worse than the burn on his hand that the skillet had left—as he remembered how it felt the day Jessie, his one true love, had left. The throbbing in his hand served as a reminder that he always got burned when he started to get comfortable with someone.

He knew it would sting if Miss Louise Parker rejected him, too. One rejection was as much as his pride could take, and Jessie had already taken care of that.

Best to stay to myself. Keep my word. Hold onto my pride and my honor. Let the chips fall where they may.

He gazed up at the sky, wondering if it might open up with a sign. Why not? God spoke to Moses through a burning bush.

"How 'bout it, Lord? You got any advice?"

Sighing, Jacob sat down on the same, smooth rock he'd rested on many times before, and cracked open the Bible that had been sitting in his saddlebag. He always kept it there for trips up the mountain or down to church. His eyes fell on the book of Isaiah, chapter forty-one:

"So do not fear, for I am with you; do not be dismayed, for I am your God. I will strengthen you and help you; I will uphold you with my righteous right hand," he read aloud.

Jacob was encouraged by this verse and felt strengthened. He wanted to be fearless like the men of old—like Samson, David, and Elijah. He wouldn't mind crackin' a skull or two while he was at it. But it wasn't fighting or hard work that scared Jacob. It was the cold, hard stare of a feisty woman. He'd rather fight a giant than face rejection again.

The verse reminded him, as he often needed to be reminded, that God would be his strength. He'd been leaning on his own strength again—a problem he was all too familiar with.

"I'll do it right this time, Pop. I'm gonna lean on the Lord like you taught me. I'm gonna make you proud. I promise… and you know I'm a man of my word."

Chapter Seven

Louise sat on the porch, sipping her coffee, and enjoying the sunrise with Minnie in her lap. Her furry friend nuzzled into the crook of her arm while Louise enjoyed the quiet of the morning. She had learned to get up earlier than Jacob so that she didn't have to be startled by him bumbling around the kitchen. She laughed when she thought about how nervous and clumsy he was on their first morning together.

She had grown to really cherish these mornings with just herself and Minnie. She enjoyed the creak of the rocking chair, the birth of the new morning sun, and the gentle purring of her longest friend. It was the only time of day she wasn't having to tiptoe around the mountain man or take care of a crying baby.

She worried about the small babe. He was so tiny and frail. Would he be able to survive without his mother's milk?

She had been glad to find out there were plenty of milk-making cows on the ranch, but she also knew that cow's milk affected a baby's stomach much differently than a mother's milk, and she worried each time he couldn't keep it down.

She heard a faint cry come from inside the cabin and she knew that her short time to herself had ended. With one more sip of coffee, she stood up and went to wait on the small babe, with Minnie on her heels. She lifted him out of his cradle and thought how odd it was that Jacob had thought to build it. He didn't seem particularly thoughtful, though he was kind, and she felt it strange he'd had the foresight to create it.

She changed the baby's cotton diaper and put the soiled linen in a bucket to wash later. She tickled his tummy and enjoyed watching his shimmering eyes and chubby cheeks giggle up at her. As the baby laughed aloud, she heard her husband stir on his pallet by the fire.

Here we go, she thought to herself. *What kind of excuse will you have to escape the cabin today?*

She immediately felt bad for having such a discontented thought about him. She had come to see that her first impression had been wrong. He wasn't the brute she had feared him to be, but after nearly two weeks, she had grown weary of trying to get him to talk to her. Jacob was silent about *everything.* He was silent about the baby, silent about their modest arrangement, and silent when she asked him anything *at all.*

Louise had noticed, however, that whenever he came home from a trip up the mountain, he always seemed much calmer and more collected. She wondered what, or *who,* he might be visiting, but she had resolved to let it be his business. She was grateful that at least he was in a better mood when he returned.

Though the fact he was such a mystery to her bothered her more than anything. She could deal with the trouble she knew. She knew how to cater to the whims of the Cankers, or how to avoid the lurid stare of the old hog, but she didn't know what to do with *him.* What kind of beast was Jacob Montgomery, anyhow?

She noticed from her place in the kitchen that he was mumbling to himself under his breath as he stirred, his broad shoulders turning. What was he saying? She couldn't tell, but it sounded as if he was asking someone why they were leaving. Then, he shuddered as if a cold breeze had chilled him to his bones.

"Jacob?" she asked, a little concerned. "Are you okay?"

She reached out cautiously to touch his brow, wondering if perhaps he might have a fever. He was cool to the touch, and she realized she hadn't been this close to him since they took their vows.

He smelled of leather and fresh pine, perhaps from being in the field all day, perhaps from riding his horse or making paths in the forest. She wasn't sure, as her interaction with him so far was only inside their log cabin.

"Where do you go off to, Jacob Montgomery?" she whispered curiously. "What goes on in that head of yours?"

As if to answer her question, Jacob opened his eyes and sat up, startled. He looked wild, like a bobcat that was cornered between a cliff and a riverbed. She backed away slowly. Perhaps she'd gotten too close.

"Good morning?" she said nervously, as if she were asking a question. Louise stood up and straightened her skirts, feeling flustered. "I mean, *good morning.* You said something in your sleep, and I wanted to make sure you were okay."

"You were worried about me?" Jacob asked, looking surprised, with one eyebrow cocked up high.

"I didn't say I was *worried,*" Louise clarified awkwardly. *Perhaps I'm the cornered bobcat.* "I just wanted to make sure you weren't mad with a fever. Now that I see that you're not, would ya take the baby so I can go on and make breakfast?" Louise cringed inwardly at the quick lie she'd crafted.

As she turned to go fix their meal, the baby started to cry.

"I didn't do anything," Jacob said. "All I did was hold my arms out."

"Well, that's the problem," Louise said with a sigh. "You have to support his head." She couldn't believe he was still so helpless with the baby, but at least he acknowledged the babe now.

Louise gazed down into the babe's light blue eyes. They looked crystal-like as his tears dried and he looked up at her sweetly. Rosy, plump cheeks adorned a soft round face, while loose blonde curls tried to peek out from under the swaddling blanket. Louise's heart filled with love and pity for the helpless babe, and it ached as she wondered what would become of him.

"Were you able to find anything out in town… about where he came from, I mean?"

"I still haven't found anything about where he came from, but I'll keep lookin'… What do ya reckon we should call him in the meantime?" Jacob asked, looking perplexed. There was a tenderness in his voice and a look of concern in his eye that filled Louise with surprise.

"Well, I don't rightly know," Louise said in shock. "Perhaps it will come in time."

Louise turned back to make breakfast and hid a smile to herself. She was amazed and delighted that Jacob had brought up naming the baby as he rarely spoke about him.

She could see by Jacob's heavy shoulders drooping over the child and the concern in his eyes that the baby weighed on him more than he let on. She was elated at this discovery and mulled it over as she made their morning meal.

She wondered if he wanted to keep the baby or if he was eager to get rid of him. The thought of losing the sweet babe shot a hot flash of foreboding through her. She couldn't bear to think of it, and she poured her energy into kneading the soft dough instead.

Louise made biscuits and gravy, which she had learned quickly was an easy favorite for Jacob. If there was one thing Louise could do with her eyes closed, it was cook. She could tell as Jacob devoured the breakfast that she brought something useful to the table. She sighed contentedly as she wiped flour onto her apron.

This may just be a marriage of convenience, but it's clear he needs me. I can hold my own all right.

***

After breakfast, Jacob left to get some work done on the ranch and Louise did not mind one bit. She loved getting to arrange her day however she wanted—something she'd never been able to do in Missouri—so when Jacob left the house, she looked around. It wasn't a mess of chores, but a mess that was finally *hers*.

Even though she had a million chores to do, from caring for the babe, to the laundry, to all the cooking, it was so different than back in Missouri. Life with the Cankers was all about how much they could force her to do for them as they shamed and ridiculed her. Her shoulders tightened as she remembered words like beatings falling on her ears.

Life here might be full of hard work but at least it was work of her own making. No one was there to punish her. In fact, she got the distinct impression that Jacob was grateful for what she did, so she didn't mind working hard, washing the clothes, cooking the food, or caring for the baby, because it was all hers.

"What are we going to name you?" she asked the babe in her arms.

He felt a bit heavier now, which she took as a good sign. He was keeping more of the milk down than he had a few days ago. She sighed gratefully.

"At last, you're putting on weight, little one," she said as she studied his face.

His soft skin was so light, it was almost translucent. She could see a tiny blue vein in his otherwise spotless forehead.

Louise leaned down to kiss him on the forehead and paused to smell the sweet scent of clean baby. She cuddled him for a few minutes, relishing the tender moment that felt safe outside time, and then put him in his cradle next to the bed for a morning nap.

Minnie mewed and pawed at her skirts, reminding her she needed attention as well. Louise scooped up her cat and walked over to the kitchen. "Come on, Minnie," she said. "It's time to start preparing dinner."

She mixed some flour, water, and butter for fresh bread but realized she was out of eggs. She looked back at the babe, fast asleep in his cradle.

"You'll be out for at least an hour," she muttered to him. Acting quickly, she grabbed a small basket and walked out to the chicken coop, just a little over an acre away.

Jacob had gotten her a small parasol to use while walking in the sun, but she didn't want it today. She could tell he thought she was a delicate rose who would wilt if in the sun for an hour.

On the contrary, when she was back in Missouri, she spent all day outside when she could get away with it. And she loved getting a chance to go out and collect the eggs. She often felt stuck in the house with the baby, trying constantly to get him to keep milk own, to sleep, and to stay safe. She was ready to venture outside!

Minnie tried to follow her out the door and she gathered the wiggly cat into her arms. Louise giggled and brought

Minnie under her chin for a quick hug before lifting her up to her eyes. The curious kitty pawed playfully at Louise's cheeks as if to invite her on an adventure.

"You can't join me for this chore, my friend. I don't think the hens would be too fond of me if I brought a cat along to collect their eggs."

***

Louise breathed in the cool mountain air as she walked to the coop. At last, she was in nature. She skipped up the green hill, made lush by the creek nearby, and wished there was someone within earshot that she could converse with.

When she reached the chicken coop, she knelt to look inside the wiry structure and was glad to find nearly two dozen eggs. Pleased with the hens' contribution, she gathered the eggs into her basket.

She was surprised at how quickly she had grown accustomed to her work and how much it pleased her when it ran smoothly. In truth, she found it deeply satisfying, and her chest swelled with pride as she turned with her basket of eggs to return to the house.

She heard a horse whinny over her shoulder and walked around the coop to find Jacob in the pen with a horse. She could tell that the horse was wild and not interested in being tamed, which she herself could empathize with.

She expected to see Jacob a helpless ball of nerves with the horse, all tense and quiet—angry and frustrated—but what she found surprised her entirely. Far different from the man she saw in the log cabin every day, this Jacob was calm and relaxed. This Jacob was strong and confident. This Jacob took her breath away.

"Hah! Hah!" Jacob said as he lifted his arms and chattered at the horse. He was loud and vocal as he told the horse how it must submit to his will.

The stallion ran around the pen, eyes darting about wildly, and Louise could tell it was looking for an escape. When no escape was found, the horse reared up with his front hooves in the air and let out a blood thirsty neigh.

"Oh my!" Louise exclaimed silently, as a lump caught in her throat. She had no idea that breaking a horse could be so dangerous and she felt suddenly afraid for her husband.

Undeterred by the strong-willed creature, Jacob lifted his arms in the air and made a clicking sound.

"Hah! Hah! Down boy!" he called out. He looked about twelve feet tall with his arms lifted toward the heavens.

When the horse finally settled his hooves back down in the dirt, Jacob grabbed the reins, not angrily but confidently, and brought the horse to bare. Within a matter of minutes, this once-wild animal had been peacefully broken by the powerful and certain rancher.

Louise had never seen this side of Jacob before. She was surprised to find herself in awe of him.

She couldn't help but notice how his shirt clung to his broad shoulders. His muscles seemed to ripple and struggle to contain themselves under the flimsy cotton apparel. His suddenly cool demeanor juxtaposed to the heat sizzling through the air, and Louise's stomach did a small flip without permission.

Suddenly, she felt something slam against her ankles and she jumped a mile high. She realized too late that it was Minnie, who had managed to escape the log cabin, and she let out an accidental scream as she dropped the small basket in her hands.

The basket fell to the ground, along with the eggs that were now shattered. The two had made a big enough commotion that they spooked the horse, as well as Jacob, who headed in her direction. The horse was now tied to a post and Jacob looked fit to be tied as well.

"What in tarnation!" the frustrated rancher declared in a start. "Don't you know that it's dangerous to sneak up on a man breaking a horse?"

"I'm sorry!" Louise said, her heart twisting and her lower lip quivering. "I was trying to get eggs for supper." She dropped her eyes to the ground. "Although I don't suppose we will have any eggs now."

Jacob did not say anything else, but she could tell by the look on his face how displeased he was. The two looked at each other awkwardly for what felt like a long, cold winter, and then they turned back to go back to their respective chores.

"How dare he, Minnie?" Louise exclaimed as she held her cat and stomped back to the house. Embarrassment and disappointment intermingled in her heart. "How dare he yell at me like that? How silly was I to have a moment of attraction to such a creature?"

Chapter Eight

Jacob kicked the hard mountain dirt with the toe of his boot.

"Ow!" he exclaimed, grabbing his boot, and regretting more than one decision he'd made that day. The dust from the packed red dirt spun up into the air and reminded Jacob of the mess he had made.

What had he been thinking, raising his voice at Louise like that? He had been startled when he heard her behind him, but if he was honest with himself, then it wasn't just the bronco bucking that scared him.

The ranch was *his d*omain. It was the only place he could get alone with nature, with God, and most of all, with his thoughts—which didn't always come easy. It was where he could put all his stress and worry into his work. It was where he could feel the anxiety leaving his body as he pushed the plow to the ground.

This was *his p*lace. How dare she encroach upon it? What was she doing out there? The chicken coop wasn't that close to where he was. Why had she been watching him so? What did she think of him? Did it just prove to her how ridiculous he was?

With the deep sigh of a man who had made a mistake he knew he could not take back, he took the stallion to the barn and thought of how he might make it up to Louise. After he put the young stud up, he dusted off his pants and washed his hands in a trough of clean water before he started out toward the house for lunch.

As he walked past the small red barn that housed the milk cows, he heard a strange noise. It sounded like someone humming on the breeze.

Is it Louise? he asked himself. Hadn't she had enough disappointment on the ranch to go back to the cabin? Why wasn't she in the house where she was safe?

And yet, her song was so sweet. She was singing, "Come Thou Fount of Every Blessing," his favorite hymn, and he couldn't help but listen in.

He poked his head curiously around the edge of the rugged red barn. He stepped cautiously over some old hay and tucked himself quietly behind the thick wooden wall that separated the cows' stalls.

As carefully as he could manage, he looked over the stall, and caught a glimpse of Louise holding the baby as she fed him underneath the cow.

Why, that's one way to get the milk while it's warm.

Jacob sat as quietly as he could manage on the soft hay floor. The old pine barn was a dusty mess of broken boards and creaky boards, and he took care to not be discovered by Louise.

He was surprised to see she was braver than he had given her credit for. Perhaps he had been wrong to assume that a girl from a busy town in the south couldn't hack it in the west.

That particular dairy cow was often easily agitated, and he was impressed to see how calm she was under Louise's gentle hands. He felt momentarily jealous of the cow and wondered if she could be that type of a gentling influence for him as well. He was embarrassed at the thought of her smooth, ivory hands holding him.

He sat against the dividing wall and wondered if her gentle song was for the cow or the baby. Either way, her sweet voice worked like a salve to soothe everyone in the barn—himself included.

He stood slowly and dared to peek over the edge of the stall again. He was amazed at the warmth she showed a baby that wasn't hers. The graceful curve of her neck leaned over the baby as she cradled his head, which Jacob had never been able to do just right.

When she had first arrived, just ten days ago, he imagined her to be a frail, spoiled southerner not capable of surviving in the west, but he could see now that he had been wrong. What he saw before him was a strong, calm, and very capable woman.

His eyes followed the smooth lines of her hands, which held the baby, over to her sleek arms, which were stronger than they looked. Then, he traced the outline of her body over her shoulder and down to the small of her back.

He felt his heart twist, and he looked away, embarrassed. Who was this beautiful young woman who was constantly surprising him and how would he make himself worthy of her?

While he had originally thought to surprise her and return the favor from earlier that day, he now thought it best to leave her and the suckling young babe to their simple happiness. He walked quietly out of the barn, hoping not to disturb them.

As he walked back to the cabin, he sent up a silent prayer, filled with a hope he wasn't yet ready to admit out loud. Perhaps they might find happiness together yet.

Jacob saw some wild sunflowers as he walked up the hill to the family home. He paused for a moment to pick some for

Louise, just as his father had always brought them home for his mother. Perhaps a simple apology for the chicken coop could set them on the right path forward.

Then again, would she think the flowers too forward? Would he be setting himself up for another disappointment?

The crushing feeling of rejection rushed through him anew and he tossed the flowers to the ground. It wasn't worth the risk.

Jacob walked up the wide porch steps and into the house, feeling disheartened but still hungry. He grabbed some lunchmeat and a block of newly cured cheese out of the icebox and set it on the table. He may not know what to say, but at least he could have lunch on the table when Louise walked in with the baby.

Jacob reached into a cabinet to fetch some plates, and when he turned around, he was horrified by what he saw. The ridiculous orange cat was standing on the table, eating the meat he just sat out.

"Get down!" Jacob hollered as he waved his hand through the air, not to strike the animal but just to scare it off.

"How *could* you?" a voice whispered behind him as Minnie hissed and scurried off to hide behind the curtains.

Jacob spun around to see a crestfallen Louise, staring at him with a face redder than a robin's breast. She looked frightened, and Jacob couldn't understand why.

"How *could* you?" she repeated, with a crack in her voice. "How could you be so mean to such an innocent little creature?"

He shook his head in disbelief. What was her odd attachment to that animal?

"I mean, it's just an animal," Jacob said, without thinking, and he regretted it before it had even finished passing over his lips.

"Just an animal?" There was a catch in Louise's voice, and it sounded like she might cry.

Jacob instantly wished he could take back what he said but it was too late. In the short amount of time he had known Louise, he had never seen her this upset.

She laid the now-sleeping babe down in his cradle and walked up to Jacob with tears in her eyes.

"Well, even animals have feelings, Jacob… which is more than I can say for you!"

Jacob saw a tear roll down her cheek as she turned her back to him.

"Louise," he said gently, holding out his hand, but she only stuck up her nose.

She picked up the cat, still hiding behind the curtains, and ran out of the house, leaving Jacob alone with a sleeping babe he wasn't sure what to do with.

**

Louise clutched Minnie to her chest as she ran up the hill toward the edge of the valley. She didn't stop for the mewing cat in her arms nor the howling wind around her. She had to get out of that valley.

The tears she'd been struggling to hold in fell like a hard rain from dark clouds. She cried for the unmet expectations and the man who she had thought would love her. She cried for the baby who she wanted desperately to survive. She cried for an entire childhood that was already lost and fear of the unknown future that stretched out before her.

When she finally reached the top of the hill and the log cabin grew smaller and more bearable, she finally stopped to catch her breath. She was winded from the sudden sprint up the hill, and she was grateful for a large, smooth rock to sit on while she gathered her thoughts.

Minnie crawled up Louise's shoulder and mewed gently as she pushed her nose against her wet cheek. She let out a deep sigh and hugged her friend gratefully.

"I won't let anything happen to you, Minnie."

Louise had been to hell and back at the Canker's. And more days than not, the only friend she had known was Minnie. When the Cankers were cruel to her, it was Minnie who comforted her. When she had no one to talk to, it was Minnie who had purred in her ear. When she made the wrong turn out west, it was Minnie alone who had been at her side—and now it was Minnie with her on top of a mountain.

She would sooner be tarred and feathered than let anything happen to that cat. Jacob Montgomery had another thing coming if he thought he could yell at her like that.

She knew Jacob wasn't a cruel man, and she felt embarrassed for running out of the house, but when he'd raised his voice, it had triggered something in her. She could hear the hollering of Maw and Paw again, something she hadn't heard these last couple weeks. She could feel their withering stares and the cold sting of hatred she'd grown up with.

She knew good and well that Jacob wasn't the Cankers, but in that moment, all she could think of to do was run.

As her tears dried and her pulse steadied, she looked out over the ranch. Her ranch, she realized.

She was glad to have a baby, freedom, a home, and land, but she couldn't quite figure out what to do with the puzzling man that came with it. She hugged Minnie close, her furry orange friend pawing at her nose and nuzzling against her cheek.

***

A cool, fall breeze passed over her shoulders as she watched the sun set, and it turned icy cold in the evening air. Louise shivered as a chill went through her.

"We better get on home, Minnie," she said with a sigh. "We can't stay gone forever."

She held Minnie as they walked back to the house, but when the cabin came into view, the small cat suddenly jumped from her arms and raced for it.

"Minnie!" she called after her, but the cat didn't listen. Louise ran after her friend all the way to the front door.

When Louise finally reached the porch, the cat was pawing at the door, no doubt ready to go in and sit by the warm fire.

"Minnie, you scared me half to death running off like that!" she said, realizing she must have also scared Jacob when she ran off. "Oh well, at least we made it home."

Home. Such a strange word, but did it really feel like home? Minnie certainly thought so.

She paused at the door and wondered what she'd find on the other side. Would the baby be crying? Would Jacob be frustrated with her?

As she slowly cracked open the door, the warmth from the fire rushed out—a welcome comfort to her cold bones. It was quiet in the house and Louise walked in quickly, concerned for the baby. She turned the corner and was pleasantly surprised with what she saw.

Jacob had his back to her as he sat on the floor by the fire with the baby in his lap. He was covering his face with his hands and then popping out from over the top with a *"Peekaboo!"*

Louise was shocked to see him playing with the baby. Who was this man? She stood quietly for a moment as she observed the odd pair who had not noticed her enter the home.

Each time, Jacob would pull his hands up and over his eyes, the baby would look worried, as if Jacob had stopped existing for a moment. As soon as Jacob popped over the top with his silly expression and another *"Peekaboo!"*, the baby would giggle and so would Jacob.

He knows how to giggle?

Louise was amused to see the strong beast of a man behave like a sweet and gentle child. Her heart warmed at the sight of them, and she decided to tiptoe away so as not to disturb them.

She was just about to draw a bath when she heard the baby start to cry. She ran back into the room to see that Jacob was trying to rock the baby but had forgotten to support his head again. Instead of getting frustrated, though, Jacob was speaking tenderly to the baby. She took a deep breath of relief to see him so calm and gentle.

"I'm tryin', little one," he said as he tried to fold his burly arm in awkward positions to support the babe. "I'm not as good at this as she is. Work with me here."

So, he does care. He just has no idea what he's doing.

She let out an accidental chuckle and Jacob turned around with eyes wider than a fox.

"Louise! You're back," he said. "I didn't hear you come in."

She saw a look of insecurity and anxiety creep back over his face. Was he just that way around her? Why did she make him so nervous?

"I just needed to clear my head," she said quickly. "You're doing a good job... with the baby, I mean. The trick to supporting his head is to prop it up against the inside of your elbow, like this."

She lifted the baby's soft, fuzzy head and laid it on Jacob's large, muscly arms.

"There you go," she said gently. "Just like that. That's how it's supposed to be."

As she released the baby's head, her hand accidentally pressed the outside of Jacob's large forearm, and he looked up at her with a look of surprise.

"Thank you," he said, sounding like he had a frog in his throat. "I... I'm sorry about earlier."

"It's okay," she said. "Me too. I shouldn't have run off like that."

They stared at each other for a few seconds, and she was touched by the tenderness in his eyes. Louise suddenly found herself in the very rare predicament of not knowing what to say, so she smiled gently and turned to go make dinner.

What a strange day, she thought as she made supper. This new place was full of surprises and none more confusing—or interesting—than the mountain man himself.

Chapter Nine

Jacob sat in the old wooden wagon and stared at the young woman walking toward him. She wore a long yellow dress, the same one she'd worn the day she arrived, but this entrance was different. Her long, wavy blonde hair cascaded down over her shoulders all the way to her waist. The white bonnet on her head did little to shade her delicate blue eyes from the sun's fierce rays, and it made Jacob want to protect her.

She wouldn't have to squint if she had the parasol, Jacob thought, but that would require her being less stubborn. He shook his head with a chuckle as he watched her.

Determined she was, and while it had bothered him at times, he admitted that it was her determination that might make a rancher's wife of her yet.

After she had seen him break the horse a few days ago, she had spoken of little else than getting to see the ranch, the horses, and all the excitement it offered.

Jacob had been surprised initially that she had taken an interest in his work, but truth be told, it made him swell with pride.

Once she heard George mention they had gotten new horses in, Louise had talked of nothing but wanting to meet them. She had inquired about it enough that Jacob thought it was best to give into her—lest she talk his ear off about it.

George's wife had been kind enough to offer to keep the baby for the day, so the time had finally come for Louise to venture out onto the ranch.

As she walked toward him and the wagon, Jacob couldn't help but notice she moved with a new bounce in her step. He hadn't seen her excited quite like this before, and it made him feel proud he could be the one to give her some adventure.

Jacob stepped down and offered Louise his hand as she climbed into the tall, brown wagon. He had never found the wagon to be particularly tall, but when Louise stood next to it, she looked like a small child.

"Mind your step, Louise," Jacob said with a grin as he hoisted her into it.

"Oh, I can get along just fine, Jacob Montgomery," she said with a smile that nearly knocked him to the ground.

He went back to his seat in the front of the wagon, feeling a bit flustered. He lifted the reins to take off when he heard a noise coming from over his shoulder.

"Don't forget about me, partner," George said, just as Jacob was about to pull off.

"I work this ranch too, you know!"

Jacob had gotten so distracted by Louise he had nearly forgotten his best ranch hand. He felt embarrassed and thought it best to just ignore it.

"Well, come on, then! Best hurry up!"

Relieved he had dodged an embarrassing moment, Jacob lifted the reins once more, and the crew took off toward the ranch. As they traversed the bumpy road, Louise nearly lost her balance and reached out to steady herself on Jacob's strong arm, causing a warm glow to erupt on his cheeks—something he hoped stayed with him for a long while yet.

***

Jacob offered Louise his arm as she stepped down from the wagon and onto the wild and dusty dirt of the ranch. The touch of her hand made Jacob's heart skip a beat. She looked so out of place there—like a bluebonnet amid a cactus patch. He had the constant instinct to shield her and keep her safe, which was part of the reason he had not brought her to see the ranch just yet. It was just a mile from the house, but it was long enough to take the wagon, lest the southern belle succumb to the heat.

He saw her eyes light up like a child at the state fair when she caught sight of the new horses running around the corral. He wondered where she got that sense of adventure and that fire in her eyes as she pranced toward it.

"Thank you for bringing me," she said, looking around the beautiful meadow with a lovely smile.

"'Course," he replied shortly. He wasn't sure how else to respond.

Jacob wasn't used to her being this friendly, if not altogether sweet. He wondered what on earth had gotten into her. Perhaps it was because this was the first time she hadn't had a baby on her hip.

He found her disposition inviting, if not a bit confusing, as he walked to catch up with her.

Jacob opened the heavy wooden latch to the corral and then swung the door wide for Louise.

"After you," he said.

He thought she looked like a queen arriving at her crowning as she glided gracefully past the gate, and he kicked himself for not bringing her sooner. He regretted not giving her the chance to explore the ranch with him before, and he could see now that she fit the place like a glove.

A short and stocky ranch hand named Michael walked a horse on a lead. Louise listened intently as the ranch hand introduced her to the different horses and explained where they came from.

"I best head down to town to get some more feed," George said suddenly, looking at the ranch hand. "Michael, why don't you come on with me?"

"What's that now?" Jacob asked concerned. He knew they had plenty of feed in the red barn and wondered what George was getting at.

"Oh yes," George continued. "I'm certain we're almost out of food for the horses. Y'all can manage brushing out the horses, can't ya?"

"Of course," Jacob said roughly.

George motioned for the other ranch hand to join him, and they headed off toward town.

Jacob's chest started to pound as he realized what this meant. He was about to be all alone with Louise. Whenever they were at home together, the baby was there, needing to be tended to. Aside from eating meals together, they tended to their own chores, and spent most of their time away from each other.

Truth be told, he stayed gone as much as possible to escape her many questions and attempts to spark conversation. Now, that would be tough—if not altogether unavoidable. Jacob felt his shoulders tighten rigidly as he realized this was perhaps the first time they had been really and truly alone.

He dreaded being forced into conversation, and his nerves started to get the better of him until he glanced down at Louise. Her warm smile both relaxed and excited him.

There she was, smiling again. What was that about anyhow? As George, Michael the ranch hand, and all Jacob's hopes for diversion drove away in the wagon, he steadied himself.

"Well, we best get to it," he said, as he grabbed a brush and handed one to Louise.

He showed her the proper way to brush out a horse, and he enjoyed watching her hang on his every word. Usually, she had so many opinions and so much to say, but now, she just looked up at him with gentle blue eyes that awaited his instruction.

He expected to have to show her several times, or for her to at least have something disagreeable to say, but that didn't happen. Brushing horses came almost too naturally for Louise. He caught himself wondering if perhaps she hadn't cared for horses before, as he admired the ease with which she brushed the domesticated animal.

Though she looked so short in comparison to them, she cared for them so tenderly, so gracefully, like a mother hen with her chicks. She was so gentle and maternal, and it reminded Jacob of how natural she was with the baby.

This must be what motherhood looks like, he mused to himself, wondering if that was what his *own* mother had been like. Louise had an elegance that didn't quite fit in the Wild West, and yet, she somehow looked like she belonged.

She was lovely, and he knew he would have to be blind not to notice. He took a deep breath and looked away, hoping she hadn't caught him staring.

They stood there silently for a while, brushing the horses side-by-side with the neighing of the animals as the only conversation. At first, it felt peaceful, but slowly, the quiet became too burdensome, and Jacob finally felt as though he had to say *something*.

"You're not half bad at this," Jacob said carefully. "Are you sure you haven't taken care of horses before?"

Louise laughed softly, which made Jacob catch his breath. He had never heard so much warmth in her voice—at least not where he was concerned.

"Well," she began slowly, "I was a governess for a while back home—back in Missouri, that is. I was responsible for teaching two young children and a rather precocious dog."

"That makes sense," Jacob said. "I mean, cause you're good with the baby. You must have done that for years."

"No," she said sadly. "I was only a governess for a couple of short months."

Jacob noticed Louise's hands clinch around the brush as she answered him.

"Why is that?" he asked carefully, eager to know more.

"My adoptive parents were..." her voice trailed off, and she turned away from Jacob for a moment before continuing, "...unkind."

"Unkind how?" he asked. Who could be unkind to such a lovely, gentle creature?

"I wasn't exactly their favorite child," she continued. "At any rate, they had work for me to do around the family farm, and they couldn't spare me working out of the house any longer."

Jacob gazed at Louise as she worried her bottom lip with her teeth. There was something she wasn't telling him, but what was it?

"How were they unkind, Louise?" he asked again, more gently this time.

He heard her take a deep breath that ended in a shudder, and she slowly looked up to him with sad, apple-shaped eyes that looked like they might cry. Jacob's heart raced and his fist clenched at his side as he thought about what he might do to anyone who could hurt such a sweet creature.

"They were always very displeased with me," she said quietly, "and they told me as much every day. Sometimes, they told me by yelling at me, and other times, they told me by not giving me supper... but they always let me know how displeased they were. I worked so hard to earn their approval, or at least their respect, but I just couldn't do it."

Her voice trailed off, and she cleared her throat quietly as she looked down. Jacob unclenched his fist and used it to reach over and gently lift Louise's chin.

"That's not your fault," he said quietly. "That's on them."

He wanted to say more. He wanted to comfort her. He wanted to assure her that he would stop anyone who wanted to hurt her. Most of all, he wanted to tell her how beautiful she was, but he couldn't bring himself to do it.

Instead, he just gazed down into her soft blue eyes, shaken by how affected he was by them.

"Thank you," she said softly. "No one has ever told me that before."

Her voice sounded like gentle rain on a warm day, and it soothed Jacob. As he looked in her eyes, he could tell there was more to the story. What was she hiding in that lovely head of hers?

"What about you?" she asked with a decidedly peppy voice. "What's your story?"

It was clear to Jacob that she wanted to change the subject. He was going to have to talk about himself—his least favorite task to undertake. He would sooner wrestle a wild hog than talk about his feelings, and in fact, he had on many an occasion.

He steeled his resolve and told her about Pop. He told her how he started the ranch when Jacob was still a babe, how Pop had raised him on his own after his mother died in childbirth, and how Pop had left the ranch to him when he died a couple years ago.

It was strange to him how easy it was to talk to Louise in that moment. While normally, he couldn't find the words, there was something about brushing the horses and her sweet countenance that made his normally awkward words come tumbling out.

He told her much of what had happened before she came, but he stopped just short of telling her about Jessie. The scar Jessie had etched into him when she'd broken his heart was too deep a wound to reveal.

Yet, as the sun started to set and they walked back to the wagon to head home, Jacob could not help but think that it was the best conversation he'd had in years—in a whole lifetime. That was all well and fine, granted she didn't expect him to be that talkative on a regular basis.

He helped Louise back into the wagon, and he smiled to himself when he saw that she sat in the seat next to him. What a strange day this had turned out to be, and what a lovely mystery of a woman it was that sat beside him in the old wooden wagon.

Chapter Ten

The late morning sun shone through the window as Louise gazed down at the sleeping babe in the cradle. His plump cheeks assured her that he was well nourished. Her heart was filled with hope each day when the baby was able to keep the milk in his belly. She swelled with pride to see that he was starting to put on weight.

"Thank you, Lord," Louise prayed quietly. "He might just make it after all."

Minnie weaved in and out of her ankles like a dance, purring contentedly. When a small coo came from the sleeping babe, Minnie turned her attention back to the cradle. Louise watched as Minnie crept over and slowly put orange paws on the side of the cradle, peeking in.

Could she trust her furry friend with the fragile child? She had previously kept the two at a distance just to be safe, but it was high time that she gave Minnie the chance to get to know the baby. She bent down and gently scratched Minnie behind the ears.

"This is your brother, Minnie," she said warmly. "You've got to be careful with him, girl. Do you think you can do it?"

Minnie put one tiny paw on Louise's face in gentle agreement and Louise nuzzled noses with her sweet animal friend. She stood up with the cozy cat in her arms, and enjoyed Minnie purring soothingly, as if she understood the need to be gentle.

"I know you can do it."

"Who are you talking to?" asked a warm, deep voice from behind her. Louise nearly jumped out of her stockings as she spun around.

"Didn't see you there, husband," she said, wondering how long he'd been standing there. "Dinner is not quite ready yet, but I'll have it ready shortly. I was just about to change the baby's diaper."

Louise set Minnie down gently and then lifted the babe from his cradle. She grabbed some fresh cotton linens and a safety pin with her other hand. She laid him down carefully on a soft white rug by the fire to keep him warm while she changed his garments.

She was surprised to see Jacob come over to watch. However, he'd been much more attentive since their time alone on the ranch last week. He hung around the house a bit more, coming home earlier than necessary for dinner.

He still didn't say much, which continued to puzzle her, but he seemed to come nearer, to sit closer, as if being in her presence pleased him in some way.

Well, if he's gonna hang around, I might as well teach him how to be useful, she thought to herself with a smile.

"Any interest in learning how to change the baby's diaper?" she asked curiously, looking up at Jacob.

"Might come in handy, I reckon," he replied, as he settled onto the soft rug next to her.

His deep, brown eyes staring down at her looked equally curious and cautious. She thought it might not be hard to get lost in them, if only the lips attached would open and speak.

Strong, defined muscles pushed through his brown linen shirt, searching for more room. She allowed herself to wonder for just a moment what it would be like to be held by them. A chill of embarrassment ran down her spine and she turned her attention back to the baby.

Louise took off the wet diaper and set it in an empty tin bowl.

"Why do ya put the soiled diaper in a bowl?" Jacob asked, perplexed. "You gonna cook it clean?"

Louise let out a short giggle, before she caught herself. She knew from experience with Paw Canker that men didn't much like being laughed at.

"Well, sort of," she began. "Later, I'll take the soiled diapers to the wash bin out back. I'll scrub them out a bit with the lye soap first, but then, yes, I'll sanitize them in some boiling water… so, I guess you're kinda right."

The two shared a laugh and Louise was pleased to find that he had a sense of humor.

Next, she showed him how to take the square cotton cloths, fold them into rectangles, and wrap them around the babe. Finally, she took the large contraption of a safety pin to secure it in place.

"This is the most important part," she said, as Jacob leaned closer. She could feel his breath on her neck. It made her unsteady, though it was not altogether unwelcome.

"It's important that the safety pin is fastened on the outside of the cloth, so that it can't poke the baby. That way, it is also out of the babe's reach…"

"So that he can't poke himself?" Jacob added with a hearty chuckle.

"Indeed!" she said with a giggle. As she wrapped the baby back up in his swaddling clothes, he slowly opened sleepy eyes and smiled up at her.

"Well, good afternoon, little one!" she said with a kiss on the forehead.

She noticed his legs were getting long enough to poke out the bottom of the swaddling blanket. He had recently started trying to crawl, and she knew that soon he would need different clothes. But today, he could still be bundled up, warm and safe in her arms.

"He's getting so big," she said as she cradled him close to her chest and looked back at Jacob. "Maybe he'll be big like his Paw," she said before she thought better of it.

Her heart sank at the reminder that they had no idea who his parents were. She wondered how that affected Jacob, as she looked slowly up at him with an embarrassed smile. Jacob looked back at her with wide eyes, and she could tell he felt awkward at the mention of him as the baby's father.

Louise hurried to her feet, equally embarrassed for the conversation she'd brought on.

"Mind if I hand him off to you while I finish dinner?"

"O' course," Jacob said quickly, and she could tell that he was eager to change the subject.

She handed the baby to Jacob, who settled into the rocking chair, and she hurried off to check on the stew.

She leaned over the wood-burning stove, grateful that the ranch afforded her such comforts. It was certainly an easier way to cook than the hearth back in Clinton. The large and black cast-iron box heaved and hissed from the heat emanating out of it. It wasn't quite as lovely as an open hearth, but it was a significantly easier way to cook.

A marriage of convenience is very convenient indeed.

But was it really *just* a marriage of convenience? Jacob had come around so often the last few days, almost as if he were interested in not just the cooking, but in *her.*

Never mind that now. I best focus on getting dinner on the table.

She threw a bit of salt and pepper into the boiling pot and took a deep whiff of the fresh concoction. The warm autumn vegetables were softening, evidenced by the delectable aroma now filling the log cabin.

Louise loved cooking. It came naturally to her, soothed her even, and it was an easy time to get lost in her own thoughts. As she stirred the bubbling stew, the scent drifted up to her nose and her mind wondered about what could be.

Would the mother, who had dropped him on the doorstep, turn up one day demanding her child back? Then again, what type of parents would abandon their child on a stranger's doorstep? She shuddered to think of the baby returning to such thoughtless parents.

Not over my dead body, Louise thought fiercely.

The bigger obstacle, perhaps, was the question of whether Jacob would be willing to keep the child—to adopt it as his own. As talkative as Louise tended to be, she was scared to bring it up, so she avoided the topic altogether. She was afraid that if she pushed her husband for such a promise, the answer would be no.

Instead, she carried on dutifully each day, handling all the chores related to the baby and hoping that Jacob assumed they would keep him. Perhaps they could become a real family. He certainly had not said otherwise, and this gave her hope.

He didn't talk about the baby much, unless to mention that he was asking around in town to see who it belonged to.

He belongs to me, Louise said to herself. *He belongs here, safe and sound on the ranch.* Oh, if only Jacob could see it!

As it was time to make the fresh bread, she turned to get flour from out of the cupboard. What she saw when she stood up nearly took her breath away.

Louise couldn't believe her eyes. Jacob was sitting in the rocking chair, a vision of fatherly love. He looked so natural as he cradled the baby in his arms. While one arm held the baby's body, another arm gently cradled his head—just as Louise had taught him to do on several occasions. Only this time, he had gotten it right.

It wasn't the way he held the baby that struck Louise, so much as the gentle look in his eyes. In her short time as a governess and nursemaid, Louise had seen many a father hold babies inattentively, with eyes fixed on a paper or a parlor guest. This was different. As Jacob peered down at the wee babe, he peered tenderly into the baby's eyes, as if he were invested in his soul.

Where on earth is this coming from? Who is this man and what has he done with my actual husband, Jacob Montgomery?

She knew from the last couple of weeks that Jacob was a good man, but she had never thought him to be a tender one, too. She continued to stare at the strange sight with a mix of wonder and hope.

She watched as the tall giant of a man humbled his large frame to lean over the babe. His shoulder length brown hair was held back by the baby's hand upon his face.

The restrained hair revealed a chiseled jaw. Though his chin was still covered by a scraggly beard, it protruded almost gracefully above his neck, making his jaw more pronounced.

Louise wondered what he might look like if only he took the time to trim his hair and beard. She chuckled silently, knowing that it was too much to ask, but even still, she could tell that he was handsome beneath all that rugged wildness.

Her heart spun with the acknowledgement, and she took a deep sigh. She had to be careful—lest she get disappointed all over again.

"Steady," she whispered to herself with her hand on her heart.

"What's that?" Jacob asked, hearing her misstep.

"It's ready," she recovered. "Dinner's ready! Best eat it while it's hot."

Jacob stood to place the baby in his cradle before walking slowly to the table, his muscles rippling under his tight sleeves once more.

Can't that man find a shirt that fits? Some of us are trying to mind our chores!

Flustered, Louise turned to fan herself over the stew. Whether the heat came from the stove or Jacob, she couldn't be sure, but of one thing she was certain. This new realization would not be altogether *convenient*.

Chapter Eleven

Jacob walked up the hill from the ranch to his cabin home, exhausted from his morning toil. He had worked all morning to break a new colt. With any luck, he'd have it done soon, but the young stud had taken all the energy out of Jacob. He trudged through autumn leaves up the slope, hoping for something to eat.

The cool October weather had grown colder over the last two weeks since his bride's arrival, proving that winter was drawing near. He enjoyed the bright fall colors that fell to the ground, but he was equally eager for the warm fire inside.

As he took an eager breath of air, he was pleased to smell the scent of baking bread floating down from the house. It was too early for dinner, but perhaps the fresh bread that Miss Louise Parker made each day would be ready soon.

Mrs. Louise Montgomery, actually, he corrected himself. *Not Miss Parker. Maybe I should start callin' her Louise aloud. I am married to the girl, after all. Besides, she already calls me Jacob freely—which I don't mind at all.*

*H*e smiled as he considered the exciting young woman cooking bread in his home. While she wasn't as mild-mannered as he might like, she amused and excited him. He had grown to really enjoy her company.

The cooking isn't half bad either, he thought as his stomach roared inside of him.

While supper was often small leftovers before bed, the midday meal was a hearty, delicious event that he always looked forward to—especially now that his young wife was the one doing the cooking.

For someone so tiny, she sure can cook a big meal!

He wasn't sure what was better looking—her or the food—but he looked forward to both and he had been coming home earlier each day for their one o'clock dinner.

The closer he got to the house, the stronger the scent of the bread was, until he could take it no longer. Eager for the delicious meal, he was ready to fling open the door like a warrior storming a castle.

At the last moment, he thought better of it, as he remembered the baby might be sleeping. Things with Louise had been much more pleasant lately, but nothing irritated her more than when he accidentally woke up the babe. He slowly pushed open the heavy pine door and looked toward the kitchen.

He didn't see Louise or the baby in the house and figured they must be playing out back by the garden. He'd pay them a visit after he had a bite to eat.

He set his gaze on the single-room cabin that looked so different than it had a couple weeks ago. The evidence of a woman's touch was everywhere.

The once dusty home was now well-swept and organized. Windows that were once empty now held a pair of sky-blue curtains. Across from the kitchen, next to the large four-post bed, stood a large folding screen that blocked off the room from the bathtub. Louise could dress and bathe behind it but left it up all the time. He could tell that it pleased her to have her own private space, as small as it might be.

That must be where they are now.

Jacob could hear a woman's song and child's laughter outside the back door that led to the garden. Eager to get outside to his Louise and the baby, he tried to step around the folding panel that blocked his path. He walked eagerly toward the door, hoping to see the woman and babe in their natural habitat, playing and laughing together outside. But what he saw when he walked to the edge of the folded screen froze him in his tracks.

To his shock, Louise was sitting in the bathtub with her back to him, a vision of bubbles and beauty. Frozen in both fear and awe, the hunger in his stomach dissipated as his eyes drank her in. The dainty curve of her bare shoulders was elegant and looked porcelain in their perfection. His eyes followed the curve of her neck down the line of her back, until the water hit her waist. The water below held secrets not accessible to him, and he averted his gaze with haste.

In the span of a split second, he'd seen more of a woman than he'd seen his whole life, and he felt embarrassed for them both. Wife or not, he knew his gaze was uninvited, and he was determined to be a man of honor. He thought of how he might escape without being seen, so as to spare them both the embarrassment.

Please Lord, get me out of this situation.

The only one who could possibly give him away was the small orange cat sitting next to the clawfoot tub. She sat with her back to him, the same as her mistress, as she licked her paws. Neither seemed to notice him yet.

Jacob raised his right foot carefully and set it behind him, as slowly as he could manage. A wave of relief came over him when the floorboards did not give him away. He held his breath and took another step back.

This time, however, the old wooden boards were much less forgiving. The creak of the old pine gave him away. Minnie turned with a hiss and Louise shrieked a scream that froze him dead in his tracks.

"What are you doing here!"

Jacob covered his eyes and held out his other arm to shield Louise from his gaze.

"I.... I'm sorry!" he stuttered, stunned.

He couldn't see anything, but he heard water slosh out of the tub, as the sound of small feet pattered quickly to the other side of the room.

"Get out!"

Humiliated, he turned and tried to exit the house with his eyes closed and walked into a beam that held up the wall next the kitchen.

Dazed, he reached for the door and was met by a kind voice.

"Easy there, Mr. Montgomery! Is everything okay? I was out back in the garden with the baby when I heard a mighty scream."

He opened his eyes to see George's daughter, Sarah. The slight girl of sixteen was a mess of free-flowing, shaggy brown hair and a sincere face. She stood at the door with a kind smile and a baby on her hip.

"'Scuse me," Jacob said, as he darted out the door.

"It's all right, sir," Sarah called behind him. "I will help Mrs. Montgomery. I'll holler to ya as soon as it's safe to come in."

Jacob took off down the hill and paced back and forth like a prisoner awaiting execution.

I've gone and done it again. I scared off another perfectly good woman.

Memories of rejection flooded his brain as he stormed across the pasture, furious with himself.

He kicked himself for being so thoughtless and the shame was almost more than he could bear.

"What an oaf," he could almost hear Jessie say. The cold voice of his last betrothed shot an awful heat through him that started in his face and spread to his legs.

The urge to flee to the ranch until nightfall was strong but something kept him there. Perhaps it was the hunger in his stomach or perhaps it was a small voice saying, *Peace, be still.*

***

At long last, Sarah stuck her head out of the door of the log cabin and invited him back in.

"Dinner's ready, Mr. Montgomery!" she called with a cheerful smile.

He walked warily through the door, unsure of what he would find.

Louise looked cool and pristine, sitting at one end of the long table like a queen admitting the company of a commoner. Though she appeared aloof, perhaps in defense of her honor, he was relieved to not find her angry. Minnie, on the other hand, sat in Louise's lap and mewed in an irritated way when Jacob walked up to the table.

They ate a polite but quiet dinner. Jacob spent the meal looking mostly at his food.

Aside from the frustrations of the first day and his accidental intrusion into her bathing, she wasn't much the yelling sort.

Indeed, while Jessie had been prone to fits of rage and yelling that made Jacob take off for the hills, Louise wasn't that way at all.

He only hoped that he hadn't messed it up for good with this current embarrassment.

He had started to feel a heat boil up inside of him at the thought of her, and today's accidental viewing just exacerbated his longing. His heart pulled in the direction of the feisty but warm young woman, and he was drawn to her.

He could not bring himself to look in her eyes from the embarrassment of that afternoon—afraid of what he might find there.

What must she think of me? Have I lost all honor in her eyes?

As he ate the leftover stew and fresh bread in front of him, he took comfort in the delicious warm meal. Remembering the freshly churned butter that Louise had made the day before, he allowed himself to look up briefly to scan the long farm table for the homemade spread, and then looked quickly down again.

As he reached out for the butter, their hands accidentally touched. Startled, he looked up and met surprised, round eyes, as large and warm as a fresh blueberry pie. The sweet intensity of her gaze triggered something deep inside of him. His heart turned in his chest and started to beat wildly. He could not let her see the passion in his eyes. He had to get out of there.

"Pardon me," he said, as he rose from the table. "I best be gettin' back to the ranch. Still a few good hours to work before the sun sets this evenin'."

Jacob grabbed his Stetson hat, sitting in the chair by the door. Without another word, he sprinted out the door, longing for the oasis of his ranch and leaving the embarrassing scene behind him. What he could not manage to leave, however, was a fierce and boiling heat brought out by one thought only… *Louise.*

Chapter Twelve

Louise held onto the side of her seat as the old wagon made its way down the hill toward the ranch. With her free hand, she held the sleeping baby in her arms. How he snoozed on such a bumpy ride, she had no clue.

"What's your secret, little one? How do you sleep so peacefully while the rest of the world clambers about?"

She gazed down into his gentle face, which was blissfully unaware of the turmoil swirling in her heart.

The last couple of days had been fearfully awkward between her and Jacob. She could tell that he was avoiding her at all costs. The truth was, she had started avoiding him, too. Louise had no idea what to say to him. It had become much easier to not cross paths than to risk the conversation that neither of them wanted to have.

While Jacob accidentally walking in on her might have been embarrassing, it wasn't half as bad as the silent game of avoidance they were both playing.

She had been quite surprised when Jacob had asked her to come help him at the ranch that day. She'd been a ball of nerves ever since George came to pick her up mid-morning with the wagon.

The wagon went over a tree root in the small dirt road, jolting Louise into the air.

"Oh my, George!" she declared as she clung to the baby and drew him closer to her chest.

"Sorry about that, ma'am," the friendly ranch hand replied. "These scarcely tread dirt roads can be a might dangerous at times. At least you didn't get thrown!" he said with a chuckle. "It's happened more than once to me!"

"No kidding!" she said, settling back into her seat with a soft laugh.

"It'll be just a couple minutes, Miss Louise," George encouraged.

She smiled gratefully at George, who turned back to drive the rig onward. Louise always felt safe with George and his wife—two of the kindest folks she'd met this side of the Mississippi.

Now on a smoother patch of mountain road, Louise allowed her attention to drift to the beautiful land around her. Green grass was rare this high up in the mountains, especially in the desert land of Nevada. She was grateful for the small trickling stream that fed their land, allowing it to nourish small patches of wildflowers among the otherwise arid ground.

She gazed at the meager brook, pleased that at least some small sprinkling of water fed their land.

So, there was no private place to bathe in the mountains, she wondered with a chuckle of embarrassment as her cheeks blushed afresh. Would they ever move on from that embarrassing day?

"Here you are, ma'am," proclaimed George, as the small rig came to a sudden stop. "Told ya it wouldn't take long!"

George held out his hand and assisted Louise as she stepped down from the wagon. Before she had a chance to look around, there was Jacob, as if he had come out of nowhere.

"Right this way," he said quickly, as he turned toward the large red barn.

"What are we doing?" Louise asked anxiously. She was equal parts excited to see the horses and nervous to talk to Jacob.

"We're gonna be trimming horse hooves," Jacob called over his shoulder.

"Trimming horse hooves?" she asked, unsure. "Won't that hurt?"

"What?" Jacob asked, stopping cold in his tracks. He laughed with his eyebrows raised in surprise, turning to face Louise.

"We aren't cuttin' their *feet,* just their hooves. It's kinda like our nails here. They need to be trimmed so that they don't split, crack, or hurt the horses."

A lump caught in Louise's throat, and she looked up at Jacob, realizing that this was the first time he had looked her in the eyes since their awkward encounter.

"I see," she said carefully, feeling vulnerable as a mouse caught by a cat.

"Tell you what," George cut in, "Why don't you let me take the baby so that you two can focus on the ... um... *horses?*"

Louise blushed as she handed over the still sleeping babe to George. She wondered what would happen, indeed, if any words passed between them at all—once they were left alone.

"You don't have to do that," Louise insisted, but it was too late.

"Now y'all don't worry about a thing, ya here?" George said with a grin. "I'm going to take the baby just over yonder to meet the chickens. Y'all take your time. I'm sure you have a lot to work on, with the horses, I mean."

George walked off with a chuckle, leaving Louise to turn back to Jacob with a blush rising to her cheeks.

"Best get started," Jacob murmured. Motioning for Louise to join him, he turned and continued to the barn.

Louise walked beside him quietly, a ball of nerves. What was she supposed to say to the first man who had ever seen her without being fully clothed?

What must he think of her? Did he think perhaps that she had lured him there purposefully to get a hold on him? No, that would be silly. They *were* married. But they'd certainly never had relations and she didn't want him to think her forward, or worse yet, a loose woman.

She shivered at the very thought of the phrase. She had taken care, ever since she was just a girl, to make sure that her honor and reputation were intact.

She knew growing up with the Cankers that she had very little to her name and little to offer in marriage, other than her chastity and honor. That was something that no one could take from her. Wedding vows or not, that would be the one thing that was still her choice to surrender.

Another thought lingered in the recesses of her mind, brought on by years of insults at the hands of the Cankers. What if he simply found her to be ugly? What if that was why he stayed gone these past two days? The sting of that possible rejection was enough to keep her quiet.

She knew that it really had been just an accident. Jacob would never have humiliated her like that on purpose. She could probably move past it—if only she knew that Jacob didn't think less of her.

She was painfully aware that a conversation needed to take place, but she dreaded it. That was the conversation she had taken great pains to avoid the last two days.

She looked down at the dirt and hay covering the floor of the large red barn. A small mouse scurried in and out of a horse stall, virtually unseen, and she wished that she could trade places with it.

***

Jacob was kind as he explained, in a surprising amount of detail, how to trim the horse's hooves. She could tell that he was in his element here, and his sudden talkativeness helped to distract Louise from the other conversation she was dreading.

"This is the wall of the hoof," Jacob said, as he straddled a silvery horse's back right leg. He bent over, holding the foot aloft in his hands. The horse seemed oddly relaxed, as if he knew that his hoof was safe in the rancher's capable hands.

"This here hoof grows about half an inch every month, come rain or shine. If we don't cut off enough, it's liable to crack and hurt old Gus here."

The horse huffed and swished his tail, as if to agree, and it made Louise smile.

"Then again," Jacob continued, "if we cut off *too* much, his foot will grow a might sore and be prone to infection."

"You do it so carefully. I can tell that he trusts you," Louise replied, impressed with his knowledge of the steeds in his care.

When Jacob was done explaining the process to Louise, he handed her a pair of iron nippers. He held the horse's foot for her while she tried her hand at trimming the hooves.

Louise was careful to not nick the tender inside of the horse's foot. She worked diligently, but she could tell she wasn't taking quite enough off. She looked up at Jacob as if to say sorry, but her voice caught in her throat when she saw his warm, brown eyes looking down at her.

"Louise," Jacob said slowly, "I'm, um... I'm sorry about your bath the other day."

"Sorry about my bath!" She looked up in a start. "What on earth is that supposed to mean?"

"I didn't want to see you in the bath," he stuttered clumsily.

Didn't want to... The words hung in the air awkwardly.

"Well—not that I wouldn't *want* to or... or that I *did* want to... just... that I didn't m-mean to."

"Anyway," he continued, "I didn't see anything, other than your shoulders and back."

"Of course," she said quickly. "It's all right. I think I better go check on the baby."

She walked quickly out of the barn, embarrassed anew. Her heart pounded and her brain buzzed. She was eager to get back to the baby, back to the log cabin, and back to Minnie—any excuse to avoid Jacob Montgomery.

***

Once back in the old log cabin, Louise busied herself making dinner, grateful that she had her work to keep her busy. Her chores proved her value and secured her place in a marriage where she was growing more suspicious that her husband wasn't interested in her.

That's fine with me, she thought, as she stirred the potato soup.

She could cook. She could make a home. She could raise a child and be safe in the beautiful Nevada mountains, even if she didn't get the romance her heart longed for.

She turned from her work when she heard the baby cry. Minnie, whose paws were on the cradle, turned with a look of surprise. Her ever-curious friend had accidentally rocked the cradle and woken him up.

"Minnie, did you wake the babe, you silly kitty?"

Minnie ran over to Louise and mewed as she rubbed up against her legs. She begged to be pet while the baby cried in the background.

"It's all right. I got him," Jacob said, as he lifted the small babe.

"Oh! Thank you, but he usually needs..."

Louise's voice trailed off as she realized that the baby had stopped crying. Jacob gently rocked the babe in his arms and Louise lifted her eyebrows in surprise to see that Jacob had calmed him down.

Louise went back to the kitchen to spoon up the soup into clean, metal bowls. She glanced over her shoulder at Jacob, who sat by the fire with the baby's head on his shoulder. Was he asleep? She couldn't believe it.

"Dinner's on the table," she said in a hushed tone, as she carried their bowls of soup to the fresh bread and ham hock waiting on the table.

She watched her husband carefully set the baby back in his cradle before he came to the large table. She shook her head in disbelief.

As they sat quietly, she wondered how he'd learned to be so good with the baby. Louise couldn't help but wonder how he would be with babies of their own.

She turned her attention to the ham hock on the table, sliced some for their soups, and ate quietly, enjoying the work of her hands.

"Mmmm... This is good," Jacob said under his breath as he ate. His voice was low and warm, like fresh honey off the comb. It made Louise's stomach tickle.

"Good job putting the little one to sleep," she said, trying to turn her attention away from the feeling in her belly.

"Thanks," he replied, with a spoonful of potato soup in his mouth.

His table manners were still lacking but that was to be expected of a man who grew up without a mother. Louise wondered how hard that must have been for him, and her heart swelled in compassion.

She was distracted by a tickly feeling at her ankle and looked down to see Minnie mewing and begging for food. She gave her a small piece of bread to satisfy her. Then, the cat strode away to the other side of the table.

Why on earth would Minnie go over there? She wasn't likely to find much help on that side, Louise chuckled to herself.

Without saying a word, Jacob tore off a piece of ham and gave it to the little orange cat. Louise dropped her mouth in shock.

Now he's feeding the cat, too?

Since when did he give a lick about Minnie?

As Jacob dug into his soup ravenously, like Esau when he had been hungry enough to give away his birthright, she stared in wonder and downright confusion at him. Questions that she couldn't answer swirled through her mind.

What sort of man was this? Was he fierce or tender? Mountain man or gentlemen? Or was he something altogether different? What sort of man was this that could tame a wild horse and soothe a crying babe, and what was this feeling growing inside of her that she couldn't quite name?

Chapter Thirteen

"Got any more o' those, George?" Jacob asked, as he hammered another nail into the fence of the horse pasture.

"Here you go," answered George. He handed Jacob a handful of nails and then propped up the fence while Jacob hammered away.

"How's Louise settling in?" George asked, pausing. "For what it's worth, Pop would'a loved her."

That might be true, but Pop isn't here, Jacob thought as he looked up from his work and gazed at the sprawling acres of ripe ranch land that Pop used to work. Jacob looked farther up to the mountaintop to where his parents' graves laid. His heart sank when he realized it had been too long since he last visited.

"She's doing just fine, George. But that reminds me... I haven't been to see Pop lately," Jacob confessed to his friend.

"Well, why not?"

"Don't rightly know. Just busy, I guess."

The truth was that his thoughts of late had been solely fixed on Louise. He was both bewildered and bewitched by her. She was maddening at times—the way she talked incessantly and disagreed with him passionately—but her fieriness also piqued his interest. Then there was her elegance and her gentle warmth that drew him to her like a moth to a flame.

"*Ow!*" Jacob cried out, looking down at his hand now pulsating in pain. He'd failed to pay attention to the task before him and his left thumb bore the brunt of the consequence.

"Did you just hit yer thumb with the hammer? Where's your head today, Jacob?"

"I'm fine," Jacob retorted gruffly. "Hand me another nail and let's get this finished."

"No way. That looks just awful. Go home and put somethin' cold on it."

Jacob tried stubbornly to move his thumb but winced in pain.

"Like I said, you've no business holding a hammer today. Why don't you go up to the mountain and visit your Pop? Maybe you could take Louise with you, introduce her to both of your parents' graves… and to you, for that matter."

"Not a good idea."

"Whataya mean?"

"You know my history with women, George."

"You mean, *lack of history?* Except for Jessie, that is."

"Exactly. Best to keep things simple. No reason to make a mess of it all. No point to it."

"No point to it? Now, you listen here, friend, and you listen good. I knew your Pop well. What he wanted more than anything in the world was for you to be happy with a family of your own. What's more—I recall you promisin' him that you'd do just that. If you wanna honor Pop, you'll do this and give your marriage a fighting chance."

***

When Jacob walked into his home, he was determined to take George's advice, but when he saw Louise, his heart skipped a beat and distracted him.

Jacob watched as his wife spun merrily around the kitchen, truly at home. Her curious orange cat jumped at Louise's skirts as if trying to catch a fly. He could tell that both pet and owner had finally come into their own here, and he wondered how Louise would take new information about his past.

"You're home early for dinner," Louise said with a laugh. "I got fresh bread by the stove if you like."

She stopped in her tracks when she caught a glimpse of his thumb, now swollen to nearly twice its original size.

"Jacob! What happened?"

"I hit my thumb with a hammer. Pay it no mind. I'm fine."

Louise hurried about the kitchen looking for something to help his hand. He admitted to himself that he enjoyed her fussing over him. She grabbed some cold venison from the ice box and placed it on his thumb, looking down at him with worried eyes.

"Keep this on there for about thirty minutes. It'll keep the swelling down."

The concern in her eyes emanated a warmth that melted Jacob's heart and he could've kissed her for it.

George is right. Pop would've loved her.

It was time to make good on his promise to his father.

"Louise," Jacob began unsteadily, "I'd like to take you somewhere today—somewhere important to me. How soon can you and the baby be ready to go?"

***

Jacob was surprised, as he traveled up the mountain with his family in tow, that Louise had agreed to go silently—not daring to bombard him with a million questions about where they were going.

He felt his nerves start to turn in his belly. Was this a mistake? He hadn't told her where they were going yet, so it wasn't too late to change course.

He could take her to town, take her to church, take her anywhere but his most private spot. What was he thinking?

"If you really want to honor Pop," George's words flashed through his head, and he remembered why he was doing this. He steadied his nerves, determined to honor his father.

They rode uphill into cloudy skies that mirrored the confusion present in his heart. He took a deep breath and peered at the woman sitting next to him.

Louise was a picture of grace in a blue cotton dress that matched her eyes. She held the baby close to her and wrapped her shawl around him to protect him from the wind.

Jacob was in awe of her beauty, as well as how natural she was with the child. Perhaps one day he would have the courage to tell her.

He heard an eagle's call in the distance and looked up to see it flying above the hilltop where they were headed, as if it was beckoning him onward. He turned his attention back to the path in front of him and lifted the reins to urge the horses forward.

***

"Here we are," said Jacob as he brought the wagon to a halt at last.

"And where might that be?" asked a curious Louise. He could tell by the furrowed brow on her forehead that she was somewhat confused.

"I wanted to show you the place I come sometimes to think. It's my parents' graves."

He helped Louise down from the wagon and motioned toward the granite headstones labeled, "Frederick and Rebecca Montgomery," resting under a giant, flowering cactus. The thick leaf-like spines sprouting out of it almost shaded the headstones as the sun peeked out around them.

Past the hill, the clouds floated away and opened up to blue sky, and sunshine that lit up the valley below. The peaceful scene filled Jacob's heart with hope, and he turned back to Louise to gauge her reaction.

"Oh!" said his wife softly. "It's lovely. I mean, is it okay to say that it's lovely?"

She blushed as if embarrassed by her response, and Jacob chuckled softly.

"It certainly is. It's why Pop buried Mom up here, and why he wanted to be buried beside her. This is where he would bring her on picnics when they were courting."

Jacob was surprised that he was so comfortable talking to her today. He wasn't sure if it was the surroundings or the gentle, welcoming look in her eyes that urged him to continue.

"It's where they fell in love. He came every day after her death. And it's where I feel most at home... Not that I don't feel at home in the cabin..." Jacob trailed off, his cheeks flushing.

"No," Louise comforted him as she set her hand on his shoulder. "It makes sense, and it is lovely here. It's no wonder he brought her here to fall in love. Thank you for bringing me."

She gently took the baby back into her arms and sat near the cactus, next to the graves. Jacob caught his breath at the lovely site. She fit right in. A picture of peace and serenity.

Jacob sat next to her on a smooth rock and had the strangest sensation. As he gazed into her gentle eyes, he realized that he was falling in love with her, too—just like his Pop.

His heart beat fast like the hooves of a wild stallion as it pounded the earth. He had the sudden urge to kiss her, to grab her and make her his, but something stopped him short.

I'm not worthy of her. The thought fell on him like a ton of bricks.

He looked down in the dirt, tracing dark thoughts, when Louise's lovely voice broke through the noise in his brain.

"Tell me more."

"What do you mean?"

"Tell me more about yourself, Jacob. I want to know more."

He couldn't deny her. For a reason he didn't understand, it suddenly felt natural to open up.

He told her what it was like growing up without a mother, and how his father had been his only confidante. He told her how the two did everything together—how Pop was his truest friend. He told her how crushed he had been when he'd passed from a heart attack, and how he wasn't sure the guilt would ever leave.

"But why?" asked the lovely girl sitting at his side. "Why would you feel guilty? It's not your fault his heart gave out."

Jacob released a heavy sigh. It was time that she knew the monster that he really was.

"I knew that Pop's heart was weak."

"What do you mean?" Louise asked.

"The doctor told Pop that his heart would give out if he kept working as hard as he was. The doc told him not to ride anymore but I couldn't make him stop. There was so much work to do on the ranch, and Pop was determined to make the ranch a success. If I had made him stop, if I had stood my ground, Pop would still be alive today."

Jacob's voice started to crack, and he looked away. He wouldn't cry in front of the poor girl. He might have been too weak to save Pop, but he wouldn't show her his weakness. He'd be strong for her.

Then, he felt the warm touch of her hand on his, and he turned his attention to the sweetest blue eyes he'd ever seen.

"Jacob," Louise began gently, "it's not your fault."

"It's kind of you to say so, but…"

"No, Jacob," she insisted. "You are the strongest man I know, but you can't stop the hand of time. If the Lord decided it was time to call your Pop home, there's not a thing in the world you coulda done to stop it."

She moved her hand up to his cheek. He tried to wish his beard away so that he could feel her hand closer on his skin.

"It's not your fault," she continued. "You've got to stop beating yourself up about it. Well, you've just got to."

She was close enough to smell, close enough to kiss, and he let his senses drink her in. She smelled like fresh bread and honeysuckle, and he longed to make her his. He slowly leaned toward her as his heart picked up speed.

Suddenly, the baby in her lap started to cry and they both looked down in a start. Louise lifted the child from her lap to her shoulder and leaned back against the tree as she patted his back.

Jacob turned away and looked out over the valley, his heart still pounding in his chest. What was he thinking? No doubt the girl must've been relieved that the baby interrupted them. He knew he'd better pull it together before he did something he couldn't take back.

"He's okay now," Louise said as she set the baby down. "Just had a bit of gas in his tummy."

Jacob turned back to her, relieved for the change of subject.

"Poor thing has been doing a heckuva job getting by on cow's milk," Jacob said. "But he's keeping it down and starting to gain weight. You've seen to that. He's lucky to have you."

"Why, Jacob Montgomery," Louise said with a giggle. "Did you just give a compliment?"

"I compliment you plenty."

"Cooking compliments don't count," she said, ribbing him with a wink.

"Ah well, there you have it. That's what I wasn't clear on," Jacob answered in kind as the two laughed heartily. "I thought for sure it was the cooking compliments girls wanted. Next time, I'll just tell you how lovely you are."

Jacob stopped suddenly when he realized what he'd said. Now he'd really messed up. How would she respond now that he'd showed his cards? He felt vulnerable, like a wolf pup rolled over on its back, belly in the air. He didn't like it. Not one bit.

Louise paused and smiled ever so slightly, an innocent blush on her face.

"You know, I don't think you're the cold mountain man that the townsfolk say you are. I think they got you wrong."

"I wouldn't be so sure," Jacob said coolly, trying to gather his wits about him.

"What happened with you and the people in that little town anyway?"

The uneasiness started to grow in his belly, and he felt too exposed. He wished that she'd just leave well enough alone.

"Nothin' much to tell, Louise. What's for supper tonight?"

"Why are you changing the subject?" Louise asked. "Whatever it is, you can tell me."

What did she want him to say? That the whole town saw Jessie run out on him when she went to the train station? That some laughed and murmured about the way he chased after her, begging her to stay? Jacob wouldn't put either of them through the pain or embarrassment of that story, and he wasn't about to relive it.

The walls that Jacob had let down grew back instantly, like molten lava cooling to stone. He'd clearly made a mistake opening up to her and had quite nearly paid the price.

Best to keep it simple, he reminded himself.

"Nothin' to tell. I just like keepin' to myself. Some folks can't handle that."

He stood up and walked back to the wagon as a breeze blew through and brought a chill in the air.

"Best be gettin' back for dinner. 'Sides, my thumb is better, and I've got more to do on the ranch this afternoon."

Jacob hopped into the wagon and grabbed the reins, as Louise walked over to him looking confused, if not a bit hurt.

He didn't want to hurt the girl, but he knew that a slight sting now was better for them both than a heartbreak later.

Chapter Fourteen

The afternoon sun trickled through the cabin window, a welcome warmth now that winter had arrived. Soft rays of sunlight fell on the white fireside rug that held the sleeping baby.

Louise watched from the kitchen as he slept soundly, and Minnie crept curiously toward him. She had given Minnie more opportunities to be around the baby little by little over the last couple of months, and it came as no surprise that her furry best friend was doing well with him.

Now that the baby was about three months old, he could lift his head and flip over onto his stomach. The happy boy loved to lay on his tummy and reach for the cat while she pranced and purred in front of him. When he slept, Minnie would walk around, inspecting him curiously, like she did just now. Sometimes, she would even nap beside him.

Louise walked over to her beloved feline friend and scratched her lovingly behind the ears. Minnie purred and rubbed her head deeply into Louise's palm, embracing the ear scratching. Then, she resumed her spot on the rug where she stretched and warmed herself by the fire.

Louise took a moment to admire the adorable pair. She wished that she could sit and watch them all day, but she had to prepare the baby's bath. She boiled some water that she'd fetched from the creek to make sure that it was rid of any bacteria. Then, she poured it into a large basin to cool and waited for the baby to awake. A few minutes later, she heard a soft cooing by the fire, as the babe started to stir.

"Hello, little one," she said as she gathered him into her arms. "It's time for your bath."

Eager arms reached up for her face as she prepared him for his bath.

Every night for the last two months, she'd prayed a silent prayer that whoever dropped him on their porch would never return. So far, nobody had come around to claim him, and Jacob hadn't had any luck finding out about him from the townsfolk. Each day that passed made her feel more grateful and more certain that he wouldn't be taken from her. It was high time that they named him.

As Louise set the baby down in the warm water, she propped him up with one hand behind his back and got to work bathing him. She mused about what they might name him and laughed at the thought of him running the ranch one day and still being called "little one".

"Now, that won't do," she chuckled, as she gently poured water over his hair. "But what will we call you?"

Louise thought about the different men that she knew and different names she could give the growing babe. She sighed, as she realized that there were not many men she trusted, nor that she wanted to honor—least of all Paw Canker. She was at a bit of a loss until a new idea struck her.

What if she named him after Jacob's father, Fred?

"Frederick Montgomery, now that's a nice name," she said, as she watched the baby splashing in the water.

"What do you think, Fred?"

The soapy babe looked up at Louise with a giggle and splashed the water her way. Louise laughed heartily, as she picked up and dried off the wet baby.

"Well, that settles it. We'll call you Fred, as long as Jacob likes it."

And why wouldn't he? The longer that the baby was with them, the more that it felt like he was their child, and the more it felt like they were a family—or at least that they could become one.

There was no denying the look of affection in Jacob's eyes when he held the baby, which happened daily now. What better way to honor him, and perhaps secure the baby's future with them, than to give him the name of Jacob's late father?

Louise lifted the newly named boy and spun him about the room as her heart surged with excitement.

"Come on, Fred. We gotta get you dressed. Your papa will be home soon."

***

Louise could barely contain her excitement as she prepared their evening supper. She gathered the leftovers from dinner that day and added fresh rolls and homemade butter.

She set them on the table before preparing a kettle of tea on the iron stove. A bag of sugar left over from a trip to town the week before would make an excellent addition to the fresh brew. She mixed the sweet substance into the warm tea and set it in the ice box to cool.

Sweet tea was Jacob's favorite. It would do nicely as a treat to celebrate the baby's name. She hurried to set the table and dressed Fred in a new frock she'd recently made. Last of all, she put on her soft blue dress that she saved for special occasions. She had noticed Jacob eyeing her in it. She wanted everything to be just so for this special occasion.

When Jacob walked through the door, the smiling faces of his family were waiting for him at the table.

"Welcome home!" said Louise in an excited declaration. The cat at her ankles jumped a mile high from the loud, high-pitched tone. The baby on her hip bounced and laughed at his friend. The merry trio awaited Jacob's response.

"Hello," said Jacob, with an oblivious yawn as he passed them by.

To Louise's disappointment, Jacob walked away from them to the fireside, without noticing the special spread on the table or his well-dressed family. He walked over to the fireplace, kicked off his boots, and sat in the rocking chair. He held out his feet and warmed them by the fire without so much as a look over his shoulder to Louise or the baby.

"Dinner's ready," said Louise, standing her ground, ready to be acknowledged.

"Course," said Jacob as he arched his back and leaned into the deep rocking chair. "I could use about five minutes of shut eye if ya don't mind."

"What's wrong with you?" Louise asked, half-concerned and a half-irritated at her husband.

"It'll be all right, I reckon. I had a rough mornin' with a couple of new colts that aren't keen to be broken," he said with a weary sigh. "I just need a minute to rest my bones."

"Actually, I had something I wanted to talk to you about," Louise said impatiently. Sure, Jacob was tired, perhaps even a bit grumpy, but when he heard the good news, it would certainly put him in better sorts.

"Everything okay?" he asked over his shoulder, as if picking up on the tension in her voice, but he didn't bother to turn around.

"No," Louise laughed, as she poured Jacob a mug of cold tea from the icebox. "Everything is fine. Better than fine, even! I've come up with a name for the baby and you're gonna love it, I reckon!"

Louise watched as the man with his back to her in the rocking chair tensed. He didn't say anything, but she could tell by the tension in his shoulders and hands that grasped the chair that he didn't yet understand the good news. If he would just turn to see her special dress or the lovely feast, then he would realize the celebration. She rushed on to reassure him.

"Well, I was just thinking while I was bathing the baby today, that we've had him for a couple months now and we can't just call him 'baby' forever. Anyhow, it stands to reason that the poor thing needs a name, and well, what better name to give him than Fred? Isn't it just perfect?"

Jacob stood from the rocking chair, still facing the fire without a word. For what felt like years to Louise, Jacob stood there, a pillar of silence. Finally, he turned to face her with a look of deep pain in his eyes. He looked like he had just taken a swift kick to the gut.

"What makes you think that I would give my father's name to a stranger's baby?" Jacob spoke in a hushed tone but the message hit Louise louder than a grizzly bear's roar.

The words hung in the cold winter air like an icicle refusing to fall.

"A stranger's baby." Not his. Not hers. Certainly not *theirs.*

Louise's heart sank as she turned away from Jacob, devastated. She set his cup of tea down hard on the table and then sat to feed the baby without a word. There was no use arguing. If that was how he truly felt, there was nothing to say.

***

Dinner was silent. When her husband tried to apologize, she would have none of it. He complimented her cooking and thanked her for the sweet tea, but she could not have cared less. Louise had no need for lackluster apologies and just wanted to be left alone.

When Louise was done eating, she stood up to clear the table, ready to do the dishes so that she could get on with her day and get Jacob out of her hair.

After she put the dishes in the sink, she came back to pick up Fred, but Jacob stopped her gently.

"I don't mind tendin' to him while you do the dishes."

"If that's what you want," Louise said, filled with confusion.

She turned her attention to the work of cleaning dishes and tried unsuccessfully to put Jacob out of her mind. She added a bit of lye to her cooking pot, which still held hot water. One by one, she added the dinner plates and scrubbed them by hand in the soapy water. She wished she could scrub away the memory of that afternoon as easily with the scouring pad.

What am I to do now, Lord? she prayed silently. She felt helpless as she lifted her prayer to heaven.

Louise took a deep breath as the comforting words of another of her favorite verses washed over her, and she finished rinsing off the dishes.

Louise felt something push firmly against her ankles and she glanced down see Minnie trying to get her attention.

"I've got to finish the dishes, girl. I'll hold you soon."

Just one more dish to go, she thought to herself. Then, she could get some fresh air with Minnie and the baby and Jacob could go back to minding the ranch. *The only thing he truly cared about.*

"Louise," a deep, rich voice called out right behind her ear. She spun around, startled, and dropped a tin bowl to the floor. Louise and Minnie jumped, the cat mewing her discontent. But it was only Jacob, standing there, looking uneasy.

"Yes?" she asked, feeling a bit trepidatious.

"I, um, I just wanted to say that..." his voice trailed off as Louise stared at him like a kettle that was set to boil.

"I don't understand you, Jacob," Louise said in the silence that followed his words. She took the opportunity to have her say. "You sit here, holding the baby and talking to the sweet thing every day, but you don't want to give him a name?"

"Louise, I—"

"I know that you're upset with me but I'm not sure why. I honestly thought you'd like it if I named him after your Pop. I was trying to do something nice for you is all."

"Louise," Jacob said more firmly. He raised his eyebrows with an urgency that caught her attention. "I'm just trying to say that I'm sorry."

She blinked, surprised. "You are?"

"I overreacted. I do that sometimes. Look, you were right. Fred's a good name—a strong name."

"Why did you say that, then? About him being a stranger's baby?"

"I... thought we might have our own someday, I guess, and it might be nice to have my Pop's name to pass down... or at least to have a say in the matter." He chuckled slightly.

"Oh, I see." Louise felt heat flood her cheeks and she wondered if Jacob could see how flustered she was.

"But you're right. If we're gonna keep this here babe, he needs to have a proper name. What better name than Fred? Pop would be proud."

A wave of relief flowed through Louise like cool air on a hot summer's day.

"So," she started slowly, "We're keeping the baby?"

"I'm not sure what else we'd do with him. Nobody's claimed him. Besides, if the Lord brought him here, then He wants him here, I reckon."

Suddenly, Minnie popped up on the table, refusing to be ignored any longer. She reared up playfully on her back feet with her paws in the air and then purred and rubbed up against Louise's arm. Fred giggled and reached out for his friend eagerly. His unsteady hand accidentally popped her on the nose. Minnie shook her head and sneezed, which just made Fred laugh harder.

"I guess we'll have to keep Minnie, too," Jacob said, "especially now that Fred's attached."

Louise feigned shock and laughed, as she ribbed her husband gently with her elbow. The young couple chuckled together. *Just like a real family,* Louise thought and smiled.

Chapter Fifteen

"Come on, Fred! No time for dawdling. Sarah will be here any moment!"

Louise picked up the growing babe, who was much more interested in crawling around with Minnie than putting on a proper frock. Louise hurried to change Fred's diaper and got everything together as she prepared for her friend's arrival.

She was so excited that Sarah was coming to visit again at last!

Occasionally, Sarah's mama would give her the morning off so that she and Louise could have a proper visit. Today was such a day, and Louise could not wait to spend the morning catching up with her dear friend.

A knock on the door brought Louise back to the present. Her heart surged with joy, and she opened the door to greet her friend.

"Sarah, I'm so glad you're here! I've been looking forward to seeing you all month. But what happened? Are you all right?"

The slight girl stood in the doorway a mess of dark curls and dried out tumbleweed pieces in her hair. She looked like she'd lost a fight with a spring storm.

Sarah blew the leaf-strewn mixture of hairs from her face and revealed a wry smile underneath.

"Oh, I'm just fine, I reckon! Just took a small tumble down the hill. I was fighting with a sunflower root that didn't want to come up. I almost had a nice flower to bring ya."

The pair giggled as Louise ushered her inside. Louise was always so relieved and calmed by Sarah's presence.

The two friends embraced and jumped around in a fit of excitement as they discussed what they might do that day. Now that spring had finally arrived, Louise was eager for a walk in the wildflowers and Sarah quite agreed. They bundled up the baby and meandered toward the stream where the best bluebonnets grew.

Louise carried Fred on her hip, while Minnie scampered gleefully along beside her. The friends chatted as they walked, and Sarah's voice filled Louise's heart with warmth.

"Mama took me to town last week, when she needed to get some new fabric, and I saw some lovely new patterns that the dressmaker has in the store."

"I wouldn't mind making a new spring dress now that the cooler weather has gone away," Louise replied wistfully.

"Oh, I don't mean just a dress for the spring, Louise. I want to make a new dress for the county fair! Why, it's coming up in just a few months. It'll be here before you know it once the summer hits."

"I didn't know that we had a fair! Oh, that does sound fun! Perhaps we could all go together?"

Sarah giggled as she bent down to pick a buttercup and place it in her wicker basket.

"I don't know, Louise. Don't you think that you and Jacob might like to spend some time alone on the dance floor?"

"I doubt it," Louise laughed in reply. "Jacob's about as likely to dance as he'd be to give a public oration. Besides, I would have way more fun with you."

"Don't be silly! I bet Jacob's strong arms could be downright fun to dance in."

"Well, I wouldn't know," Louise answered, her smile falling as disappointment filled her. She might not mind being held in Jacob's chiseled arms, but he certainly hadn't hinted that he wanted that. She tried unsuccessfully to banish the thought from her mind.

"All I know is that if I had a husband as fine as Jacob, I would grab him and kiss him as often as I could."

Louise laughed and gently shoved her friend's arm. "Why, Sarah! If I didn't know better, I'd think you were in the market for a husband yourself!"

"Never said I wasn't," Sarah said with a generous laugh as the two continued to the creek.

***

The late morning sun danced on the tops of the trees as the two young women finally reached the creek. The gentle bounce of Louise's footsteps had lulled Fred to sleep, so she wrapped him in a woolen blanket and laid him in her wicker basket.

"What's wrong?" asked Sarah, as Louise stared sadly at the baby in the basket.

"This is the basket that Jacob found Fred in on the porch," she said pensively. "I brought it with me because it's so easy to carry him in, but I just keep imagining him being abandoned. I can't understand it, Sarah. I could never leave Fred. What kind of mother would do that?"

"Probably a desperate one." Sarah replied with a hint of pity in her voice. "At any rate, he's asleep now, Louise, and you should enjoy the time to yourself while you have it."

"Of course," Louise said, turning back to her friend. "He won't stay asleep for long!"

The friends filled Sarah's basket with bluebonnets, butter cups, and Indian paint brushes, until the basket would fit no more, and Fred appeared more like a flower himself. Then, they sat in the soft grass, fed by the luscious stream, and fashioned spring wreaths for their hair. They braided together chains of the long, tender grass and bent it to their will, weaving the wildflowers through them.

"There now," said Sarah, as she placed one of the lovely flower wreaths onto Louise's head. "You look like a right lovely princess. Jacob will be just dyin' to dance with you if you wear that at the fair."

"We'll see," muttered Louise, as she stood up from the soft grass. She tossed a smooth stone into the creek and watched it skip down the current.

"After all, who knows what's around the bend."

***

When the women got back to the cabin, Louise boiled a kettle of fresh tea to share with her beloved friend. They sat in the rocking chairs by the fire, swapping stories and sharing laughter, while Fred and Minnie played on the soft rug at their feet.

When their cups were empty and their hearts were full, Sarah stood up. "I really should get going," she said with a warm sigh and a smile. "It'll be dinner time soon."

"Nonsense!" protested Louise. "You can have dinner with us. I made plenty."

"Thank you, friend, but Mama will expect me home, and she worries when I'm late."

Louise let out a sigh of acquiescence. "I understand," she relented, as she leaned in to hug Sarah goodbye. "Promise you'll come back soon?"

"As soon as I can," Sarah agreed.

With one last hug, the friends bid farewell, and then Louise looked for her next chore. Since she knew that Sarah was coming, she had set a pot of stew to boil that morning, and it was all ready for dinner. Fred and Minnie had both fallen asleep on the rug, the house was already clean, and Jacob wasn't home yet. Louise found herself in the rare predicament of having extra time.

She settled into her favorite rocking chair, from where she could see the door and most of the house, gazing thankfully at the pair sleeping by the fire. It always made her feel so relaxed and satisfied to watch Minnie sleeping, but now she had two sweet little ones to watch as they slumbered. Both slept soundly with a smile on their faces, as if they knew that they were home.

Home, Louise thought to herself.

Yes, somehow in the last few months, the large log cabin had somehow become home. Things had changed so much in the last few months, and she felt the need to process it.

She picked up the woven basket sitting by the fire, that Jacob had given her to put her special things in. It held her Bible, journal, quill pen, a coal pencil, and now, her lovely new flower wreath. She fished through the basket until she found her journal and pencil. She settled back into the rocking chair and flipped open the journal, grateful for some time to herself.

And since she knew this rare quiet would not last long, she put pencil to paper to ease her mind. At first, she wrote about Minnie and Fred, and their peculiar friendship that warmed her heart. Then, she wrote about Sarah and the time they'd enjoyed that day. At long last, her mind turned to her husband, the quiet but kind man—the strongest she has ever known.

Suddenly, the door creaked open and in walked the very man. He walked in slowly with the look of hush across his face, and she was grateful that he took care not to wake the baby. He carried a large sack of flour in one arm and a sack of sugar in the other. The flour was balanced precariously on his firm and ample shoulder.

The strain from the heavy bag forced his muscles to flex in their confident strength. Her heart twisted and she couldn't help but wonder what it might be like to get held firm in those arms.

He turned slowly and smiled at her. She lifted a gentle finger to her lips, reminding him to stay quiet. He looked at the baby, and then back up at her with a nod of acknowledgment.

"I got more to fetch outta the wagon," he whispered cautiously, before heading back out the door.

She turned her pencil back to her journal and scribbled her feelings urgently, lest she accidentally say them out loud.

That puzzling husband of mine came home a mess of sweat and flour today. My heart sways a bit when I see his muscles ripple under his shirt, after he's carried something much too heavy for an ordinary man. I confess I wonder what it might be like to get lost in those arms... but I can't think of a ladylike way to let my affections be known. Perhaps one day he'll understand. He's taking me to the fair soon and Sarah says there will be dancing. Will he ask me or is that too crazy a thing to hope for?

Chapter Sixteen

The summer heat beat down on Jacob's back as he led a pair of colts to the barn. So much had changed in the last year, but the hard and honest work of the ranch remained the same.

It had been almost a year since he had placed an ad in the *Gazette* for a mail-order bride—nearly a year since he received Louise's first letter. He couldn't believe how much his life had changed in the last ten months that she'd lived with him.

He was still alone in certain marital ways, and while he yearned for what might be one day, his heart was full that he had a family to protect and provide for.

"There you are, Jacob!" a familiar voice called from behind, and he turned to see his friend, George. "I was starting to think those colts had done you in once and for all. Glad to see you're still in one piece."

"For now," chuckled Jacob.

George took the reins of the smaller colt, and the two friends walked together to the horse barn. Jacob was grateful for the company that came with George's help, although he talked a bit more than Jacob would've liked.

"How's the baby?" George asked. "Sarah said that when she came 'round the other day that he was crawling everywhere. What do you think about that?"

"I think it's a normal thing that babies do, George. Why do you ask?" Jacob could tell from the tension in George's fists and the way he shifted his weight that something was weighing on him.

"Look, there's no easy way to say this." George's countenance changed suddenly, and Jacob leaned back, wondering what was wrong.

"There's been some rumors in town, Jacob—rumors about a gang leader come looking for his son."

"His son?"

"His baby, actually." George averted his eyes to the ground when he said the words, and Jacob knew why. It felt like a millstone dropped in his stomach as he grasped the weight of the words.

"Why would an outlaw be missing a baby?" Jacob asked, not wanting to know the answer.

"Well, supposedly he had a woman that was carryin' his child, a prostitute that went and run off on him, and the gal worked at the saloon in Austin. Rumor has it, she dropped the baby on a doorstep somewhere in town. Anyhow, the outlaw's been around, looking for his son."

Jacob lifted a hand to his head and grasped his hair in disbelief. Sweat gathered on his brow and he felt short of breath. He bent over at the waist to put his hands on his knees and steadied himself. He couldn't believe it. Nor could he imagine a worse possibility.

"Now, Jacob," George went on, "This don't mean nothin'. It's just a rumor—a story that shopkeepers tell to interest nosy customers. Plenty of babies get left on doorsteps all the time. Even if the rumors are true, it don't mean Fred's his baby."

Jacob stood up and sucked in a hurried breath. He paced back and forth in the old barn, trying to process the information. He had to get home to tell Louise. Sarah was supposed to come by later, he remembered, and it was important that he be the one to tell her. Maybe he could soften the blow for her somehow.

"I best be getting home for supper," Jacob said, as he headed toward the large opening at the front of the barn.

"Don't think nothing of it, Jacob," George called after him. "It's just a rumor!"

Just a rumor that could change everything.

***

Jacob walked the mile-long path from the horse barn at the ranch back to the log cabin that overlooked the valley. Normally, he would have taken his horse, in a hurry to get home for supper, but he needed the time to think things through.

If he was going to tell Louise about this, he had to do it the right way. He needed to have his ducks in a row and have a plan in place, so that the poor girl didn't fall apart. He knew that she would be upset, and though he entertained the idea of not telling her, he knew that wasn't an option. He had to be a man of honor and tell her the truth—regardless of the results.

He could only imagine the way Louise might react if you told her that the baby was in harm's way—that their young family was in danger.

A family. Is that what they were? Jacob swallowed hard, and the meaning of such a responsibility washed over him. His heart softened as he confessed to himself that he truly *did w*ant them to be his family. He would certainly protect them as such, come what may.

He marched up the steps of the log cabin, ready to tell Louise the full truth, as gently as possible. She had a right to know, but when he opened the door, what he saw took his breath away. On the far side of the large single room, atop the grand four-post bed, lay his sleeping family, and that's exactly what they were.

Louise slept propped up on a pillow against the cherry oak headboard. She was nearly sitting up, and he chuckled softly that she must have fallen asleep accidentally, pausing briefly between chores.

In the crook of her left arm slept the beautiful blond boy. Now nine months old, his light hair was finally starting to fill in. Though he had grown so much bigger, he still lay curled up against her side, like the newborn baby he used to be.

Snuggled somehow in between the two, in between Louise's knees and Fred's feet, was Minnie the cat. She had fastened herself into a tight ball, and her body was nestled firmly against her mistress and her baby friend.

Jacob's heart warmed at the site of the cuddly crew. He refused the urge to curl up behind Louise and hold his family in his arms. The irony that these three had taken over the bed, that once belonged to him alone, was not lost on him.

Indeed, it was still *his* bed, but he would not go into it uninvited. He would wait until such a time that his wife might invite him into his bed to be with her—

their bed. However, he would not encroach upon her without her request.

Jacob looked out the window by the fireplace, covered by soft blue curtains that Louise had sewn together. The curtains were pulled back on the sides by white, lacey ribbon, and they framed the most beautiful sunset. He walked over to the window to get a closer look.

When he walked up to the window, his arm brushed against something on the rough wooden windowsill. He looked down to see Louise's journal, laying open with a pen in the spine of the book.

He couldn't help himself as he lifted the small book, and the pages turned, as if begging him to read it.

October 11th,

Am I crazy to be getting married today? Jacob is respectful and kind, but I barely know him, and I can't get him to say more than a few words.

I'm driven forward by the firm belief that the Lord brought me here on purpose. Like Esther was brought to King Xerxes to save her people, perhaps I was brought here for such a time as this. Could the Lord use me, an unwanted doorstep baby, to help this precious baby boy grow up in a loving home? Help me, Lord. I trust in you.

Jacob shut the book, shocked at what he had just found. Louise had been a doorstep baby? Her instant connection with Fred made sense in this new light, and he could see that the Lord had certainly brought her there to mother the boy.

His heart fell for a moment, thinking of the leader of the outlaw gang who might be coming for Fred. It would crush Louise. He would do whatever he needed to do to protect her. He started to walk away from the journal, feeling like an intruder, but then he turned back, eager for more.

He flipped through a couple of pages until the words, "mountain man," leapt up at him. With a deep sigh of foreboding, certain that she would express her disgust for him, he read on:

March 18th,

The Mountain Man

He's rough around the edges to be sure, but also very handsome and kind. I confess that lately, it's his rugged strength that draws me to him. He smells like leather and pine from working with the horses and chopping wood, and he has the muscles to prove it.

Jacob leaned back with a half-cocked smile, proud of himself for a moment. So, it wasn't all in his head. She noticed him as well, perhaps even longed for him, as he longed for her.

He stepped closer to the little book, ready to devour it whole. He wanted to know everything that was in that mysterious head of hers. As he turned the page, he heard the creak of the four-post bed as someone woke up. He knew he'd been found out. Quickly, he shoved it back onto the windowsill.

"Jacob, is that my journal?" The sleepy voice of his wife turned incredulous with each word.

"I... I..." he stuttered, his cheeks brightening with embarrassment.

"You, what? You read my journal? My most private thoughts? Jacob, how could you?"

Wide awake now, Louise grabbed the book from out of his hand and held it to her chest, like it was a baby in her arms.

"To be fair, it was sitting wide-open on the windowsill, begging to be read. It was practically an invitation, Louise."

Jacob watched as her face grew bright red, as fury filled her cheeks, and he knew that he'd said the wrong thing.

What have I done?

"How dare you not respect my privacy?"

"My apologies, Louise. Truly. I'm sorry."

Jacob didn't know what else to say. In fact, he did feel bad for reading the journal, as he was hungry for Louise—hungry for her thoughts, hungry for her charms—and if a journal was the only way to get it, he'd probably do it again.

They were interrupted by Fred, who had woken up, crying on the bed.

"Now look what you've gone and done! You've woken the baby!" Louise said, looking fit to be tied.

"I'm not the one that woke the baby. I might've read your journal, but I'm not the one hollering in our house."

Louise took a deep breath as if to settle herself, but it did not work.

"You lucked out, Jacob Montgomery," Louise said, as she went to pick up the baby. "But know that we are not done talking about this."

***

The supper table was a little quieter than normal that night. To Jacob's surprise, he was the one who wished that Louise would talk, and he was eager to break the silence.

"Louise," he said gently, "I got carried away with curiosity. I really am sorry. Please don't be mad at me."

His wife cracked a slight smile and sighed as she passed him the butter.

Must be my rugged good looks or the smell of leather and pine getting the best of her, he thought, chuckling to himself. As he sat sipping on the warm stew and enjoying the fresh bread, he felt a hunger much deeper growing inside of him, a hunger for the warm and fiery blonde sitting across the table. He determined right there that it was high time to woo this woman.

Chapter Seventeen

"Shall we, Mrs. Montgomery?" Jacob asked his young wife as they exited the little country church. Louise smiled and gave Jacob a small sigh.

"Yes, Mr. Montgomery, I think we shall."

The two walked arm in arm to the wagon. The traveling preacher had been through town again and the whole town had turned out to see the man of God teach the scriptures. It always did Jacob's heart good to hear a sermon, and he always seemed to receive just what he needed from the Good Book. Louise was downright giddy to go to church and worship with other believers from the town. She had lifted her voice louder than the rest as they sang hymns of joy and hope.

Jacob was relieved that going to church had put her in a better mood, because he'd had to do some fancy footwork the last day or so to get Louise to forgive him for looking in her journal. It looked like he'd finally gotten on her good side. After a day of him doing penance and then attending the traveling preacher's sermon on forgiveness, Louise seemed ready to let bygones be bygones and move on.

He was relieved when she agreed to take his arm. It was a good thing, too, because Jacob intended to woo the girl. He may have apologized for reading her journal, but he couldn't take back what he knew.

His heart had swollen in pride when he read what she really thought of him. He held his chin a little higher, walked a little more intentionally, and had noticed her eyes on him when he was lifting things around the house. Now that he felt sure that she was interested in a mountain man like him, he didn't want to let anything get in the way of their future relationship.

Jacob was full of confidence and hope as he walked to the wagon with the lovely girl on his arm. When they could walk no further, he put his hands gently around her small waist and lifted her into the wagon. He noticed out of the corner of his eye the way Louise looked at him as he lifted her effortlessly up and into the rig, and he thoroughly enjoyed it. Then, with one large step, he pulled himself up beside her.

"See you at the picnic, George," he called out to his friend across the street. Afterwards, he lifted the reins and snapped them across the horses, urging them forward.

***

"Over here, Jacob!" George hollered from the top of the hill as he waved to his friend.

The hot July sun was fierce on such a summer's day, but George's wife had sought refuge under the partial shade of a Yuca tree. She had already set about preparing their picnic. George smiled and waved back at his friend with a sense of ease he was not always afforded.

Most days, Jacob's time was filled with horses and cows, and rarely a break presented itself. The upside to the heat was that most of the animals preferred to stay in the barn and nap in the hot summer weather.

Since they had already taken a trip to town for church, which was a rare pleasure, Louise and Sarah had convinced the two families to stop for a picnic on the way back up the mountain. Jacob had protested, knowing that there was work to be done, but when he saw the look in Louise's eyes as she requested a family picnic, he could not refuse her.

"Whoa, boys," Jacob said, as he eased his steeds to a halt.

As the rig came to a stop, an orange ball of fluff leapt past Jacob out of the wagon. Fred giggled in approval from Louise's lap, and his wife laughed along with the baby.

"Silly kitty!" she called after her furry friend.

Jacob was glad the orange tabby had joined them for this venture. While it might not have been easy to keep her hushed during the church service, he knew that her presence brought Louise so much joy.

"Never hold back when you set to woo a girl," Pop had told him several years back. "If you want to win her heart, and not just her hand, you gotta be generous with your time, your attention, and most of all, your gentlemanly behavior."

As if right on cue, Louise stood and cleared her throat, waiting to be helped down from the rig. She smiled sweetly at Jacob, and he hopped down to assist her.

"Allow me," Jacob said, as he took the baby from her and then offered out his other hand to help her down.

"Thank you," Louise said with a smile in her eyes. Jacob's chest twisted at the look of her sweet gaze. What was behind those eyes, he wondered, and how could he work his way into her heart?

Could he even do it? An old familiar pain shot through him when he thought of his previous rejection, and all that he was risking by offering Louise his heart, instead of simply his hand.

But as he lifted his gaze back up to meet her, he knew that she was worth the risk. Soft blue eyes fell upon his and they twinkled as if they held a secret inside of them.

When he was done helping her down from the rickety wagon, he took a chance and decided to hold tight to her hand instead of releasing it. To his surprise, she didn't try to pull away, but rather leaned against him, embracing the gentle grasp of his hand.

He could smell the sweet baked bread and fresh honeysuckle all over again, something he could only smell when he was this close to her. His heart began to beat a mile a minute and he thought he might be done for right there.

If there's gonna be a heartbreak, it's bound to be a fierce one.

Jacob could've walked with Louise like that all day, with her hand settled softly in his, but to his chagrin, the walk was soon over. They reached the picnic blankets where George's family and Minnie the cat sat waiting for them. That was when Louise slipped her hand out of his.

"Hey y'all!" Sarah said as she jumped up from her spot on the colorful quilt to hug Louise.

She ushered them to the blanket, where her mother had a summer feast laid out. Sarah opened a large picnic basket to reveal a loaf of fresh bread as long as her arm and a roasted chicken. Next, she pulled out two huge blocks of cheese, compliments of the cows, and freshly picked tomatoes from the garden. Last but not least, she brought out the crown jewel: a ripe watermelon the size of a young hog.

She lay them all out on a clean white linen blanket atop her handsewn quilt. She produced a tin bowl for each of the guests. Then, she brought out a sizable knife and handed it to George to do the honors.

"You've outdone yourself this time, my love," said George, as he kissed his wife, Martha, on the cheek. "How did I get so lucky, and more importantly, why do I have to share all the food with these folks?"

The friends all laughed heartily as they divided the feast among all their bowls. When it was time to eat, George raised his bowl and cleared his throat, ready to bless the food. Everyone bowed their heads, eager to acknowledge the blessings of their creator.

"Lord God, thank you for this bountiful food that you've given us today, and for the friends that we get to share it with. We are truly grateful. Please bless the precious hands that prepared it and keep us ever mindful that all good things come from your hand. In Christ our Savior's name we pray, Amen."

The group of friends talked merrily under the small bit of shade of the old Yuca, eating their fill. When he had eaten his fill, Jacob leaned back on his elbows and admired the lovely view.

The wind blew through Louise's hair, causing it to dance and play around her cheeks. He thought about how nice it must be to be that wind. Jacob watched, fixated as Louise laughed easily with Sarah and swept the unruly, blonde hairs from her face.

Although he enjoyed spending time with Louise, he confessed it was nice to have other people around that she could talk to. He could carry on a conversation for a minute or two, but Louise could talk for days. He enjoyed simply being with her, and he embraced the chance to rest quietly in this moment and observe the group of friends.

As Louise continued to talk to Sarah about the past week's events, Jacob's eyes drifted to the middle of the blanket, where Fred crawled around with Minnie.

Jacob could not believe how quick the baby had changed. Somehow, he had grown from a newborn infant, days old on his front porch, to the ten-month-old toddler that crawled around before him. Two weeks earlier, he had started pulling up on the furniture and scooting about the cabin. He knew that before too much longer, he'd be running around chasing the cattle.

Jacob played with a long blade of grass and held it to his lips to whistle and get Fred's attention. He knew that Fred loved it when he made strange noises or silly faces, and he enjoyed watching his reactions.

As he blew on the blade of grass between his fingers, it emitted the intended whistle. Fred looked up at Jacob with eyes as wide as the Nevada sky, and just as blue.

Jacob's heart was filled with love for the young thing, and he admitted that it surprised him. He did not know that he could love a baby that wasn't his—not in the natural way, at least. But the more time he spent playing and laughing with the babe, the more attached to him he had become.

The curious toddler started to make his way over to Jacob, crawling across the colorful quilt and empty bowls of food, but he stopped short when his furry friend distracted him. Minnie danced around the baby, swishing her tail as she went, and Fred turned all his attention to catching the kitty.

Jacob laughed as he watched the adventurous babe. He seemed determined to catch Minnie—if it was the last thing that he would do—but she always stepped just a bit out of reach. Then, Fred crawled over to Louise and pulled up on the sleeve of her dress into an unsteady, standing position.

Jacob looked on as Louise turned her attention to the babe, smiling proudly at him. She held her hands out, ready for Fred to fall in them, but to the surprise of everyone at the picnic, Fred took a step without any assistance.

Louise's mouth dropped open and Jacob joined her in his surprise, as the two watched Fred's first steps. He took another step on wobbly legs and then two more before he tumbled over and fell on his bottom with a giggle. Everyone at the picnic clapped and cheered.

"Did you see that?" Louise exclaimed as she lifted the baby in her arms. "Fred walked on his own! Oh, did you see it, Jacob?"

"Oh, I saw it, all right!" Jacob answered, his heart filled with pride over the successful baby and his happy mama.

Louise stood with the baby held high above her shoulders and twirled in a circle before she brought him into her chest. She kissed him gently on each cheek and then lay back on the soft green grass next to Jacob, with Fred on her tummy.

Jacob felt for a few moments as though he were the happiest man in the world— as though everything was just as it should be.

But in the back of his mind, a creeping darkness burst through. It suddenly dawned on him that there was something he hadn't told his wife yet, something that could take this joy away. He would have to tell her about the leader of the gang, but not yet. He'd hold onto his happiness just a moment longer.

Chapter Eighteen

The golden daffodils and bright orange sunflowers poked upward as they danced toward the sun. Louise loved the flowers in her garden behind her home. She was excited when Jacob had told her that sunflowers grow toward the sun.

When the sun rose in the morning and hovered overhead at midday, the sunflowers could be seen stretching up to embrace the golden rays. When the sun went down in the evening, the sunflowers bent toward the west to face the setting sun. They fascinated her and reminded her of how she should always look to the Lord.

The traveling preacher had spoken about forgiveness that morning in church. He said that when our eyes were on the Lord, and we remembered what he had done for us—when we remembered that we were all forgiven—then forgiveness and love would flow through us naturally.

Louise wanted to face the Lord as the sunflowers faced the sun. Just as they soaked up the life-giving rays of sunshine, she wanted to soak up the love of the Lord and give it to her new budding family.

She'd had the loveliest time at the picnic after church, and her heart was full of the warmth of friendship and family. She couldn't believe that Fred had taken his first steps!

Did I imagine it or was Jacob just as excited as I was?

He was becoming a welcome surprise in a confusing time. The last ten months in Austin, Nevada had held a lot of changes for her, but Jacob's strong character, strong arms, and now his strength as a father, gave her such hope.

Today's picnic was delicious, but she knew that her husband would be hungry again soon. She lifted her watering can and emptied the last vestiges of water upon the petals in her garden. Then, she turned toward the house to prepare their evening meal.

Louise tiptoed quietly inside and set the watering can next to her special basket of private things by the windowsill.

Well, at least they *used* to be private. If Jacob knew what was good for him, he certainly wouldn't go rifling through her diary again.

"Forgive as you've been forgiven," she reminded herself aloud. The pastor's words from the sermon that day echoed in her brain.

Note taken, Lord, she prayed silently. She took a deep breath, determined not to throw the journal debacle in his face again.

She turned toward the kitchen to make dinner, but the sight of her husband stoking the fire stopped her cold. His furrowed brow bent toward the fire, and he was whispering something angrily to himself. His back was bent over, and his muscles were tense, as if clutched in a desperate wrestling match with an unseen entity. He jammed the stoker into the fire over and over again.

"What's wrong, Jacob?" she asked, frowning. Then, she realized with horror that the baby wasn't with him. "Why aren't you watching the baby?"

She turned in concern and ran to Fred, who was fast asleep in his cradle. Her heartbeat slowed down a little bit. She took a deep breath before she turned back to Jacob.

"What on earth is the matter?"

Jacob turned to Louise and let out a heavy sigh that released his anxiety into the room. She could feel his tension like a knife, and it hit her squarely in the chest. Something was deeply wrong.

"Louise, come sit with me by the fire for a second. There's something I've got to talk to you about."

He held out his hand and spread out a forced, feeble smile across his tanned face. Louise could tell the news was bad and she had no time for such pleasantries as handholding.

She shook her head. "Jacob, you're making me nervous. Would you please just tell me what's going on?"

"Please sit," asked Jacob gently and Louise acquiesced to his request. She sat in the rocking chair nearest the fire. Jacob pulled the other chair over to sit across from her. He reached for her other hand, and she gave it to him willingly, unable to remove her gaze from his. She could no longer bring herself to utter a single word, as a foreboding fear flowed through her.

Jacob took Louise's hand in his and looked down at her with sorrowful eyes. Louise had never seen him like this before. She'd never seen him *afraid*. Fear struck through her like a bolt of lightning.

"What is it?" she asked, much quieter this time, although she was not sure that she wanted to know any longer.

"Louise, you know how I've been asking around about the baby these past months?"

"Yes," said Louise, defensiveness building up in her heart. "But it's been nearly ten months now and nobody's come around. Don't tell me that Fred's no-good momma is wanting him back now!"

Fury grew in her belly, and she was ready to go to war to protect her child.

"Well, no, not exactly," Jacob continued slowly, "but the father's come around lookin'."

"The father?" Louise asked incredulously. "I'm not giving this baby back to a man without a wife. Fred needs two parents. He needs us!"

Louise lifted Jacob's hands close to her as she tried to convince him that they were the right parents for Fred.

"But he's not an ordinary man, Louise."

"What do you mean?"

"When I was working with George on the ranch yesterday, he told me that the leader of a gang of train robbers has been coming around town looking for his son. The whole town's been talking about it."

Louise was in shock. How could Jacob keep this from her?

"The whole town? Why am I the last to know, Jacob? I mean, George told you yesterday and I'm just now finding out!"

"I'm sorry, Louise," Jacob said, looking flustered. "I just found out yesterday, but when I came home to tell you, you were fast sleep. I didn't wanna wake you so…"

"So, you looked through my journal instead? How convenient! Look here, Jacob Montgomery! I don't care who it is looking for this baby. They can't have him."

"Louise, would you just listen to me for a sec? He's a very dangerous man! He's known for leaving trains empty of money as well as life. Supposedly he's been coming through Austin, and some other nearby towns, looking for his son, and he's made some threats."

Jacob's eyes narrowed intensely as he looked down at Louise.

"I won't let anything happen to you. I promise."

"And what about the baby? What about Fred?"

"I think we might should consider givin' him to the sheriff and lettin' the law work it out. Might be safer that way."

Louise couldn't believe what she was hearing. Panic flooded her heart and moved from her hands down to her feet. She could choose between fight or flight, and she chose to fight.

She dropped Jacob's hands as she rose from her chair, furious. She stormed to the other side of the room in front of Fred's cradle, turning back to face Jacob. She felt like a mama bear ready to protect her cub no matter the cost.

"How could you say that to me, Jacob Montgomery? *How could you?*"

Jacob rose from his chair, looking defeated. She'd never seen him so downcast before. He walked over to her with outstretched arms.

"I'm sorry, Louise. Truly, I am. Please don't look at me like that."

"We can't let Fred go back to that terrible man. He won't go back unless it's over my dead body!"

Jacob looked like a broken man as he lifted his eyes to hers. Pain struck her heart as she saw something that she never thought she would see. Tears welled up in her hard husband's eyes.

"Okay," he conceded quietly.

Her heart went out to him, and she wanted to comfort him, but she couldn't risk Fred's safety—not for herself, not for Jacob, not for anyone. She placed her hands firmly upon Jacob's chest and gazed up into his warm brown eyes.

"There's something that you don't know, and it's high time I told you. I was left on the doorstep as a baby. Sometimes, I think I would've been better off out in the cold than with the Cankers. I can't let Fred suffer the same fate. I can't let him go to cruel people. I just can't."

Tears started to fall slowly from her cheeks. She failed, try as she might, to hold them back.

"Promise me you won't let them take him. Promise me!"

"I promise," he answered hoarsely.

Louise's heart broke when she saw the tender state of her husband. She buried her head in his chest and wept.

She wept for how she'd upset the strongest man she's ever known. She wept for the fear in her own heart, but mostly, she wept for the babe asleep in the cradle and wondered what would happen to him.

Jacob wrapped his arms around her and laid a scraggly beard on top of her head. He didn't say anything further, but simply held her as she cried.

Time passed and whether it was minutes or hours, Louise wasn't sure, but slowly, the anxious beating in her heart calmed down, until at last, she rested calmly in Jacob's arms.

"Louise?" Jacob asked tenderly, at last.

"Yes?" She looked up at him, awaiting some profound reply. What would he say? What must he think of her now?

"Louise, there's a cat on my shoulder that I think is trying to get to you," Jacob said, chuckling softly.

Louise looked up to see her favorite furry friend. Minnie stood on Jacob's shoulder and peered into Louise's eyes, as if she were looking straight into her soul. Her furry friend lifted one tiny orange paw and reached out to touch Louise's cheek.

"Oh, Minnie!" Louise said with a deep sigh. She gathered her best friend into her arms. Louise nuzzled into her soft fur, while Minnie licked her cheeks.

They stayed like that for a while longer, with Jacob holding Louise, and Louise holding Minnie, as she prayed a silent prayer that the Lord was holding them all.

Chapter Nineteen

Louise dangled her basket at her side as she walked through the meadow near her home. Her Bible lay in the basket, as she'd intended to come out here to spend time with the Lord, but her mind was elsewhere.

Jacob was taking her to the fair later that day. She knew that he wanted her to be excited about it, but it just sounded so silly with all that was going on.

Fred might be in danger and we're going to a fair?

A few days had passed since Louise had found out about Fred's parentage, since her quarrel with Jacob, and since he'd held her in his arms. Every time she started to worry about the baby and the outlaw, her thoughts were interrupted by the memory of Jacob's arms holding her, and how she'd melted into his strong chest.

It was nearly enough to make a girl swoon, but she hadn't the luxury. She knew that Jacob would do whatever it took to keep them safe, but a cruel and unwelcome fear had been growing in her belly. It was the fear of the unknown—and things outside of her control. *What if nothing could be done?*

It reminded her of the feeling of foreboding that she would get when she knew that Maw or Paw Canker were in a foul mood. When they would stomp around the house, hitting walls and acting ready to wage war, the fear would rumble in her belly, and she would think of how she might either appease them or escape.

She hadn't felt that awful foreboding fear these last many months with Jacob in the mountains, but now, it was all around her. How could she ensure their safety? It was this fear that drove her to the meadow with her Bible, to seek the

Lord. What would become of Fred? What would become of her family?

"Be still and know that I am God."

The verse echoed through her head again like it had so many times before.

I know that You're in charge, Lord. I know You want me to be still, but I'm just no good at it. How do I get through this situation? Won't You just tell me what to do?

"Come to me, all you who are weary and heavy-laden, and I will give you rest."

The verse that her Sunday school teacher taught her to recite as a child came to her and she remembered what she needed to do. She plopped down in the grass and opened the old Bible that she'd had since she was a child.

She flipped the page to chapter forty-one of Isaiah, and her eyes fell upon verse ten.

"So do not fear, for I am with you; do not be dismayed, for I am your God. I will strengthen you and help you; I will uphold you with my righteous right hand."

Much needed peace flowed through Louise's heart like water on dry ground. She read the verse again and it was like pouring a healing salve on an old wound. She sat there for a while, meditating on the verse and remembering the faithfulness of the Lord.

Help me to trust You, Lord. Help me to rest in Your strength.

At long last, she rose from the spot, grateful for her time with the Lord, and started her walk back toward the cabin. She knew that Jacob and the baby would be waiting for her, ready to go to the fair, and she couldn't keep them waiting any longer.

***

She thought she was prepared for anything as she walked up the steps to the cabin. But when she opened the door, what she saw took her breath away. Before her eyes, sitting in the rocking chair, while Minnie and Fred played at his feet, was an incredibly handsome man.

He looked like Jacob, but he was completely clean-shaven, and his hair had obviously been trimmed by the town barber. Still full of every ounce of manliness, but now with an undeniable charm, sat Jacob Montgomery—her handsome husband.

"Louise!" he said, standing to his feet when she came in the room. "Welcome home."

And home she was. Louise was taken aback, and she looked around the room to see if someone was there, waiting to pinch her and wake her from a dream.

"Jacob?" While she normally felt confident and knew what to say, she felt speechless as she took in her husband's new look. The well-chiseled jaw that always poked out and caused the beard to stand at attention now drew attention to itself. His skin looked smooth and clean, and she had to fight her desire to kiss it.

"Well, what do you think?" he pressed.

She was afraid that if she said exactly what she thought, she'd embarrass herself completely. Instead, she walked up to her once-wild man and reached a tender hand to his cheek. It was silky and soft to the touch, just as she suspected.

"Why, Jacob Montgomery, I think you look like a gentleman who's ready to go to the fair."

***

As the rickety old wagon rolled down the steep hill into the town of Austin, the excitement of the fair rose before them on main street. Louise sat up a little taller with Fred in her arms, eager to see the colorful hubbub.

Vendors were selling their wares at booths that boasted the world's best peaches and pies, all ripe for the taking.

Aside from the tradesmen that were selling their wares, just beyond the town square was a large area set aside to showcase livestock. Louise could hear a farmer calling out awards for the prize hog, and someone stepped forward to receive the grand blue ribbon.

Directly ahead in the town square lay a wooden dance floor and a live band setting up their banjos. She remembered what Sarah had said about dancing, and she hoped that she was right. Louise had worn her special blue dress to accompany Jacob's handsome face. She hoped silently that he would ask her to dance.

"Woah, boys. That'll do."

Jacob brought the wagon to a gentle stop—the way that only a fine horseman could do. The horses halted at the foot of the hill, right at the entrance to the fair. Louise watched in awe as her husband stepped down from the wagon, looking like an entirely new man!

He carried himself differently as he went around to tie up the horses. She could tell that a few girls walking by recognized his appeal as well. Louise sat up a little taller, making sure they knew he was taken.

When Jacob returned to help her down from the wagon, she looked down at the handsome rancher, a picture of true chivalry.

"Shall we, Mrs. Montgomery?" he asked with a grin bigger than the fair, equally as grand.

"Why yes, Mr. Montgomery. I think we shall."

As he helped her down from the wagon, she smelled something new on his collar. Was it cologne? When did he have time to buy that? While it smelled nice, she much preferred his natural scent of leather and pine. Nevertheless, she could tell that he was trying to please her, and it filled her heart with glee.

The young couple walked arm in arm through the midway. Louise could tell, as they drank up the sights and sounds of the fair, that the townsfolk were taking them in as well.

It made sense, she admitted to herself. It was only natural that the locals might be curious about the mountain man and his new bride. Many of the girls smiled and winked at Jacob as they passed, brazenly unhindered by Louise on his arm.

But it was no matter. Louise could tell by the way he looked at her that she was the only one on his mind. She stood proudly on his arm as they walked through the fair together. She embraced the sweet moment of being presented publicly with her very handsome husband.

While the curious onlookers, who were clearly aghast at the mountain man's transformation, did not bother her, what did concern her was the other topic of conversation. She could hear it as she passed two women whispering to themselves in a corner, eating freshly shucked corn between gossip.

"Isn't that the baby?"

"Yes, I think that's the child; the one that the outlaw was looking for."

A chill ran down Louise's spine as she realized that it was her sweet baby they were talking about. She held Fred tighter to her chest and stood taller, refusing to let the idle gossip bother her.

They could be wrong, after all, she told herself.

Sometimes a rumor was just a rumor. Besides, there were certainly no train robbers presenting themselves at the fair today. She resolved to push the thought out of her mind and enjoy the celebration before her.

"Louise!" a voice called out just past the edge of the midway. "Louise, over here!"

Louise craned her neck up high and looked up ahead to see her best friend Sarah waving wildly and holding cotton candy in her hand. At last, a friendly face. Jacob led his family over to where George's family sat, waiting for them. The friends embraced and Louise was ready to lose herself in an evening of celebration.

***

After a couple hours of good food and conversation with Sarah, and a couple of other friends she introduced her to from town, Louise was right as rain. She was glad that she had decided to enjoy the fair and stop worrying about the gossip.

Once all the ribbons for the prize livestock and baked goods had been awarded, the band started up to play. Louise noticed Sarah smiling out of the corner of her eye, and she elbowed her friend, encouraging her to stop. If she was going to dance with her husband, he would certainly have to be the one to ask, clean-shaven or not.

The band struck up a familiar tune that Louise used to dance to as a child, and she couldn't help but tap her foot just a little.

"May I have this dance?"

Louise was surprised to see that it was George doing the asking and she laughed out loud.

"Whenever I see a girl ready to dance, I always say it's a shame to not lead her onto the awaiting floor. What do you say?"

"Why, I'd love to, George!"

Louise noticed a look of surprise on Jacob's face as she handed the baby to Sarah and followed George onto the floor. They weren't halfway through the first song, when a familiar, deep voice spoke from behind her.

"Mind if I cut in?"

Louise turned, surprised to see her newly fashioned and thoroughly handsome husband. He was holding out his hand with a nervous, wide-eyed look. Her stomach started to twist, and she couldn't turn him down.

"George, I do hope you'll forgive me, but I believe my husband requires a dance."

"If you must," George chuckled.

He bowed graciously as he danced off, but not before winking at Jacob and giving him a hearty pat on the back.

Louise turned, expecting her husband to be the nervous sort of dancer, but the look on his face told a different story. She looked up into brown eyes that were simultaneously fierce and warm. They held a hunger that she hadn't seen before. She felt her stomach leap in anticipation.

Suddenly, a calloused, warm hand was at the small of Louise's back, pulling her toward him. She thought she might fall into him, but then his left hand stopped her, catching her hand in his. Between his right hand on her back and his left hand in hers, she was perfectly poised as he spun her around the floor.

She danced breathlessly in Jacob's capable arms. She couldn't help but think that they were one body, moving together flawlessly.

When the song came to a crashing halt, Jacob turned her gently to his other arm and dipped her back. His face leaned over hers and she thought for a moment that he might kiss her. She knew that if he did, she wouldn't refuse him.

Then, suddenly, it was over, and people were leaving the dance floor, but Louise stayed, looking up into Jacob's sweet brown eyes. She lifted her face to his, aching to be kissed by her husband.

"Louise," the rich, deep voice spoke. She was pressed against him and could feel his heart racing in tandem with hers.

"Yes, Jacob?" Whatever he was about to ask her, the question would be yes.

"I…" She leaned in, eager for his next words, hoping that he might forget them altogether and just kiss her.

She was about to say as much when a calloused elbow dug into her arm, brushing past her roughly. The steel edge of the stranger's boot knocked her off her feet and she fell into Jacob's arms.

"Mind your step!" Jacob shouted at the stranger. He spun Louise behind him, putting himself between her and the man.

Louise looked out from behind Jacob's arm to see cold green eyes glaring ominously at her. The stranger's face held a wicked grimace. Although Louise didn't know him, she could tell by the look in his eyes that he knew her. The old foreboding fear that she knew so well started to rumble again in her stomach, warning her of who he might be. She hoped against hope that she was wrong.

Chapter Twenty

Hot Nevada dust flew up through the air. It stung Jacob's nostrils as he clung to the young stallion that churned up the dirt.

"Not today, Jonah!" Jacob chuckled, cinching up on the reins and leaning into the horse as it reared back on its hind legs.

The last couple of days had been a whirlwind, more so than the dry dirt that spun around him. He was grateful to be back on the ranch doing what he did best—breaking wild horses. When Jacob was riding a bucking bronco, he could completely lose himself in the moment, and rightly so, for it demanded all his attention.

He didn't have to worry about the outlaw wandering around town. He didn't have to worry about keeping his family safe. Perhaps the biggest relief of all: he didn't have to worry about how exactly he would woo the beautiful wild rose that he had wed.

He dug his boots deeper into the stirrups and braced himself as the young stallion reared up again.

"Whoa, Jonah! Easy boy! The sooner you realize that I am in charge here, the better."

But true to his namesake, Jonah showed no plans to submit to his master. Jacob could feel the hot muscles of the wild beast churn furiously beneath him as it ran toward the edge of the fence at full speed. Jacob hunkered down against the animal's shaggy red mane and braced himself for whatever might happen next. If this horse was going to jump, he was going to be ready.

Jacob caught his breath when the angry stallion stopped short just inches from the cold metal gate. Without warning, the horse kicked up his back legs with all his might, catapulting Jacob through the air.

He landed hard on his right arm and felt the ground shake beneath him. His arm ached and screamed for relief, as Jacob rolled over with a groan.

Could be worse, he thought with a chuckle. It wasn't the first time he'd been thrown. He thought he might be ready to give it another go, but his throbbing arm demanded attention and he knew he couldn't ignore it.

"Jacob, are you all right?" Jacob turned to see George running toward him.

"O' course."

"I've seen my fair share of men gettin' thrown from horses but that looked a might rough."

"Nah. I think he just took it sorta personal that I put a saddle on him for the first time." Jacob chuckled. "No matter though. He'll break."

"As long as he didn't break *you*. Can you move your arm, my friend?"

"Not without it hurting pretty good."

"I think I should take you in the wagon on up to the house to let your wife look at it," George encouraged until Jacob relented at last.

He sighed. "I think I might just let you."

***

The door cracked open, and Jacob groaned with it as he stumbled through the cabin door.

He looked up to see soft blue eyes peering up at him from across the room. Louise sat in the rocking chair holding Fred, who she was lulling to sleep. Jacob's heart turned within him when he saw the beautiful pair by the fire, but it was interrupted by the pain throbbing inside of his forearm.

"Oh, Jacob! What happened?" she asked, suddenly alert.

Jacob watched as Louise jumped out of her chair, clinging to the baby in her arms. Her eyes shimmered in concern and Jacob couldn't help but secretly relish it. The sight of the beautiful woman worrying about him as she held the child would've been a perfect moment if it weren't for the nagging pain in his arm.

"I'm all right," he said as he watched Louise place the baby in the cradle and rush over to him. The normally gentle sway of her hips was hurried as she bustled toward him.

"Well, you don't look all right!" his beautiful wife protested. She placed two gentle hands on his forearm, and he tried not to wince from the pain. His arm was sorer than he realized, but he didn't want to worry Louise.

"Can you stretch it out?" she asked with a deep look of concern in her gentle eyes. Jacob complied, and he stretched his arm out and brought it back in to assure her that all was well. However, the pain surprised him as he brought his arm back into his shoulder and he let out a groan, worrying the girl anew.

"Now, you sit right here, Jacob Montgomery," she said as she hurried about the room. "I know just what you need."

Jacob sat back blissfully in the rocking chair as Louise pulled some fresh cloth out of a boiling pot of water. She waved it effortlessly through the air to cool it off for a moment before she wrapped it around his arm.

"Hold still a second," she said. "I'm almost done."

Almost done, he thought to himself. *I wouldn't mind if this took all day.*

He smiled to himself and hoped that Louise didn't catch him, as if he would get in trouble if he enjoyed it too much.

As Louise carefully wound the cloth around Jacob's arm, he relished the touch of her hand. Her hair fell over her face and tickled the edge of Jacob's cheek. It sent a chill through him, and he longed for more of her touch. He gazed upon the dainty lashes that highlighted her fair eyes, and her freckles.

Oh, but that's a woman, Jacob thought, as his breath caught in his chest.

His heart swelled with love, and he realized he would do anything for her, if only she would have him. He was so wrapped up in the moment that he didn't realize when she was done. The cloth blanketed his arm effortlessly, easing the pain from his wound.

Jacob realized suddenly that although the work of winding the cloth around his arm was through, Louise's hand remained. He looked down quickly at his forearm and the small, porcelain hand that still lay upon it. He looked back to her eyes and saw that the smile had widened deeper than before.

When he realized that her hands had stopped moving, he lifted his gaze up to hers and noticed a curious look in her eyes. Was it concern or something else? *Did she feel the same way?* Jacob was almost ashamed of the thought as he looked away, averting his gaze.

"Courage, man," he could almost hear Pop say.

He lifted his eyes back to hers and his body radiated with heat at what he found. Her eyes shimmered with the secret of a smile, and one end of her mouth turned up, inviting him to ask her what her secret was.

Should he kiss her? More importantly, did she *want* to be kissed?

"How are you feeling now?" she asked him, as she hovered above him like an angel.

"Oh, I feel just fine. My arm feels fine, I mean."

A lump cut in Jacob's throat and he swallowed hard, unsure of what to do.

Just then, Fred started to cry, and Jacob watched with disappointment as Louise turned to get the baby.

When she returned with the child in her arms, Jacob noticed a look of fear in her eyes that shook him out of his daydream. She was biting her bottom lip again, which she only did when she was upset, and a fresh look of concern swam in her expression. Was she worried about his arm or was it something else?

"Louise, what's wrong?"

"Well," she began, "I can't stop thinking about the man that we met at the dance the other night. The one that bumped into me, I mean. I think he's the outlaw, the one looking for his son. I can just feel it in my gut, Jacob."

"Even if he is, it doesn't mean that Fred is his son. There could be other babies left on doorsteps, Louise."

"I know," Louise said. "But I can't shake the feeling that Fred is his son. I can't bear the thought of what would happen if he took him away from us. Perhaps we should keep Fred at home and not take him out in town until we know for sure."

Her voice broke off and her chin dropped, along with Jacob's heart. He decided then he would protect her at all costs.

Jacob reached out with his uninjured left hand and used two fingers to gently lift Louise's chin. He smiled gently and put his arm around her waist, bringing her to him.

"Louise," he said gently, trying not to think of the way her round hip felt under his arm. He cleared his throat and continued, determined not to let his desire distract him.

"You and Fred are my family now. I'm not gonna let any harm come to either of you. I will protect you. You got my word on that."

He felt Louise's tensed muscles relax under his arm as she settled against his shoulder.

"I know you will," she said as she looked up at him with a soft smile.

Her faith in him sent a rush of pride through his chest and he turned to look up at the young woman once more. Her face, still worried, looked hopeful, and he felt the full weight of his responsibility for this young family. He would do whatever it took to keep them safe. Whatever it took.

Chapter Twenty-One

Jacob closed the rusted metal gate with his left hand, and it creaked shut. The colt inside huffed and whinnied, eager for the fresh straw to be placed in his trough.

"Don't whinny at me, ya fool of a horse. It's your own fault that it's taking so long."

Jacob chuckled begrudgingly as he lowered the food into the trough for the rebellious stud. He patted his head through the gate as he bent to devour his meal.

The last couple of days had been challenging, as he had to do everything with his left arm. But Jacob was just relieved that his right arm was not broken.

Louise had fashioned a makeshift sling out of fresh linen and twine. While he was grateful for the material that held his arm in place, it was still frustrating having to do everything with just one arm.

George had offered to take care of the horses while he rested at home for a couple days, but Jacob had no intention of staying home when there was work to be done. Nevertheless, George had delegated the care of the cows to another ranch hand for the day so that he could help Jacob with the horses. Jacob had protested out of pride but was quietly relieved that his friend was coming to help.

"Hey, Jacob," George said as he sauntered up with a fresh bale of hay. "Mind that Jonah doesn't get your other arm while you're in there feeding him."

George laughed as he went around feeding the other horses in the same amount of time it took Jacob to feed two.

When at last they were done, the two friends sat down on a wooden bench that Pop had made outside of the large red barn. The venerable old bench trembled as the tall rancher settled himself upon it. Once he was satisfied that it would not give away, Jacob took out some bread and cheese that Louise had wrapped up for him.

George cleared his throat as he shifted his weight from side to side. It was clear to Jacob that he had something to say.

"I heard some news in town, but I thought you might want to hear about it from me first," George said.

"Oh yeah, what's that?" Jacob asked, half-amused and half-concerned.

"Well," George said as he stood up and rubbed his hands together nervously. "It's about the other night—at the fair."

"George, I already told you, but I'm not upset about your dancing with Louise. I know what you were doing, trying to get us to dance together, ya old cod."

"No, Jacob," George said seriously, "not that. I'm talking about the man that bumped into Louise. I think that that's the outlaw looking for the baby."

Jacob's mind reeled as he remembered how upset Louise had been by the stranger. She had been certain that it was that outlaw and he had done everything in his ability to convince her otherwise. Jacob rolled his shoulders back, trying to settle himself as he turned back to George.

"How do you know?" Jacob asked, as heat and dread flooded his chest. "Could've been anyone." At least that's what he'd told Louise.

"The whole town is astir that they saw him at the fair. Rumor has it, a tall lanky man with blond hair, green eyes, and black leather boots was bothering everyone at the fair, looking for the child. He asked anyone who would listen if they'd seen a baby boy with blond hair and blue eyes about ten months old."

Jacob grunted in assent and his mind raced, trying to figure out what to do next. He looked down at the bread and cheese in his hand and thought of the sweet woman that had made it for him. How would she handle this new information? He had to figure this out before she caught wind of it.

"That's him, all right," Jacob conceded with a sigh. "I should've laid him out flat when I had the chance."

"His name is Roy. Roy Clint. He's the leader of the Clint Gang, it turns out. They are the ones that robbed that train last month; the one that didn't leave any survivors."

"Where is he now? Anyone seen him since the fair?"

"Just Mr. Mercer at the general store. When I was there this morning, he said that Roy came in yesterday making threats and all kinds of promises about what he would do if he didn't get the baby back. He scared poor Mrs. Mercer half to death, and she reported him to the sheriff."

"Oh yeah," he replied. "And what did Charles do?"

"You know Charles," George said. "That two-bit sheriff isn't gonna do anything unless he sees someone shot in the middle of the street. Roy and his gang have been smart enough *not* to do that, so Charles can't do a darn thing."

Jacob's mind spun and the wheels started to turn as he thought of the danger that Louise and Fred might be in at this very moment. He felt his muscles start to clench as fury filled his body. *If that useless sheriff isn't gonna do anything, I'll have to take care of the bandit myself.*

"I best get to town and talk to the sheriff. I need to take care of this if he can't do his job!"

He stood up from the bench in a rush of determination but winced in pain from his badly bruised arm.

"Hold on a second, partner," George said as he stood to meet Jacob's eyes. "You're in no shape to ride down that mountain today. Much less to face an entire gang of bloodthirsty outlaws."

"I've got to take care of Louise and Fred! No one else is going to do it. It's gotta be me."

Jacob turned without another word and marched toward the barn to get Gus saddled up and ready to head to town. His boots beat the ground with the intensity of a bull ready to fight. There was no time to lose.

He needed to talk to the sheriff and fast. If he left now, he could get there before dusk. He could bypass the main road so that he didn't run into anyone from the gang. If he did meet them, he only had one good arm, but that's all it took to shoot.

As he walked up to the heavy door on the large red barn, the sun shone off the hot metal handle. He reached up with his good hand to grab the iron lever and pull open the barn, but he was stopped short by George, who pushed his hand onto the barn door.

"What do you think you're doing, Jacob? Are you trying to get yourself *killed?* You've got a wife, you know."

"I know. That's who I'm trying to protect!" Jacob hollered at his friend. "Her and the baby."

"I'm not gonna let you do this!" George yelled back. Jacob could tell by the angry upturned eyebrows that George meant business.

"Well, what exactly do you suggest, then?" Jacob bellowed back.

"Why don't you just give the baby back to the church?" George said with a sigh. "The pastor's in town and he'll know what to do. Besides, no outlaw in his right mind is going to attack a preacher with a church next door to the sheriff. He'd be safe there. And you and Louise would be safe as well. Just give him to the preacher. He'll keep the boy safe."

Rage filled Jacob's bones and he lunged at his friend, pinning him against the wall with his left arm. His boots dug into the ground as his arm went against his friend and he looked into surprised eyes. Embarrassed, Jacob relented and backed away from the wall with a sigh.

"It ain't gonna happen, George," he said as he backed up slowly. "I can't do that to Louise. It would break her."

He expected his friend to yell at him for pushing him against the side of the old barn, but instead, George started to laugh.

"You're in love with her, aren't you?"

"Don't be ridiculous!" Jacob retorted. "I'm just trying to keep all of us alive."

Jacob was a ball of emotion and stood in shock as his friend set his arm on his shoulder and looked at him seriously.

"There's worse things than falling in love with your wife, Jacob Montgomery."

Jacob sighed in concession and plopped down on the ground against the barn. He felt completely lost, like a frightened child stumbling through the woods. He couldn't give the baby back and he couldn't confront Roy on his own, but he couldn't do *nothing.*

"What are we gonna do, George?"

"Well, we're gonna be smart about it for one thing. Roy may have a gang of bandits, but we have a town full of ranchers and farmers that aren't eager to be robbed or pillaged. The townsfolk, Jacob. We use them and we can utilize the town."

"Are we talking about the *same* town?" Jacob asked, aghast. "I hear the things they say about me on the rare occasion I wander onto Main Street. They're not gonna want to help me."

"That's where you're wrong. You may not trust them, but you also don't know them—just as they don't know you—but that's about to change. It's time to round us up a posse."

Chapter Twenty-Two

While she had done nothing wrong by being present as she gathered their daily batch of eggs, Louise knew that the conversation had not been intended for her. Jacob was only trying to protect them and there was no reason to make his plight harder. She did not want to make this situation more difficult, especially with Jacob sounding unusually hot-headed. Perhaps if she could forge a plan, then she could take some of the load off him.

Still, it was hard to hear. Louise fell back against the edge of the splintered wooden wall, as if she'd been punched in the gut. She allowed herself to slide down the barn wall until she plopped on the ground, her heart pounding as she tried to make sense of what she'd just overheard. Her worst fear was confirmed.

So, it's true, she thought. The aggressive stranger at the fair was the outlaw, and apparently, Fred's real father.

She was worried about Fred to be sure, but she was surprised to find herself equally worried about Jacob.

The realization of the danger that she and Fred had brought to Jacob landed heavily upon her and her heart went out to her brave husband. He didn't ask for any of this and now it was on him to protect them all.

She leaned against the outside wall of the barn and stared desperately at the cool blue sky, as if she could somehow ascend to the heavens—as if she could somehow escape.

Louise's hands clutched her stomach, trying to keep her heart from falling out.

What would they do? How would they survive this? Who could she talk to that would help?

Sarah! She would know what to do, or if not, at least she could provide a kind ear. If there was one thing that Louise had learned about her dear friend, it was that she was a determined fighter. Whether she needed help learning her way around town, discovering new berries, brushes, and herbs, or just cooking with a lack of supplies, she knew she could count on Sarah.

Good news, too—she was already in their single-room cabin, watching Fred for her as she picked eggs. Talking to Sarah about all of this would be as easy as returning home. Louise poked her head around the edge of the barn, waiting to see if the men had yet gone. George and Jacob were still there, but their backs were turned, and she waited until they walked off to make her departure.

Finally, the two men walked inside the barn and closed the door hard behind them. Louise stole that moment to take off to the cabin as fast as her feet would carry her.

***

Louise burst into the cabin and threw open the door like an escaped convict knocking down a cell wall.

"What on earth is the matter? You got a snake in your bonnet?" Sarah asked, with eyebrows as high as the sky.

Louise bent over and put her hands on her knees as she sucked in as much air as she could manage. She had somehow managed to run all the way to her cabin, and now that she'd arrived, she couldn't manage to slow her breathing. Somewhere between the running and the worrying, her heart had beat faster and faster until she couldn't slow it down.

"He's here, Sarah!" she said between gasps of air. "What are we... what are we gonna do?"

"Who's here? What are we doing about what now? Louise, you've gotta slow down. Catch your breath and take a second."

Sarah sat Fred down on the carpet by Minnie and then walked to set a soft hand on her friend's back. Louise was grateful for the comfort, and as Sarah gently rubbed her back and hugged her, Louise felt her breath slowly return to her.

"This happens to me sometimes when I get to worryin.' It happened a lot in Missouri. Not so often here. You must think I'm so silly," Louise said when she had finally caught her breath and was able to stand up.

"Not at all," Sarah said with kind eyes, as she smiled sincerely at Louise. "We all have our burdens to bear, Louise. That's why God gave us friends to make the carryin' a little bit easier. Now, what's going on?"

Louise paused to collect her thoughts before she replied, "Do you remember the man at the fair that bumped into me when Jacob and I were dancing?"

"You mean that no-good stranger who spoiled your kiss? I almost gave him a piece of my mind but then decided it wasn't very ladylike," she said with a giggle.

"I had a feeling that he was the outlaw looking for Fred and just now, I overheard that it's true. His name is Roy and he's going around town, with a band of outlaws, telling anyone who will listen that he'll do whatever it takes to get his son back."

Sarah put her hand on her hip in defiance and Louise was grateful to have her on her side.

"Him lookin' for a baby don't mean nothin'. Babies are abandoned in these parts all the time. What makes you think that Fred's *his* baby?

"All the townsfolk say he's looking for a baby with blond hair and blue eyes, around ten months old."

The two women looked at each other knowingly and then at the baby crawling and toddling around the floor. Fred held onto the swinging rocking chair as his legs jiggled and wobbled. Undeterred, he leapt merrily and reached out to grab Minnie's tail.

Minnie whirled around, but instead of hissing, she pushed her head gently into his tummy as if trying to steady him from falling. At last, Fred plopped down on top of Minnie, who wriggled out from under the toddler and nestled up against him as he laughed.

Louise's heart swelled with joy. It was a pleasant distraction, but it was quickly overtaken by a foreboding fear and a reminder that this sweet slice of happiness could be plucked away at any moment. She wouldn't let that happen.

Her love for Fred gave her a fresh determination and she turned back to face her friend.

"I won't let him take Fred. What do I do, Sarah?"

Sarah sighed and wrapped her arms around Louise, giving her a gentle hug.

"It's going to be okay. We know that Fred is the outlaw's son, but he doesn't know who has him. We've got that on our side."

"That's a good point. But he's bound to find out if he asks enough people."

Sarah hesitated. "Nobody's claimed this baby officially and you've had him for the better part of a year. You've got every right to adopt him legally. Oh, that's it! You and Jacob can adopt him, Louise! You just need to talk to the sheriff as soon as possible about making it official."

"How am I going to do that without the gang knowing about it? I can't exactly bring Fred with me into town!"

"Of course not. I'll stay here with him. If the gang hasn't been here to get Fred yet, then that means they don't know where he is. They won't be fool enough to stop you in the middle of town in broad daylight. Go now! Take the wagon. If you leave now, you can get home before it's dark."

"You're right, Sarah! I just knew that you'd have a good plan!"

The two friends embraced once more. Then, Louise grabbed her frock and headed for the door. Nothing was going to get in her way.

***

Louise walked down the rickety steps of the sheriff's office, content. She'd been careful to explain the details in as ladylike a way as possible and the sheriff had been respectful in kind. She wondered why Jacob spoke so foul of the old sheriff, but that was a concern for another day. He agreed to pass along her request for guardianship to the judge. There was nothing more that she needed to do. In the eyes of the state of Nevada, she and Jacob were Fred's guardians until further notice. She took a deep breath of relief, enjoying the cool autumn air as her boots hit the dust.

She looked around the little town and savored it, perhaps for the first time.

The town might be simple, but the people are decent, she thought with a smile.

The sheriff had been sweeter than a piece of pie, and it had gone so much easier than she expected. She wondered if it was because she was a woman, or perhaps she was just nicer to him that Jacob. It really made her appreciative for the small community and what it offered.

Across from the sheriff's office was a tall, narrow building. An orange sign hung on it that said, "Dressmaker." She recognized with glee that there was a new business in town and enjoyed the growing community around her. Outlaw or not, the times were changing, and she felt secure here in Austin.

She turned back to her wagon and walked right up the small iron steps that Jacob had attached for her benefit. A smile spread across her face and spread through her as she thought of her wild husband, now somewhat tamed and chivalrous.

He might just become a gentleman yet, she chuckled to herself. As she settled onto the wooden bench at the front of the rig, where Jacob normally sat, Louise couldn't help but fight the concern of what her husband would think if he knew she had come to town by herself. Women might have more freedom in the west than down south, as she'd seen women occasionally go through town unattended, but with everything going on with the gang, she knew that Jacob would be worried sick.

Never mind that now. He'll be glad when he sees that I've got everything settled.

"Ho, Gus. Let's head back up the hill," Louise said as she snapped at his reins. "It's time to go home."

As the wagon headed up the road toward the outside of town, a cold wind blew in and sent a chill down her spine. Off in the distance, she heard a low rumble. She looked up in horror to see ten men on horseback just over the horizon. Their steeds were galloping furiously as they rode straight toward her.

The sound of forty hooves pounding the earth at full speed made the ground beneath her rumble and her heart shook in unison.

What have I gotten myself into? Help me, Lord!

She could tell that Gus agreed with the sentiment as he reared up on his hind legs and whinnied in protest.

"Woah, Gus. Easy boy," she said as she pulled him back and guided the rig over to the church.

She looked around wildly, unsure of what to do as the horses in the distance drew closer, their galloping hooves sounding more like approaching thunder. She noticed people coming out of every door and heads poking out of every window to see what the fuss was about. The traveling preacher came out of the antique church. He spotted Louise, huddled in her wagon, and hurried to join her.

The only person in town that didn't bother coming out was the sheriff. Louise frowned. *Maybe that's why Jacob doesn't like him. Strange.*

"Where on earth is your husband, lady?" the preacher said with a concerned air of authority.

The jovial man who had married her and Jacob looked much more somber now. His brow was furrowed in concern and the right edge of his mouth puckered as he muttered something under his breath.

Louise opened her mouth to speak, and perhaps answer his question, only the preacher cut her off. "Listen, Mrs.

Montgomery," he began, "You were brave to come here but also pretty foolhardy."

"What do you mean, preacher?" Louise asked as her whole body grew tense.

"That's the gang coming there, that is. Now, I need you to do exactly as I tell ya. When I give you the signal, I want you to snap those reins like you've never snapped them before and don't look back until you get to the ranch, you here?"

The gang was here? Already? Louise didn't feel prepared at all...

"You mean—right now?"

"No, child. If you rode out right now, he would follow you and you wouldn't make it up over that hill. We're going to have to pull them in close and talk loud enough to get the sheriff out here. Follow my lead and by the grace of God, we'll get out of this alive."

"Whatever you say, preacher," Louise replied shakily as sweat dotted her brow.

At that moment, a skinny boy with red shaggy hair ran up to the preacher. He could not have been more than eight years old, but Louise could tell that he had all the courage of a cowboy. He held a wooden toy gun at his side and held it in the air as he ran.

"I'll protect you, preacher," the boy said, a determined look in his eye.

"You'll do no such thing," the preacher said as he pointed the child's toy gun toward the dirt. "I need you to run to the sheriff's office as fast as you can. Let him know he's needed at the church this instant. Can I count on you?"

"You can count on me, sir!" the boy saluted at attention with all the grit of a Yankee soldier. Without another word, the boy turned and took off, true to his word.

As the gang got closer to the small church where Louise and the preacher waited, they slowed to a trot and then stopped about ten yards away, in front of the saloon. To Louise's surprise, she picked out the outlaw, who she only knew as Roy. She spotted him instantly from the same green shirt he'd worn at the fair, the Stetson hat that sat on his head, slightly crooked, and those sharp green eyes. While the crew waited across the street next to the saloon, Roy and one of his men sauntered over on their horses.

Louise was determined to stay calm, to stay focused, and to listen to the preacher. She sat frozen as a block of ice and couldn't find a reason to move. Her eyes were fixed on Roy's as she wondered what he was going to do.

As the unwelcome stranger walked up to her, Louise was able to observe more of him than the last time that they'd met. She could see that his emerald, green eyes had wrinkles on the side, whether from age or sun exposure, she did not know.

His right eye also had a scar just above it. No doubt received during one of the many train robberies that they were known for. Roy was lanky and tall but hunched over, as if he were trying to accommodate those shorter than himself, or perhaps had a bad back. His body posture was relaxed, but Louise could not help but notice that his cold green eyes looked like they could kill.

"Howdy there, y'all," Roy said as he stopped just a few feet from the edge of the wagon. "And just who might you be?"

Louise knew that she was expected to say something in response, but she couldn't bring herself to do it. She was still frozen solid in fear.

"That's none of your concern, Roy," said the preacher loudly with a smile as he stretched back his shoulders. "But if you wanted to talk about the good book, why don't you hop off your horse and come on into church and we'll chat a bit."

Louise could tell that the preacher was trying to make enough noise to get the sheriff's attention, and she hoped that he was successful.

"Oh no, that won't be necessary," Roy said with a smile. His lips pulled up into a sneer, and Louise wondered if he was amused by the conversation.

"I'm not sure how we can help you then, son."

"I'm not your son!" Roy snapped at the preacher before he turned his cruel gaze to Louise.

"But I do *have* a son, and this little lady here knows exactly what I'm talking about, don't ya', darlin? Where is my baby, *Louise?*" His voice sounded more like a growl than human speech, and Louise could tell that a beast bristled inside of him, wanting to come out.

White hot fear that Louise had been trying to hold back permeated her skin and flooded her chest. How did he know her name? If he knew who she was and that she had the baby, what else did he know? Did he know where they lived, too?

"My baby is none of your concern, sir," Louise answered shakily. She felt courage rising inside of her in defense of the child she'd grown to love.

"No need to lie, Louise," he said her name again, and she could tell that it was spoken more aggressively this time. "It ain't fittin' to lie, not for a good church-goin' lady such as yourself, ain't that right, preacher?"

"There's nothin' for you here, Roy," the preacher responded calmly, "Unless of course, you'd like to step down off your horse and discuss repentance. It's not too late."

Roy cackled in response. His crew joined in, mocking the preacher.

Louise pressed her lips tight. She would not give anything away to this man. She owed him *nothing.* Instead, she sat silently and prayed for help.

"I know you've got my son. Now, you and your husband can do this the easy way or the hard way, but mark my words, I will have what belongs to me."

"He doesn't belong to you!" Louise said sharply, surprising herself. She knew she should stop talking but she surged forward confidently. "I've already been to see the sheriff and seen to it that I'm Fred's legal guardian now."

As soon as she said it, she wished she could take it back. She saw the green eyes that had previously stayed cool and collected behind a thin veneer of calm suddenly turn violent. She watched as Roy's eyes shook with fury and he squeezed the reins of his horse as if the leather might crack.

"It looks like you've already chosen the hard way," he said roughly as he leaned forward on his horse.

"Now, what seems to be the problem here?" a voice called out from behind Louise. She turned to see the sheriff amble up behind them at last with the red-headed boy at his side. She smiled gratefully at the man who had helped her secure Fred's place just a few minutes prior.

Perhaps Jacob was wrong about him. He'd shown up, after all. That's not something a coward would do. Even if it was at the last minute.

"Well, howdy, sheriff," Roy said as he sat up nice and tall in his saddle. He smiled ruefully, putting on airs. "There's no problem here. I was just telling Mrs. Montgomery that I was looking forward to paying her family a call, just as soon as someone lets me know where I might visit them." Roy laughed as he spoke, and it sent a harrowing chill through Louise's body.

"No, Roy," the sheriff replied. "I don't believe you will be." The sheriff placed one hand on the gun at his hip and tapped it ever so slightly with his thumb.

"Now, we don't want any trouble here, sheriff," Roy said as he leaned back in his saddle with a chuckle. "We just want to be friends with the Montgomery's. Real good friends."

"I tell you what," the sheriff said slowly, as he walked up to Roy and placed his hand squarely on the outlaw's saddle, "Why don't you come on down and we can go inside and have ourselves a chat. What do you say?"

"Well, I sure would love to," Roy said as he cocked his head to the side and nodded at the sheriff, "but I don't know if my men would look too kindly upon that. What do you think, boys? Should I go sit a spell with the sheriff?"

"Afraid that doesn't work for me, Roy," chuckled a giant of a man, with shoulders as broad as his horse.

"Don't work for me neither," growled a short but stout man at his right.

This got the attention of the band of outlaws at the saloon, who hopped on their horses and stared at Roy, as if awaiting his next command.

"Charles!" a high-pitched voice hollered behind them. "Charles Daniels, you come over here this instant!"

The entire party turned to see a slight woman with bright orange hair running to fetch the boy standing by the sheriff. The trembling woman bent down and gathered her son into her arms.

"Come along now, son," the mother said as her voice shook with fear. "We don't want to bother these fine gentlemen."

The shaking woman curtsied and smiled in Roy's direction before grabbing her son's hand and hurrying away.

Louise couldn't help but notice that as the woman and her son ran off, the only person that watched their departure was Roy. She noticed a hint of pain in his eyes as he stared at the boy and his mother, and Louise felt a brief and momentary sympathy for the outlaw.

Was it possible he really cared for Fred? From his expression, she couldn't help but wonder. Would he have been a good father if he weren't on the wrong side of the law? Her heart ached, for a reason she couldn't understand, as her thoughts drifted to her own childhood.

Memories of being ignored and then yelled at filled her mind in an unwelcome flood and she shook them off, but it begged the question: Could the cankers have been decent parents if she had been their natural child instead of just a burden on the doorstep? Her heart sank at unfathomable questions she could never answer.

"Now, Louise! *Go!*"

Louise nearly jumped out of her seat when she heard the preacher's words resounding like a bell in her ear. Without a second thought, she jerked the reins as hard as she could, and Gus took off like he was at the races.

As she passed the band of outlaws standing outside of the saloon, one tipped his hat at her with a laugh while another twirled his gun with a sneer. It was clear they would do nothing without their boss, who was still being detained by the sheriff.

She heard Roy call her name, but she didn't dare look back. She leaned over the reins and urged Gus forward. She and Gus raced toward the ranch, like lightning flung from heaven. She didn't stop to think or look back in the time it took them to flee up the mountain. True to her word, she obeyed the preacher's directions. She pushed onward like a sailor desperate for the shore. She didn't blink once until she saw the lights of her home light up the dusk.

She saw something move in the twilight and squinted to see what it was. She could just barely make out the figure of a man running up the hill toward her with all his might.

Chapter Twenty-Three

Jacob couldn't believe his ears as he stood in his cabin with Sarah and George. He paced, trying to get his bearings.

"What do you mean she went to town by herself?" he questioned Sarah.

"Well, Mama sends me to town sometimes for one thing or another," Sarah insisted. "Besides, she was going to meet with the sheriff. Isn't that the safest place for her to be?"

Jacob watched in disbelief as the naive young girl rubbed the palms of her hands together and fiddled with her thumbs nervously.

"You should have left it to us," George said as he put his hand on his head. "But we know you were just trying to help, don't we, Jacob? ...*Jacob?*"

Jacob looked past Sarah to see Fred asleep in his cradle. Minnie sat next to him with her back to the cradle, facing Jacob, as if guarding the baby from the argument. He smiled briefly, grateful that Fred was safe and sound with a friend by his side. But he had to find the baby's mother.

"This is madness. I've got to go get Louise. Sarah, can you stay with Fred a spell longer until I get back?"

"Of course," Sarah said sorrowfully, and Jacob could see the tears building up in her eyes. There was no time for him to comfort her now. Her father would have to do that.

Jacob grabbed his Stetson and flung open the door with one hand.

It was nearly nightfall and he saw that the haze of dusk was falling over the valley. He could see the sun starting to duck down behind the trees in the distance, while on the other side of the sky, a pale blue moon started to show.

If he was going to find her before it was pitch black outside, he had to be quick. He looked to saddle Gus, as that would be the quickest way to get to town, before he realized that Louise had already taken him.

To drive the wagon, of course.

That woman never failed to surprise him and occasionally infuriate him, but this time, the only thing driving him mad was not knowing where she was—and wondering whether she was alive or dead.

With Gus gone, the rest of the horses were about a mile away in the stables. If he took off now, he could get there on foot in about eight minutes, give or take.

He started to run in the direction of the stables, when he heard a noise, almost imperceptible at first. It was the rumble of wheels rolling over the ground and horse hooves pounding the dirt.

*Louise! H*e turned toward the sound and started to run up the hill that led out of the small valley.

Finally, the wagon rolled over the edge of the little hilltop. Gus and Louise came barreling down the hill as he raced to meet them.

"Louise!" he cried out.

The wagon turned toward him then and started in his direction. Whether it was because of his wife steering the rig or simply his horse following his master's voice, he couldn't be sure. But at last, the rig reached Jacob and came to a sudden halt.

Jacob raced around to the side of the wagon to fetch his bride. He would never be so foolish as to let her be in harm's way again. He helped her down from the wagon and gathered her into his arms as she fell against his chest.

Her body was shaking, and her chest was heaving as she breathed irregularly, like a drowned man who had just come up for air.

"Louise, are you okay?"

He sat back against the hillside with the woman in his arms, as she shivered and shook against him.

"He... He found us! He knows who we are! Jacob, I'm so sorry."

He did not need to ask who she was talking about. He already knew. He was just glad that she had made it home safely.

"What happened? Did he hurt you?" Jacob looked around like a lion defending his pride. He was ready to fight at a moment's notice to defend this girl with his life.

Louise told him what had taken place in town. Jacob's heart surged with a mixture of rage and fear, not at his young wife, but on her behalf.

I should've been there to protect her. I never should've left her side.

"We need to get you inside before you catch your death of cold."

Jacob stood with Louise in his arms and carried his shivering bride into the cabin. He kicked open the door and found a surprised George and Sarah staring at them with eyes larger than the sky.

Jacob walked over to the bed and laid Louise upon it, who immediately curled into a ball. Minnie the cat jumped up on the bed no sooner than Louise had touched it. Jacob looked on fondly as the orange tabby buried her nose into Louise's hair and purred softly as she cuddled against her, warming her up.

Without thinking, Jacob bent down to kiss her forehead and tuck her into bed.

As he kissed her on the forehead, he felt a cold, trembling hand on his cheek. Even when she was terrified, she was still gentle and thought of others. His heart melted for the woman, and he wished that he could take away her trauma from the day.

"I'm so sorry, Jacob. I never should've gone to town."

"It's okay. You're home now. Just get some rest. I'll take care of it from here."

With one more kiss, Jacob tucked her in and turned to talk to Sarah and George.

"Sarah, would you mind watching over the baby while I talk to your Papa?"

"Of course not, Mr. Montgomery."

"George, can I see you outside for a second?"

The friends walked outside, and the porch creaked with the heaviness of the situation, as if it understood the burden it was about to bear.

"It's time to round up that posse we talked about."

"Great; let me grab my hat and I'll come with you."

"No, it's gotta be me. I need you to stay here and protect my family. Will you do that for me, George?"

"Jacob, you know I will," George said as he placed a strong but reassuring hand on his shoulder.

"Good. At the first light, I'll head for town. I'll gather the ranch hands together and let them know to be on guard. We will probably need some men from the nearby ranches as well. I won't be back without a posse big enough to stop Roy once and for all."

***

The next morning, as the sun began to rise and peek its golden head above the treetops in the valley, Jacob was already on his way to the ranch.

He didn't usually come out quite this early, as he preferred Louise's biscuits and coffee to anything the boys could cook up in their smaller and much less elaborate cabins, but he couldn't lose a moment. For all he knew, Roy and his men could be on their way even now.

As Gus trotted past the red barn that held all the horses, Jacob spotted the tiny cabins in the distance. The smells of fresh biscuits and bacon floated on the breeze. Now would be the best time to talk to them when their stomachs were full, and they were all gathered in one place.

"*H'yah,* Gus! Let's get this done. We've got a long way to go today, and this is just the beginning."

Jacob nodded at the ranch hands as he rode into their camp. They all looked up, one by one, surprised to see their boss coming to take breakfast with them. A few of them sat up straighter.

"Morning, boss!" said one of the newer hands as he hurried to buckle up his overalls. He ran out to shake Jacob's hand and offer him a cup of coffee.

"It ain't much but you're welcome to it," the young man said with an unsure smile.

"Thank you," Jacob said, as he took the coffee and gave it a swig. The taste of old, burnt coffee cooked in a rusty tin tasted sour, and it took all his self-control not to spit it out.

He knew that Louise's cooking was good, but he had forgotten just how good he had it. Less than a year ago, this was how all his coffee used to taste. She had brought so much goodness into his life, so much blessing, and the sour coffee in his mouth now was a bold reminder of that.

"Listen up, men," he said, as he stepped up onto a log near their morning campfire. A dozen or so men came out of their cabins, eager for what the boss man was about to say.

"The outlaw we were warned about is in town with his band of outlaws and train robbers. I need all of you to keep a rifle or a pistol on you at all times. Gotta be alert. We don't know when they're coming but we do know that they'll regret the day they tangled with this here ranch crew."

The ranch hands cheered, lifting their coffees and firearms in support. Jacob went on to explain that they would take turns guarding the main house in shifts, two at a time. It was at the front of the ranch and the closest part of the land to town, so more than likely it was where they could expect to see Roy's men pop up first.

When he was done speaking to the men, they came up one at a time to shake his hand and Jacob was pleasantly surprised to find how well received his speech was. While he was glad that it had gone well, he knew that he had to get to town and round up more men to help.

He had to form a larger posse, and not just the dozen or so ranch hands that worked for him. Everything hung on this. He knew he could count on his ranch hands if for no other reason than that the ranch was their bread and butter, too. But could he count on the townsfolk? And how would he get them to trust him when he had stayed so far away for so long?

Fancy talking had never been his strong suit, but he might have to give an inspiring speech to convince men to risk their lives for his cause.

Help me, Lord. Show me how to do this.

Jacob shook off his fears and decided to focus on the task at hand. He kept his eyes fixed on the horizon and urged Gus onward into town.

As Jacob rode Gus down the main street into Austin, Nevada, he could feel the stares of the townsfolk poking out of their windows.

They've come to see the mountain man. This is what I get for not coming into town that often.

Jacob pulled Gus to a halt and swung one leg over the saddle as he hopped down. He grabbed the leather reins and walked Gus over to the saloon entrance of the inn.

As he tied Gus to the fence out front, a cool morning breeze blew past and smelled of bacon and grits. He was just in time. Perhaps a quick cup of coffee and some bacon would give him a little bit of courage for his next speech.

***

Talking to the men in the saloon had gone better than Jacob expected. While they'd had plenty of questions, it turned out that most of the shopkeepers, minors, and farmers around town were none too keen to see a gang of bandits take over their town that they worked so hard to build. It probably didn't hurt that Jacob bought a round of drinks on him. Either way, he was elated they were willing to join. All the men promised to be ready and said that they would send word next time Roy was sighted.

Jacob walked out of the saloon and allowed the mid-morning sunshine to warm his weary face. Things in town had gone far better than he expected, and he had a bit of time left in his morning before he headed back to the cabin for dinner.

He made a quick stop at the general store and picked up a handmade fountain pen and some ink for Louise's journal. He had not forgotten that he was attempting to woo her, no matter how crazy the situation around them might be. He wanted to do whatever he could to bring her some happiness, short-lived as it might be in the middle of all this chaos. Besides, he was bringing back a bunch of good news—good enough even to write down.

***

When Jacob walked into his home, he was relieved to find a gentle fire crackling in the hearth and his friend sitting beside it. True to his word, George had stayed to protect Louise and the baby, and he sat in a rocking chair by the fire, reading his Bible.

Sarah sat in the rocking chair with Fred in her arms. The two looked up and smiled at Jacob as he walked in and then gestured toward the bed where his wife lay sleeping.

Louise was still curled up in bed, no doubt exhausted from her terrible adventure the evening before. Minnie the cat had not left her side. She was curled up in a tiny ball against her mistress's legs where she had found a cozy nook in which to cuddle.

"Louise," Jacob said, as he knelt next to the bed where she slept soundly.

Her soft blonde lashes fluttered as he said her name. They softly opened to reveal pale blue eyes that smiled sleepily up at him.

Jacob enjoyed this simple moment, watching his beautiful wife, and he wondered if this must be what it was like waking up next to someone you cared about.

I could get used to this.

It would be an upgrade from the pallet on the floor to be sure. Louise let out a yawn as she looked up at Jacob.

"Good morning," she said with another yawn. Jacob watched as she stretched her arms out behind her and sat up slowly, rustling the sleeping cat at her knees.

Jacob watched Louise look around the room and come to the realization that it was nearly mid-day.

"Oh my!" she said, sitting up with a jolt. "I didn't intend to sleep in so!"

Jacob chuckled gently and set his hand on Louise's knee.

"It's understandable. You had quite a fright last night. But that's no matter. I've got it sorted."

"You've got it sorted? Already?"

"Well, nearly sorted," he said. "At any rate, I have a plan of action in place and it's going to take care of everything. Never mind that now. I have a gift for you."

Jacob reached into his jacket pocket and produced the handmade fountain pen along with the fresh jar of ink.

"Why, you didn't have to do this. Whatever is this for?"

"It's for a talented woman who's good at writing. Anyhow, I reckon you should keep writing in your journal. Don't let my being nosy stop you. I won't look inside of it again."

A smile spread across Louise's face, and she leaned toward Jacob as she wrapped her arms around his neck gently.

"Thank you," she whispered softly into his ear. He could feel her smiling as she kissed him on the cheek. It brought warmth and courage to his heart.

Now, that's something worth fighting for.

Chapter Twenty-Four

"Here you go, Jonah," Louise said, as she held out the grain in her hand to the ornery young horse.

Jonah greedily gobbled up the grain there. Louise giggled as the horse's lips tickled the palm of her hand. She made sure to keep her hand flat as Jacob had taught her so that Jonah didn't accidentally take a thumb with it. But she had a feeling, as the hungry stallion gobbled up the food, that he was being gentler than usual.

Louise smiled back at Jacob with a slight smirk on her face, letting him know that she'd done it right.

"Now, why is he so good for you?" he asked with a smirk on his face. "He's always right awful for me and I'm the one who knows how to train horses. That ain't right, I tell ya!"

Louise laughed as Jacob winked at her. She enjoyed the banter that they had shared lately, and she decided to give him a clever jab of her own.

"How do you know it's Jonah that's been no good? Maybe the problem is with the trainer." She winked back at him and jabbed him gently with her elbow.

"No, not that horse!" Jacob went on. "He's no good, but you seem to have a way with him somehow. He must like pretty girls."

Louise blushed and shook a finger at Jacob before turning back to the stallion.

"Aw! Don't listen to him, Jonah. I know you're a good horse. Jacob is just jealous that you get to kiss my hand."

As soon as she had mentioned kissing, Louise blushed again and wished she could take back what she said. Her pale white wrists flashed hot pink and she hid them behind her back, embarrassed.

In truth, after they had nearly kissed at the fair, she had thought of almost nothing else. She longed for his arms to be around her again, for his face to be close enough to kiss, but it wouldn't be ladylike to say so.

She hoped that her sweet smiles and tender glances would let him know that she wanted more. But she was starting to worry he wasn't going to take the hint.

She'd gotten carried away this time and kicked herself for mentioning it. She would just have to be patient and wait for him to make the first move.

"Well, I best go get some more feed for Jonah here. When he's done kissing your hand, he might want some more."

Louise's mouth dropped open in embarrassment as Jacob winked at her and walked away with a kick in his step.

She turned back to Jonah and patted him on the head while she waited for Jacob to return with the food.

Jonah poked his head through the bars of the fence and whinnied as he pushed his ears toward Louise's hands.

"Oh, so you want another scratch behind the ears, do ya?"

Louise accommodated Jonah and scratched his ears as she thought about the last few days. Aside from the terrifying events in town, everything at the ranch had been right as rain.

She had been pleasantly surprised that Jacob wasn't angry with her for sneaking off to town, and she couldn't stop thinking about how romantic it was that he'd brought her a fountain pen.

She didn't know if it was because of the gift or if the two of them were simply bonded together in the midst of trouble, but things had gone so well between the two of them since then. They sat by the fire each night, talking and laughing. She'd heard more words from him in the last three days than in the entire last year that she'd lived here. Far from satisfying her, now she wanted to know more—wanted to be closer—and longed for his kiss.

"What do you think, Jonah? Is he ever gonna kiss me?"

"Sure, darlin', I'll give you a kiss," a snarling voice said behind her. The voice was gravelly like a sick dog, and she knew it didn't belong to Jacob.

She spun around to see a stranger standing on the other side of the fence near the barn. She pressed her body back against the gate between her and Jonah, wishing that she was on the other side with the horse.

The stranger held a gun lazily at his side and that could only mean one thing: He was part of Roy's gang. That would explain his confidence.

"You best get out of here," she said, as she put a shaky hand on her hip. "My husband's around and he's going to be back… Why, he's gonna be back just any second now."

"Doesn't look that way to me, darlin'," the mangy looking man said. "Looks to me like you're here all by your lonesome."

"Afraid not!" a furious voice called out from behind the barn. She heard the cock of a gun right before a shot rang out and the outlaw ducked.

"Her husband's right here!" Jacob bellowed. He walked out from behind the barn with the smoking barrel of his rifle pointed dead at the outlaw.

"There's a lot of other ranchers around these parts that don't take too kindly to outlaws, you know," Jacob said as he walked closer to the stranger. "If you hang around a little longer, you just might meet a few of them."

"Naw, that won't be necessary!" the once-confident man said shakily. "Anyhow, there's no need to shoot the messenger. I just came to deliver one."

"And just what might that message be?" Jacob asked in a low growl. He cocked the gun once more, and Louise watched as a gun shell fell to the ground, warning of more to come.

"Take it easy!" the outlaw said. "I just came to let you know that Roy knows you're here, and he said that he'll be 'round to visit shortly."

The man tipped his hat and ran backwards, toward a sandy brown horse tied up at a nearby cactus. He was nearly there when he slipped over a rock and landed square on his rear end.

"I won't be causin' you folks any more trouble," the stray dog of a man said as he climbed onto his horse. "What's between you and Roy is no business of mine. I don't have time for the fight and that's about to follow."

Then, with a quick flick of his reins, the man dug the heels of his boots into his horse's side and took off down the mountain.

Louise leaned against the fence and let out a giant sigh. It was over. At least for now. She watched the usually composed rancher run to her with wild fear in his eyes.

"Are you okay?" he asked as he gathered her into his arms. He turned her around, looking at her as if she might secretly be full of bullet holes.

"I'm okay, Jacob! I'm fine! Because of you. You... you saved me."

She placed the palms of her hands onto the full, firm muscles of his chest. She could hear him breathing quickly, almost panting for air, and her hands could feel the rhythm of his heart beating out of control.

Was it because of her? Or simply because of what just happened? She looked up into his eyes, wanting to ask the question, but when her eyes met his, she caught a lump in her throat.

His eyes were tender in their strength and beautiful even in their pain. She knew that she was safe with him, and she gently rested her head on his chest.

They had to return eventually, but she wanted to drink in this moment for a minute longer. She might not be able to initiate a kiss, but certainly it was acceptable to rest in a man's arms that just saved you from a rifleman, especially if he was your husband.

She knew that they couldn't stay that way forever, as Sarah and George were waiting at home with Fred, since he couldn't leave the house.

Fred!

"Oh no, Jacob! What about Fred? Do you think there's any chance that outlaw is headed to the cabin next?"

"The cabin," Jacob said as he looked down into her eyes. "We've got to get home!"

"We didn't bring the wagon! We walked here. What were we thinking?"

Jacob pulled her hand onto his chest, and she wondered what he had in mind.

"We don't have the wagon, and most of the horses are out in the pasture right now, but, well, we do have Jonah here."

"Jonah? Are you out of your mind? He's too wild to ride!"

"Hey, I thought you said he was a good horse?" Jacob asked with a smirk. "Besides," he continued with a more serious look in his eyes, "he's the fastest chance we got of gettin' to the house. If I ride him, can you sit on the back of the saddle and hold on tight?"

Louise's stomach did a small flip. Whether it was from Jacob riding a wild horse or worrying about Fred, she couldn't say for sure. But one thing she did know: She trusted Jacob.

"If you say this is what we do, then this is what we do. Now, hoist me up. We gotta get home!"

Chapter Twenty-Five

Jacob raced to the house as fast as the wild stallion's feet would carry them. Fear flooded through him, though not because of the wild horse, as he wondered what might be taking place at their home.

Had the stranger headed for the cabin? Or worse yet, had Roy sent other men to their house?

The feeling of Louise's tiny arms holding him tightly around his chest filled him with a mixture of love and concern. Her grasp reminded him of his responsibility and his heart ached at the duty he hoped he could fulfill.

When they finally arrived, Jacob slowed Jonah to a trot when he saw that no one was there guarding the front of the cabin. Where were the ranch hands?

The stallion tried to run in another direction, and Jacob jerked the stallion's reins hard and fast to the right, bringing him to bear. The horse finally relented and took them around the back of the house as his master commanded. Jacob knew that if anyone was there, he needed to be aware of it before they were seen.

"What are you doing?" Louise asked. "We've got to get inside and make sure that Fred is all right!"

Jacob turned to look at Louise and held a finger to his lips, motioning for her to hush. The girl looked at him with terrified, round eyes. He knew that it wasn't her safety she was worried about but the babe's. While Jacob was also eager to ensure Fred's safety, he wasn't willing to risk Louise's life in the process.

He looked for horse tracks around their small garden and pointed past Louise as he looked. The cold hard dirt at the back of the house lay bare, with not a single footprint on it. Either no one had been there, or they had taken special care to make it appear as if they were not there.

He could hear Fred crying inside the house, but no adult voices accompanied him. Why was it so eerily quiet?

He leapt off the stallion and then reached up for Louise. He lifted her gently down from the horse and motioned for her to follow him. He pressed his back to the outside of the cabin, and Louise followed his lead.

He laid a gentle hand on her cheek and leaned into whisper in her ear. Being so close to her sent his heart to racing, but he commanded his body to slow and focus on the task at hand.

"I'm going to look inside. Wait here for me. If things go sideways, I want you to climb on the horse as fast as you can, and ride like fire until you reach the next ranch. Can you do that?"

Teary blue eyes stared back at him as she nodded her head.

Jacob hugged Louise tenderly and turned back to the door. He approached the window from the ground and peered slowly over the windowsill. The window was open, but he didn't see anyone inside. All he could hear was the sound of the crying baby.

He drew the pistol at his side and put one hand on the back door. He took a deep, slow breath to steady his breathing before he flung it open.

"Jacob, what's the matter with you?"

After rushing into the house, Jacob found George, and Sarah sitting by the fire with Fred in her lap, crying. Sarah was holding him close and whispering sweet nothings in his ear as she tried to soothe him.

"I think you can get that gun out of our faces!" said an irritated George.

Jacob swallowed hard as he lowered his pistol, speechless.

Suddenly, there was a clang from the other side of the room as bowls hit the ground, and Jacob spun around, pulling out his pistol once more.

He saw the two ranch hands, who should've been guarding the house, sitting at the table eating some stew. They were shaking in their boots as one of them bent over to pick up a bowl he dropped on the floor.

"For crying out loud, Jacob," George said, "why would you come in here with guns blazing? Are you going to put that thing away or do I have to make you do it?"

George stood up, looking protective as he glanced at his daughter sitting in the rocking chair.

Jacob's heart started to slow, and he lowered his gun, putting it back in its holster.

"Sorry, George," he said in a rush as he walked over to his friend. "These fools should've been outside guarding the door instead of sitting in here, slurping down soup, when there could be an entire band of outlaws riding here at this moment!"

"I was looking out the front window while these guys ate. Everyone's got to eat sometime, you know. What do you mean by coming over here at any minute?"

Louise ran past Jacob then, gathering Fred into her arms. Immediately, the baby stopped crying once he was held by his mother, causing Jacob to breathe a sigh of relief.

"We got a lot to talk about, George. Right now, I need you to come with me to the ranch. We've got to gather the ranch hands, minus these two, of course."

"We were just finishing up here, sir. We'll be back outside, keeping a lookout."

"Good," said Jacob, a bit harshly, "because we might be having more visitors soon."

***

When Jacob and George rode out to the ranch, more ranch hands began to gather, coming back from their dinner for the latter half of the day at work.

George helped Jacob round up the men and they explained what was going on. Jacob enlisted the men to help them look around the area to see if they could find where the straggling outlaw had come from and where he had gone.

"Jacob," George called out from the outside of the red fence that hemmed in the barn. "I found something that you're gonna want to see—footprints, just there."

George pointed at not one but six sets of human footprints, all different sizes.

"This was more than one straggler wandering through," Jacob said. "This was a small crew of men that were staking out the area."

Jacob followed the footprints etched into the dirt to a line of trees. Around the trees were footprints belonging to six sets of horses. There was still a lead tied around a tree where it looked like one of the horses had been held.

They must have left in a hurry.

Jacob's blood began to boil. This was Roy's doing and he knew just where they were.

"What do you want to do?" George asked with a heavy hand on his friend's shoulder.

"We're going into town. That sheriff has got to be good for something."

***

"Charles! You've got some explaining to do!"

Jacob pushed into the sheriff's office like a bull in a China shop, startling the sheriff, who was sitting at his desk, drinking his morning coffee.

"What's the problem here, Jacob?"

"You know perfectly well what the problem is. Why am I coming here to tell you that outlaws have been at my ranch and wandering all around these parts when you should be the one warning *me?* You should be coming to tell *me* what's going on, not the other way around. What are our tax dollars paying for, anyway?"

"Take it easy now," the sheriff said as he stood from his chair and walked toward Jacob. "I can't abandon my post and high tail it up the mountain every time a rumor floats around. Anyhow, I stopped Roy and his men from following your wife outta town yesterday. You're welcome for that by the way."

"Welcome?" Jacob fumed. He took a step forward, standing nose to nose with the tired old sheriff.

"That's right," Charles replied. "You're welcome. And I'd thank you to remember who you're talking to." Charles stepped back and tapped the edge of the silver badge on his chest. "You'd be wise to remember it."

"And you'd be wise to remember that the people of this town have every right to form a militia if you don't do what you're supposed to do! Either get rid of Roy or I will!"

"Okay fellas," George said as he stepped between the two, placing a hand on each of their shoulders. "Let's all slow down and take a deep breath. We're all on the same side here."

"Well, you might want to remind your friend of that," the sheriff said, "before he ends up arrested for disorderly conduct."

"Before *I* g*e*t arrested? *Ha!*" Jacob laughed. "Why, you got some nerve! There are outlaws running all around these parts, and you're threatening me instead of going after them? You're about as useful as a lame horse!"

Jacob's blood burned like lava as he stormed out of the sheriff's office.

He realized he must look as furious as he felt because the moment he slammed the door, he noticed people poking their heads out of stores across the street, gawking at him.

Jacob paced outside the office, waiting for George. What was taking him so long? He was wasting time if he was trying to get that no-good sheriff to help.

After what felt like a year, George finally came outside. While George did not slam the door and kept a calm look on his face, Jacob could tell his friend was angry—perhaps as angry as he was—but he was better at not showing it. Hide it as he might, Jacob could tell by his tight jaw and his clenched hands that George was ready to go to war—just as he was.

"Well, what happened?" Jacob asked as his friend reached the wagon. "Did you have any better luck with him than I did?"

"Sort of," George said with a sigh. "Charles reminded me that he did approve Louise's claim on Fred after all, but he clearly doesn't want to get involved in this. He didn't say it, but it was written all over his face. The only way he's going to get involved is if the gang draws blood first."

"We can't wait for that to happen, George. I got a wife and baby at home right now that could be in harm's way. We don't have time to waste!"

"Oh, I agree," George added quickly. "We're going to have to handle this on our own. We have every right to legally form our own militia, a posse if you will, and that's exactly what we're going to have to do."

"Works for me," Jacob replied eagerly.

"I'm glad you feel that way," said George, "because we're going to need the help of all the people in this town, and we can start right over there with the owner of the general store."

"It's funny that you should mention that," Jacob said, laughing, "because when I was down here yesterday, I talked to a bunch of men at the saloon about joining our cause—other ranchers and local townsfolk. They were a lot more eager to help than I thought they might be."

"Why, Jacob Montgomery," George said, looking honestly surprised. "Is it possible that your love for this woman has brought you out of your shell enough to talk to the *townsfolk?*"

"You might say that," Jacob said, his cheeks flushing red with embarrassment. "Tell ya what, I gotta get back and make sure that Louise and Fred are okay. Why don't you go around town and let them know that we need to meet up? It's about time to hunt ourselves an outlaw."

"Sounds good," said George with a slight smile. "I'll see what kind of help I can rustle up and I'll be by your house in the morning."

Jacob nodded to his friend, and without another word, took off for home. He had to get back to Louise and the baby. He'd already been gone too long, and as he didn't see any of Roy's crew in town, he knew they could be anywhere.

As he urged Gus forward, racing to get back to his family, he let out a silent prayer asking for the Lord's protection. He knew he was going to need it.

He would do whatever he had to do to protect his family—lay down his life, even. The only thing that was left to do was find that no-good outlaw.

Chapter Twenty-Six

Louise paced in front of the window anxiously. When would Jacob be home?

She leaned out the window and felt the cool breeze on her face. In the dark of night, there was nothing to see except the stars in the sky and the torches of the two ranch hands that guarded her door. Fear flooded her belly and reminded her of the night she escaped Clinton, Missouri.

She remembered vividly how terrified she had been to leave, and how fleeing was the only way to escape the danger that had surrounded her. Now, however, it was quite the opposite. While she knew she was in danger, there was nothing she could do except to stay in and wait—everything she loved was here.

She heard Fred giggle behind her and turned to see him playing with Minnie on the soft carpet in front of the fire. The innocence and sweetness of the two friends brought a smile to her face and allowed her heartbeat to slow.

She sat with them, and Fred and Minnie climbed into her lap. She gladly accepted them into her arms and hugged them tightly.

"What would I do without you two?"

Just then, Louise heard the rumble of horse hooves on the hill and her heart jumped inside her chest. Would it be Jacob or someone from Roy's gang?

She set down Fred and Minnie, and her breath sped up as she ran to the door, flinging it open. Whoever was coming down that hill, she needed to know what to expect.

When she saw Jacob's broad shoulders and warm brown eyes come out of the darkness into the light of the torches, her heartbeat slowed, and her breath returned to her.

"Jacob!" she cried out. She wanted to run to him, but he'd told her firmly that she needed to stay inside the house. It wasn't safe for her outside where men could be stalking the grounds, lying in wait. But he said nothing about the doorway. She stood there, waiting for him, until he tied up Gus and walked inside.

She flung her arms around him, unable to contain herself, and gave him a soft kiss on the cheek. Would he ever get the hint?

"What's wrong, Louise? Are you and Fred all right?" Jacob asked as he looked around her and into the house.

"Yes," she said as she let out a relieved laugh. "Everything's fine now that you're back. It always feels safer when you're here—more like home."

Home. There was that word again. Yes, they had definitely made a home for themselves, and now that Jacob had returned, Louise could finally relax and go work on finishing supper.

She released her arms from around his neck, slightly embarrassed that she had thrown herself on him so completely. Flushed, she looked up into his eyes, wondering if he thought her foolish. But what she found there told her a different story.

As she looked up into his warm, brown eyes, she saw tenderness and longing there. She felt his hands on the small of her back gently pulling her toward him. It reminded her of when they were dancing, and her chest heaved in remembrance and anticipation.

"You were waiting for me," Jacob said as a sly smile spread across his face.

Louise rolled her eyes, smiling. She had the sudden urge to cover her tracks and salvage her pride, lest he think her silly—or worse yet—*desperate.*

"Well, I wanted to make sure I wasn't wasting my efforts on a hot dinner if you weren't going to be here to eat it. Anyhow, I best get back to finishing supper."

She turned and went to the cast-iron stove to check on the chicken she had stewing, but as she turned to look back at Jacob, she could tell that he didn't buy her story. He smiled at her out of the corner of his mouth and nodded as he walked over to the fire to polish his gun.

She looked at her family while she made supper, relieved they were all back together. As she admired the warm scene before her, she thought they looked like a normal, happy family… if it weren't for the guards talking outside the door, or the gun that Jacob polished in his lap.

Louise pulled apart the stewed chicken and set the bones aside as she placed pieces of the meat into the fresh broth. She took a pinch of the herbs and spices that she'd grown in her garden and had ground by hand. She sprinkled them into the soup proudly, admiring what she had created.

She leaned over the soup and let the aroma rise to meet her. She took a slow whiff of the simmering concoction and felt the sweet satisfaction of success. It calmed her as it filled up her senses and she felt safe in her element.

"It's almost ready," she said as she stirred the soup, gazing at her family.

Fred and Minnie were both locked in a wrestling contest, as they rolled across the floor together.

She couldn't believe how much Fred had grown. He looked every bit the ten-month-old as he toddled around the room with Minnie at his side. She followed him everywhere he went, and she was gracefully undeterred by his falls.

It wasn't as easy to contain him as it had been a few months before, when he was only crawling. Louise knew it was only a matter of time before he was opening the door and going out to help Jacob on the ranch… granted nothing got in their way.

Reality crashed back in, and her heart sank as she pondered that there was someone out there who wanted to break up her family and the simple happiness they'd found here.

She wished that she could freeze this moment and keep them safe in it forever. She realized that she would do whatever it took to protect them and keep them together.

Fred came over and pulled on her gown; she bent down to meet him. "Hello, my darling. How can I help you?"

Fred reached out to touch his mouth, showing her the sign he made when he was hungry.

"Have your way," Louise chuckled as she scooped him up into her arms. "Supper's ready!"

***

When the house was dark and quiet, the only sound that could be heard was an owl off in the distance. Everyone was asleep. Everyone, that is, except for Louise.

Try as she might, she could not stop thinking about the band of outlaws who only wanted one thing: to break up her family. She knew that there were ranch hands outside guarding the door. She knew that she had a perfectly capable husband sleeping on a pallet with a gun by his side. But neither of these things served to soothe her weary mind.

She stood slowly from her bed, and tiptoed past Fred's cradle. He was still fast asleep, blissfully unaware of the storms that brewed around their home.

She stepped carefully past Jacob's pallet on the floor. He had previously kept it by the fire, but tonight, he positioned it directly in front of the door. She chuckled quietly to herself, admitting that his ample frame was a decent tool to use to barricade the door.

But... how long was he going to sleep on the floor? Was he ever going to come to their bed? What did he want, a formal invitation? She shook her head, smiling at the handsome rancher, who was still so mysterious to her. At least in some ways.

She walked to the window and looked outside. There was still nothing there but stars and ranch hands guarding the door, but how long would that quiet last? She felt like any moment they could be bombarded by a band of murderous outlaws, and she had no idea how she could sleep through that.

She needed something to distract her, something to help her mind rest, and she looked for something to do with her hands. She reached into her basket by the fireplace and found a piece of the toy she'd been crafting into a teething ring for Fred.

She sat in her rocking chair, where she could see out the window, and started working the wood. She could keep watch and make a teething ring for Fred at the same time, certainly.

She worked steadily on the supple piece of Cottonwood bark, bending it to her will, relieved to let out her frustrations in a way she could control. She was so focused on the toy, that she didn't notice her best friend jump up on the arm of the chair.

"Minnie!" Louise whispered happily in a hushed surprise. "You're awake, too, I see. Come here, you curious little cat."

Regardless of the stressful situation she found herself in, Louise was grateful that Minnie was there with her still, as she had been since the very beginning. She hugged her to her chest and felt comforted by the warm and gentle purring of her longest friend.

When Minnie had enough of the cuddles, she licked Louise on the nose and jumped off the chair, but she didn't go far. Her caring cat walked around the fire, sniffing the air, and then settled by her feet.

Louise took a deep breath, appreciative that some things still hadn't changed—like the loyalty of her cat and the perfect love of the God that had never left her.

She realized then that she hadn't prayed recently, and she knew this was adding to her anxiety.

Help me to lean into You, Lord. I know I need to, but I can't seem to find the time or the energy.

"If we are faithless, He will remain faithful, for He cannot disown Himself."

The verse hit her heart powerfully and she thanked the Lord for his faithfulness to her.

"You're so good to me, God. Thank you for being always by my side. Please help me to remember that."

She continued to work on the teether and dwell on the faithfulness of the Lord as the minutes ticked by. She yawned as she stared out the window, the toy falling into her lap.

Everyone had to rest, after all—even a wife in the Wild West up against a gang of outlaws.

She closed her eyes and finally drifted off, until Fred started to cry.

Chapter Twenty-Seven

"Come on, Fred," pleaded a weary Louise. "You've got to stop crying, little one."

Fred had been crying for over an hour and she'd tried everything. She had already offered him warm milk, which he rejected entirely. She had rocked him gently and he'd pushed her away. She'd changed his soiled diaper, which appeared to make him angrier, somehow. Finally, she pulled him into the large four-post bed, thinking that that might be what he wanted, but he had continued to cry mercilessly.

She had decided that the bed was the best place to be, as it was the farthest point away from the door, where Jacob's pallet lay. She had resigned herself to stroking the babe's hair and singing to him gently, hoping that he didn't wake Jacob. She might be tired for a night, but she knew that her husband had been breaking his body all over town, trying to keep them safe. If he was going to do that, he needed rest.

"Hush, little one. Everything's okay. What on earth is bothering you?"

Minnie jumped onto the bed and walked around Fred in circles. She meowed long, slow cries as she circled him, as if to join in his anxiety, or perhaps to protect him from whatever ailed him.

It was then that Louise realized, with the two tiny friends in cahoots, perhaps they sensed danger nearby. Louise tried to remain calm, but it heightened her anxiety as well.

To calm all three of them, she pulled out her Bible and looked for words of peace.

A comforting verse came to mind, and she flipped to the book of Philippians, chapter four. She began to read from verse six:

"...do not be anxious about anything, but in everything by prayer and supplication with thanksgiving let your requests be made known to God. And the peace of God, which surpasses all understanding, will guard your hearts and your minds in Christ Jesus."

She was comforted in her heart as she remembered the promises of God and his faithfulness to her. Where there was fear just a moment before, instead, she was flooded with peace and thankfulness.

God had brought her out of a terrifying situation in Clinton to the Wild West in Austin—to a safe place—to a man she had fallen in love with. And of whom she was growing to believe perhaps loved her in return. She had a baby, and a real home, for the first time in her whole life.

If You brought me here, Lord, I know that You can take care of me. I'm sorry for forgetting so easily.

As Louise became calm, she noticed that Fred and Minnie joined her. Their cries slowly faded as she cuddled them both. Fred fell asleep on her pillow, with Minnie curled up between his arm and his side. The two were so precious that she did not have the heart to move them.

Louise curled up around the little pair, feeling grateful and restful at last. She closed her eyes and was just about to drift off when she was startled by a noise outside. The sound of dead, autumn leaves cracking underfoot struck a sense of alert through her spine, and she sat up, instantly on guard.

Was it just the ranch hands? It came from behind back, so it wasn't likely. Jacob's men would have been on the front side of the house. It could just be her imagination, or an animal walking around in the garden, but she wasn't willing to risk it. She got up as quietly as she could and tiptoed to the front window. Off in the distance, about a hundred feet from the house, she could see both guards perfectly alert. She thought she might call to them, but she knew that if someone was around back, they would hear her and get to her before Jacob's men had a chance to run around the back.

I need to wake Jacob.

Louise walked over to her peacefully slumbering husband and knelt at his side in a hurry. She placed her hands on his shoulders and bent down to whisper urgently in his ear.

"Jacob! Jacob, wake up!"

Jacob groaned slowly at first, but when he opened his eyes, he sat up with a start.

"Louise! What... What's going on?"

"I think there's someone out back. I heard leaves cracking underfoot... There it is again!"

"Stay down, Louise!" Jacob whispered, putting his arm out in front of her as they sat on the ground.

Then, in one fell swoop, he picked up his gun and headed to the front door. He lit a torch and stepped out into the night.

"Keep him safe, Lord," she whispered breathlessly after him.

Louise was on pins and needles waiting for Jacob. She sat on the floor for a moment, listening to the sound of footsteps on the side of the house. She knew that Jacob wanted her to stay hidden, out of sight, but she couldn't bear the thought of not knowing what would happen. He could be mad at her later, but right now, she needed to see what was going on.

She crawled on hands and knees past the back window, so as not to be seen by whoever may be outside. When she got to the back of the house, she carefully lifted herself up to the edge. With a deep and steady breath, she slowly raised her eyes over the tip of the sill.

All she could see in the pitch black was the back of Jacob's broad shoulders and his torch that he held out into the night. His frame was still for a moment, and then, he took a couple more steps as he bent his neck to the right, looking off at something in the distance.

Quickly, he lifted his gun and shot out into the darkness. He shot a second time and a third and then ducked behind some cacti. She could see him no longer. Louise stayed frozen at the window, her heart beating rapidly inside of her chest.

At the sound of the gunshots, Jacob's men rounded the corner with their own guns drawn. They ran to their boss's side, and she heard them mutter something quietly, and then the three of them ran off into the blackness.

Louise would've stayed at the window all night waiting for Jacob's return if it wasn't for Fred, who started wailed as more shots echoed in the distance.

Chapter Twenty-Eight

Jacob rolled over in the bed and almost knocked his arm into the sleeping toddler at his side. Curled up next to the babe was his beautiful wife, who had invited him to sleep in the bed last night. When he had come home after searching half the night for whoever was on their property, she had insisted that he sleep with her and Fred in the large family bed. They hadn't found anyone in the woods and Louise said she'd feel much safer if Jacob was right beside them.

He couldn't believe how well he'd slept in his bed. It was certainly a leg up from his pallet on the floor. Though whether this was permanent was yet to be seen.

Laying on his left side, he took a moment to gaze at his young family. Fred slept in the middle of the bed spread out with arms and legs spread in all directions, taking up more than half of the bed. Jacob shook his head with a chuckle, wondering how a baby could take up that much room.

She had said that he needed a good night's sleep with all the manhunting and defending that he'd been doing. Besides, she'd insisted she felt safer with him nearby.

Jacob grinned and his whole soul lit up as he remembered the invitation. It was almost enough to put his heart at ease and make him forget the terrible danger they were in... Almost.

Certainly, even outlaws and bandits could wait five minutes for a man to wake up properly. He lay there, enjoying the view, until Louise started to stir. She opened her eyes and looked at him sleepily. Even first thing in the morning, eyes puffy from lack of sleep, she was still the most beautiful creature he'd ever laid eyes on.

As she stared at him, Jacob felt suddenly nervous, like a simple schoolboy who fancied the girl next door. If only showing his interest in her was as simple as pulling her pigtails. But something told Jacob she wouldn't care for that much.

He swallowed hard and cleared his throat. "Mornin'," he said, more roughly than intended.

"Good morning," Louise said sweetly as she stretched. "How did you sleep?" As she sat up in bed, her nightgown ruffled around her tummy, and Jacob smiled as she tried to straighten it out and act proper.

"I slept like a babe," he answered her. "Although not as good as this one, I reckon." Jacob looked at Fred, still fast asleep on his back with his limbs sprawled in every direction. He chuckled heartily and Louise joined him.

When Louise stopped laughing, she looked at Jacob with eyes lidded with intimacy.

"It must be because his papa was sleeping in the bed with him," she said tenderly. Her voice was lower than usual. It sounded warm and sweet like apple pie, and Jacob could swear that it was laced with honey.

What was that the look he saw in her eyes? Was she simply grateful they were safe, or did he see a hint of love in those blue eyes?

The moment of heart-pounding happiness ended suddenly with three sharp knocks at the door.

"Jacob! We need you outside."

Jacob watched, crestfallen, as Louise's previously blissful gaze turned worried, and her brow furrowed.

"I better go see what it is."

Reluctantly, he stood from the bed. But once he was on his feet, he marched to the door, determined to find what was the matter.

Jacob opened the heavy front door to find the two ranch hands from the night before. Their overalls sagged along with their eyes, and they looked half-dead.

"What are you two still doing here? You should've been relieved hours ago."

"We're truly sorry to wake you, boss," the shorter of the two men said as he fiddled with his hat in his hands. "We know you need your sleep, but quite frankly, sir, so do we. The Wellesley brothers should've been here to relieve us a couple hours ago but haven't showed. It's nearly half-past seven."

Jacob put a hand to his face and rubbed his chin as he looked off into the distance. His mind reeled as he wondered what could've happened to the next round of ranchers.

"I'm sorry, boys," Jacob said in a rush, "but you might have to sit here a spell further. The Wellesley boys haven't missed a day of work since they were eighteen. If they're not here, it means that there's mischief afoot. I'm gonna go figure out what's going on and I'll send relief as soon as I can. In the meantime," he paused and pointed to the house, then back to the exhausted ranchers, "you boys stay alert!"

He saddled Gus as quickly as he could and raced to the ranch. He didn't get far before he found several tracks, at least a dozen pairs of horse hooves, and two different sets of footprints.

Jacob had to find out what kind of mischief they had caused while he slept. He kicked himself for enjoying his rest so much and lifted Gus's reins to urge him faster toward the ranch.

***

When he got to the large horse stable, he found that the giant red door was wide open, and the place was as quiet as a graveyard.

He drew his gun, prepared for whatever he might find, but he knew from the silence that he was alone. When he walked into the barn, his heart sank as his fears were realized. All the horses were gone, including Jonah.

Jacob mounted Gus in a single bound and raced as fast as the poor horse could manage toward the pasture.

He was a bit rattled about the stolen horses, but he also knew there were bigger concerns at play. What was Roy doing? Perhaps he was just trying to impoverish them by taking their livelihood.

What would be the fate of the rest of his livestock? Most of his horses ran free in the field and they knew better than to be caught by a stranger. But what else had they taken? And where were the ranch hands?

***

"George, are you and the boys all right?" Jacob asked as he stumbled up to sGeorge, and a dozen or more ranch hands.

"Sure, we're all right," said George. "We're just saddlin' up for the day, about to go feed the horses in the field and then check on the cows. Why do you ask?"

"Someone was at the house last night," Jacob said as he panted and tried to catch his breath. "There's half a dozen horse tracks between the house and the horse barn and.... George, all the horses in the stable are gone."

George lifted a hand to his mouth speechlessly. With his other hand, he took off his hat and threw it on the ground.

Jacob looked on as the steadiest man he knew turned and searched the perimeter with his eyes looking wild, like a colt hoping for a fight.

Jacob put his hand on George's shoulder, trying to calm his friend. The irony that George was the one that needed the calming was not lost on Jacob.

"George, it gets worse. The Wellesley brothers didn't show up for their guard watch at the cabin."

Jacob saw George's eyes grow as wide as the ranch itself and he could see the realization settle in.

"The Wellesley boys? I got a bad feeling about this, Jacob. Why, those boys haven't missed a day at work since…"

"I know," Jacob said solemnly, matching the severity of George's eyes. "I know."

The team of ranchers spread out through the field looking for the horses and the animals that remained. Oddly enough, all the cows and chickens were still in their place. The ranch hands fed the animals that remained while George and Jacob tried to plot their next move.

Jacob enlisted four of the ranch hands to help him find the Wellesley boys. They were about to saddle up, when off in the distance, he saw three horses riding up the hill toward them.

"Well, I'll be," George said heavily, "If that isn't the sheriff riding toward us. That could only mean one thing. Big trouble."

***

As Charles stepped down from his horse, the two men traveling with him ran up to him, trying to assist him in the process.

"I'm fine," he grumbled. "Get off me, you young whippersnappers. I've been getting down from horses since before you were born."

Charles limped toward him, and Jacob rolled his eyes as he gave a deep sigh impatiently, but with a second glance, he felt a twinge of pity for the aging sheriff.

Jacob noticed that the man's chest heaved as he ambled over to them, holding up his belt as he went. He bent over and put his hands on his knees, practically gasping for air.

"Ya all right, Charles?" Jacob asked sincerely. While he wasn't overly fond of the man, it wouldn't do any good if he dropped dead on the top of this mountain either.

"I'm fine!" the crotchety old man declared. "I just need to… just need a second to catch my breath, is all."

When the plump old sheriff finally caught his breath, he stood up with hands on his hips as if he'd come to save the day.

"I've got news that you boys aren't gonna like, but you need to hear it. A couple homes in town were set on fire last night."

Jacob and George stole a look of knowing dread and then looked back at the sheriff.

"Who did they get, Charles?" George asked. "It wasn't the Wellesley boys, was it?"

The old sheriff looked up with a start. "Well, as a matter of fact, it *was*. How did you know?"

Jacob sighed and leaned over, putting his hands on his knees.

He felt George's hand on his shoulder and Jacob was grateful that his friend answered the sheriff for him.

"The Wellesley brothers didn't show up for their shift today and they're the hardest working men we got. We afeared somethin' was wrong."

Jacob couldn't stand the idea that some of his men had gotten hurt. Roy was after him, and Jacob just couldn't stomach it if someone else got the hit of it on account of him.

"They dead?" Jacob asked, afraid that he already knew the answer.

"No, they're all right," the sheriff answered, "The Wellesley boys are just fine, but I can't say the same for their homes or ranches. Everything they had is gone and they are fit to be tied."

Jacob let out a huge sigh of relief at the realization that they weren't gone yet.

"Sounds about right," said George with a smile as he patted Jacob on the back. "Those are two of the toughest men I've ever met."

"But there's more you boys should know," Charles said hurriedly. "The gang rode through town with torches lit, screaming that there would be more trouble to come if they didn't get the baby. My guess is that they didn't burn your house down because it's a might harder to get to without being noticed. Plus, you've got men guarding it around the clock, but I'm sure you're next in line. If I were you boys, I would get home to defend your families and not waste time with these here animals."

Dread filled Jacob's bones as his mind shot to Louise and Fred. Were they safe at the cabin with half-exhausted guards at the door?

Could that be why Roy's men took the horses from the barn but didn't bother with the other animals? Had they just lured him away?

"I gotta get back to my family!"

Jacob turned back to his men briefly before he jumped on his horse.

"If you men have families at home, get to them now. The fact is, we have no way of knowing who Roy and his men are gonna hit next."

Jacob saw the terror fly into the eyes of a handful of fathers as they jumped on their horses and flew away at lightning speed. Still, most of the ranch hands were young single men and they all stayed with a look of bravery on their faces.

Jacob looked back at his men, who were waiting for his orders.

"Saddle up, boys. It's time to ride."

Chapter Twenty-Nine

"We'll burn the back house first," Roy said as he drew in the hot dirt, tracing the layout of the Montgomery farm.

"The men left out the front and they'll be coming back the same way. If we start with the buildings past the back house and use the rope as a wick leading to the main house, the woman won't know that the fire is there until it's too late. She'll be forced to come out with my child."

Roy smiled to himself as he lay out the plan to his men. He'd been patient, and now, he would finally have satisfaction.

When he had first found out that the saloon girl had borne him a son, he hadn't been particularly keen to the idea. Roy wasn't overly fond of ankle biters, but he knew one day, the boy would grow up into a man that he could pass his legacy to.

The barmaid had enjoyed his provision at first. It had gone well enough, until she decided that she wanted to quit following the gang and asked Roy to settle down.

"Ain't no time to settle down, girl," he'd told the woman. "Too much to take and claim if I'm gonna run this here crew. Besides, If I'm gonna have a legacy to leave this boy, I gotta grow our gold and our territory."

She had not been overly fond of the idea of following the crew, and when she'd told Roy that she was leaving and taking the baby, he slapped her hard once across her mouth.

"You'll do no such thing!" he screamed at the girl. "You hear me, woman? That there baby's mine and if you wanna be near it, then you're mine too."

She had submitted to his authority that night, but the next morning when he awoke, she was gone—and so was his son.

He had tracked her to Austin, where they first met, but she was long gone now. When he visited the old saloon where she used to work, it was clear that she'd hightailed it out of town. All that was left of her were rumors about a baby that she'd left on some rancher's doorstep.

All his previous reservations of having a child had halted in that moment, and his focus narrowed on one goal: finding his son.

Roy had been patient as he plotted and now it was time to fulfill his plan. *At last.*

It had been easier than he thought to blend in at the fair and overhear the gossip of the townsfolk.

When he'd seen them gawk and talk about Louise holding his son at the fair, it had taken all his strength not to snatch him right then and there.

It had been so satisfying, knocking her over on the dance floor. The fear in her eyes had brought him immense satisfaction.

Her awkward husband, though immense in size, had been easy to ruffle. While it was obvious he was protective of the woman, it had been far too easy to separate them when he took the horses.

He knew that taking the horses and burning different homes would be enough to gather the men away from the Montgomery home, but the real stroke of genius was burning the homes of the two men meant to relieve the exhausted guards.

When they attacked the house with no men to defend the babe but the exhausted guards, it would be far too easy to exact the plan.

He also knew he was lucky he didn't get caught the night before, when he'd crept up to the window, but he couldn't help looking in to see his son. When he saw him, the babe had started to cry, but it was no matter.

Once his son knew him, he'd feel safer with him than some religious ranchers in the driest part of the west. He might have cried last night, but one day, his son would appreciate being rescued from this bleak existence.

"Roy, did you hear me?" Roy's second in command asked.

"Huh?"

"What do you want us to do with the woman when she runs out of the house with the baby?"

"Throw her back in the burning cabin or shoot her where she stands. Makes no difference to me. That foul woman has had warnings a plenty."

The gang cheered their approval as they waved their hats in the air.

Roy felt a slight twinge of sympathy for the helpless young woman that his men were so quick to cheer to her death. She would be unable to defend herself. He preferred a proper challenge, and he knew he wouldn't enjoy this ignoble victory, but his spine straightened as he considered the chances he'd given her.

Had he not offered to do this the easy way? She had refused—had tried to adopt his son—to steal him out from under him. He was doing nothing except what he said he would do, and she was getting nothing but what she'd asked for.

Roy looked around at the rugged faces of angry men, thirsty for battle. He was their captain, and he would lead them to victory as he had time and time before. He would continue to build a gilded legacy to leave his son. *His* son.

He looked down at the deep valley littered with thorn bushes and tumbleweeds. He would be rescuing his son from this. The wind blew up from the valley, hitting him squarely in the face as if to hold him back from his mission, but nothing could hold him back now.

"It's time to pay Mrs. Montgomery a visit. No doubt she's expecting us and it ain't right to keep such a fine lady waiting."

***

The noon day sun beat down hard upon Jacob's neck as he raced away from the mountain and to his home. The pounding of his heart matched Gus's galloping footsteps and their panted breathing hummed in a unified rhythm. The melody of the horse and its rider, perfectly in sync, was normally a sweet sound to Jacob's ears—but this day, it was merely a painful backdrop to the morose ballad that played out before him.

Jacob regretted half of the decisions he made in the last year and all the times that he'd been angry with Louise. What would he do if something happened to her or to the baby? He thought he could never forgive himself.

Please God, keep my family safe.

As he flew down the top of the hill into the valley, he saw a bright orange fire at the bottom of the ravine.

I'm too late!

His heart skipped a beat until he realized that it was just the backyard house by the chicken coop that was on fire. It had not yet reached the cabin. He should have plenty of time before it spread across the dry dirt and tumbleweeds.

He could see a couple dozen men swirling around the fire. He urged his horse forward as he flew down the mountain, confident that he and his men could overtake them before the fire reached the house. That is, until he saw one of the outlaws lay a line of rope from the fire to the house. He soaked it in kerosene and swiftly lit the wick on fire.

"*Louise!*" Jacob screamed at the top of his lungs, soaring down the mountain as quickly as he could. "Louise, get out of the house!" He hollered desperately, hoping beyond hope that his bride would hear his cries and come outside before the kerosene-soaked rope reached the house.

As they rode down into the valley, Jacob and his men drew their guns at the band of outlaws. By the time they were within shooting distance, Roy and his men had already saddled up and were riding hard up the hill and out of sight.

Jacob's attention, however, was focused on the kerosene-soaked rope and the fire that made its way across the backyard to the cabin that held his family.

***

Jacob burst through the back door like a mountain lion escaping a bear. He just narrowly arrived before the flames and there wasn't a moment to waste.

Louise sat in the rocking chair by the window, singing to Fred while a loud and crackling fire shimmered in the fireplace. The cast-iron stove hissed and heaved from the bread baking within it. Between the noise of the oven, the fireplace, and his wife's sweet voice, it was no wonder that she was unaware as to what was happening outside.

"Louise! Get outta the house!"

Louise jumped up with Fred in her arms.

"What is it?" she asked as she looked around wildly. "Has Roy been found in town again?"

"No time to explain! There's a fi—"

Before he could finish his sentence, Jacob was interrupted by gunshots and the rumbling sound of fire climbing the side of the house.

The fire spread slowly, quickly, and all at once. Then, it was everywhere. Jacob realized too late that the outlaws must have soaked not only the rope but the outside of the house in kerosene.

Without missing a beat, he ran to Louise and grabbed her hand. He took off for the front door, the only part of the house to not be marked by fire.

"Wait!" cried Louise as she pulled back. "I don't know where Minnie is. *Minnie!*" Louise cried as she turned back toward the fire. "Minnie! Where are you?"

Louise coughed as smoke started to fill the room but still, she would not go.

Jacob looked up at the ceiling and saw golden flames start to reach their deadly claws through the beams. There was no time. They were seconds from the front of the house being engulfed in flames, and then they would have no escape. In one move, Jacob swooped his wife into his arms as she cradled Fred and barged out the front door.

Jacob did not stop running until they were twenty yards or more from the house. He set his wife gently to the ground and looked around, ready to defend her.

Roy and his men were gone, along with most of Jacob's crew, who had chased them up the hill. George and a couple of the crew remained and ran up to Jacob.

"Is everybody all right?" George asked, panting hard.

"We're okay," Jacob said between coughs, "but I think it might be too late for the ranch."

"Louise, no!" George yelled. "You'll get yourself killed!"

Jacob turned, horrified, to see that Louise had set Fred on the ground and ran back to the burning house, screaming for Minnie.

Jacob took off after her with the fear and fury of all the wild colts that refused to break. He would not lose her today.

He caught up to her just feet from the house and threw his arms around her waist, pulling her into him from behind.

"Louise, no!" he begged as she reached for the house and tried to pry free from his grasp.

"I can't lose Minnie!" she said through hellbent tears. "I just can't…"

Jacob spun her around and grabbed her by the shoulders.

"And I won't lose you! Do you hear me? I can't! Your life is too precious, not just to me, but to that babe as well."

George caught up to them and Jacob placed her firmly in George's grasp.

"Take care of my wife, George!" Jacob hollered above the sound of the roaring flames as he disappeared back into them.

***

Jacob could hear the cries and screams of Louise calling his name as he searched for Minnie inside the burning house. He tore off his shirt and wrapped it around his face, hoping it would keep out some of the smoke. But it did nothing to stop the burning in his eyes, which he could not cover if he wanted to see the orange tabby. Unfortunately, the cat's fur matched the flames, and he couldn't spot a thing. He knelt on the floorboards to get away from the smoke and to listen for her cries.

"*Meow!*" He heard the terrified sound coming from under the bed.

Jacob crawled on his belly until he reached where the sound came from. He looked behind the bedframe to find the horrified cat stuck between the bedframe, the wall, and a board that had fallen on her. She was not yet singed from the fire, but she was just a moment from it, and she was shaking with fear.

He lifted the board with one hand while he pushed back the bed with the other. Then, he unwrapped his shirt from his face and swaddled Minnie inside of it. He buried her in his chest as he bolted out the front door.

"Jacob!" Louise yelled as she ran to her husband and threw her arms around him.

Jacob coughed, trying to catch his breath as Minnie leapt from his arms to her mistress. Louise held her cat to her chest and then turned back to Jacob.

"Jacob, are you burned? Are you all right? Can you speak?"

He wiped soot from his eyes and looked up at his tearful wife.

"Well," he coughed, "as usual, I'd let you know if I could just get a word in edgewise." He chuckled, enjoying the mix of shock and warmth in his wife's face.

He tried to catch his breath in between chuckles as Louise set Minnie down and then threw her arms around his neck.

"Thank you, Jacob," she said softly as a tear ran down her flushed cheek. "You risked your life for me *again!*"

She pulled him in close, soot and all, as she buried her head in his chest and clung to him. Jacob enjoyed the embrace more than words could express and he finally caught a deep breath for the first time since he and Gus had run down the mountain.

After a moment, Louise leaned back and looked up at him with a tear-soaked face.

"I thought I lost you."

Jacob leaned his face down to meet hers, touching his forehead to hers. She ran her fingers through his hair and held her body up against his.

"I'm not that easy to get rid of, Louise," Jacob said with a satisfied chuckle. "Especially not when I've got you to come back to."

Jacob took a deep breath as his wife's fingers gently scratched the base of his neck. If there was one thing that he learned today, it was that the next moment was never promised. They might only have right now.

He steadied himself as he leaned back slightly and lifted Louise's chin to his. His heart raced inside his chest as he drummed up the courage to do what he should've done a long time ago.

"Besides," he said shakily, as Louise stared up to him with love-sick eyes. "I could never forgive myself if I died before I had the chance to do *this.*"

Louise's face was a heartbeat away from his as he lowered his lips to meet hers. She didn't pull away—didn't even flinch. Instead, she pressed forward and met his kiss with the fervor of someone who had wanted it that whole time, too. He closed his eyes and held her tighter. Her kiss was warm and welcoming, like the sun in the spring after a cold winter, and it heated him all the way through.

Chapter Thirty

As Louise melted into Jacob's arms, she was overcome with gratitude that they were all still alive. She couldn't imagine not kissing him a moment longer.

She felt the passion of his love surround her as she became completely enveloped by his strong arms. His kiss was warm, and his lips were soft—just like their first kiss on their wedding day. But this time, something was different.

She felt the passion and purpose of his original letters double one hundred times over with his willingness to lay down his life for her. She couldn't believe how she felt in this moment, her insides tingling and her skin shivering as it came alive under his touch. Her only regret was that it took her this long to realize that she loved him completely.

"Ahem," came the sound of a chuckling voice. "I hate to interrupt you guys, but y'all aren't the only thing on fire."

Louise looked up to see George's warm smile suddenly laced with concern.

"The ranch!" Louise felt Jacob's body tighten as he pulled away to look at what used to be their home.

Louise couldn't help but notice that, although he had pulled away from their embrace, his hand remained locked inside of hers. She smiled silently to herself, embarrassed to find joy in the midst of a fire, but snapped out of it when she saw the look on her husband's face.

His normally cool and reserved face was wrenched with pain. Louise's heart sank as she saw his eyebrows furrow. The fire from the cabin reflected in his face and she could tell that his emotions matched the fury of the flames.

She suddenly was back to the present. She knew they were walking through a terrible tragedy, but at least they were walking through it hand in hand.

Louise heard a sigh and looked up to see George's hand clap down on Jacob's shoulder.

"I'm sorry," was all that he said.

They stood there in silence as the walls of their home surrendered to the merciless flames. The only noise Louise could hear was the crackling of the flames and the laughter of her baby behind her.

She turned to see Minnie batting her paws at Fred's face as she jumped around in his lap. Louise couldn't believe that she'd almost lost Minnie to the flames and she felt grateful that her furry friend was there to comfort and distract her baby. At least Fred was safe and somewhat unaware of the tragedy befalling them.

She enjoyed the fleeting pleasure of her child wrapped up in the happiness of his friend as he was far out of reach of the fire. She tried to enjoy the peace of the moment until she heard a rumble off in the distance.

Who's coming over the hill? Who won the showdown?

Would it be her husband's ranch hands, returning in glorious triumph, or would it be the cruel gang of outlaws, after her child?

Louise felt a sudden panic grip her heart when she realized that if it were the outlaws, Fred was sitting nearly fifty feet away. She had to get to him before the horses pounding the ground in the distance came over the ridge.

She released her husband's hand and flew to Fred with all the protective instincts that a mother possessed. She swooped Fred up into her arms and held him to her chest, determined to protect him from whatever came over the top of the hill.

She felt the wind hit her face, and it was cooler than she expected. As she tried to wrap her shawl around them, Fred protested and arched his back as he reached down to touch Minnie.

"Mi-mi!" Fred protested, demanding to hold his feline friend.

Louise looked down to see Minnie standing dutifully at her back legs, with her front paws stretched up, as if requesting to be picked up.

"How could I forget you, my friend?" Louise said as she scooped up Minnie with her left hand and pulled both her and Fred into the safety of her shawl.

"Louise!" she heard her husband call out behind her. "What are you trying to do, get yourself killed?"

She looked up, surprised at the irritation in her husband's voice as he placed himself in between her and whoever was about to come over the hill. Louise laid a gentle hand on his shoulder and hoped that it would give him strength. She felt especially grateful for his bravery and protection now.

She watched in surprise as he lifted his rifle and pointed it squarely at the hill. She tucked her head down to cover the baby and kitten at her breast as she sent up a quick prayer for protection.

"I can't look," she whispered quietly to Jacob.

"It's all right," Jacob said roughly as he cocked his rifle. "If I say 'run,' I want you to take my horse and don't look back 'til you get to town."

The noise got louder as the hooves pounded the ground under her feet and her heart joined them in a thunderous rhythm. It got faster and faster until she felt like her heart might explode.

She tightened her once gentle hand on Jacob's shoulder and braced herself for whatever was coming toward them.

***

"It's our men!" Louise heard George cry out happily.

She let out the breath she just realized she'd been holding, and she felt Jacob's body simultaneously relax in front of her, guarding her. She lifted her head to see Jacob's men race toward them holding buckets, with what looked like half the men from town in tow.

The men didn't stop when they got to Louise and Jacob. They rushed past them like a fall wind and continued toward the fire.

Most of the men were on horseback, but she noticed five wagons barreling down the hill as well.

Why would they bring wagons when horses were so much faster?

"It's no use," she called out wearily. "The house is gone!"

As her eyes continued to follow them, she saw for the first time more flames in the distance.

Would there be anything of the ranch left to save?

The sheriff stopped in front of them, driving a wagon that held the rest of George's family.

"George!" cried out his wife as she leapt down from the wagon and into her husband's arms.

Sarah was right behind her, and she helped her younger siblings down before turning to hug Louise.

"Oh, Louise!" Sarah sobbed as she hugged her friend. "I'm so glad you're okay! When the sheriff's men came for us and told us that your house was in flames too, we feared the worst!"

Louise leaned back with her hands on Sarah's shoulders as she looked her over. Her normally tanned and smiling face was pale in shock and awash with tears.

"Too?" Louise asked. "You don't mean…?"

"Our house is gone," Sarah conceded as more tears fell down her cheeks. *"Everything's* gone. Any building we passed on the way here had been set ablaze."

Louise's heart sank when she heard her friend's sorrowful words. Louise hugged her close and stroked Sarah's hair as she cried bitterly.

"I should've been there!" George's normally jovial voice was tinged with regret and pain; Louise's heart went out to him.

"There's no way that you could've known, George," Jacob said as he placed a hand on George's shoulder. "At least everyone is safe."

"What happened, Sheriff?" Jacob asked, as Louise looked on hopefully. "Did you catch Roy and his gang?"

"Afraid not," sighed the weary old sheriff. Louise saw the lines in his face furrow and stretch wearily as he gave Jacob the news.

She imagined the stress that he must be under trying to keep everyone safe. Her heart went out to the old sheriff.

"We chased them over the mountain on this side of town," he continued. "We think they're hunkered down in the hills, waiting for night to fall."

The outlaws were waiting for night to fall? Why?

Louise's heart swelled in worry. What would become of them when the sun finished setting?

"Makes sense," Jacob said and nodded. "That's where I would go if I needed to stay concealed and have the upper ground. But where'd all these men come from? Y'all didn't have time to go to town!"

"Didn't need to." The sheriff smiled. "The Wellesley brothers put two and two together and figured out that their houses were just a distraction from the ranch. They pulled a posse together and loaded up wagons with these here buckets of water."

"Well, I'll be," said Jacob with a smile that Louise thought might just light up the sky. "Looks like it was a good idea to hire those townsfolk Wellesley boys after all."

"Any idea how much of the ranch they set fire to?" Louise asked.

"Outside the main house and the back house, I'm not sure, but if these ashes are any sign…"

Louise's eyes shifted to the house where Jacob and the sheriff were looking. The fire had done its work quickly, leaving little but ashes and dust in its wake. All that stood were pieces of the original frame standing tall, connected to nothing but smoke. She shuddered to think what would have happened to them had Jacob not showed up when he did.

She clung to Jacob's arm with her left hand, as if she might fall should she let go. She looked down at Fred and

Minnie, who were still snuggled up contentedly in her other arm, completely unaware of the day's happenings. She kissed Fred's head, grateful that he was safe... for now.

Suddenly, Louise was startled by the sound of a horse whinnying, followed by the sudden sounds of a wagon rolling in front of them. It came a screeching halt, nearly running them under its wheels. Louise coughed as kicked-up dust filled the air. When she was done waving the unwelcome dirt from her face, she looked up to see the kind, familiar eyes of her friend Alice and her husband Jethro.

"Alice!" Louise cried as her friend hopped down from the wagon and hugged her tightly. She cried quietly into her friend's shoulder. They hadn't seen each other since the wedding, and she felt deeply grateful for the solace in the middle of such a storm.

Finally, she said, "What are you *doing h*ere?"

"We were in town fetching supplies for our barn," her friend explained. "When the Wellesley brothers rolled through Main Street asking for help. We already had our wagon with us, so we thought we'd fill it up with buckets and come assist!"

"Just tell us where to help and we'll get started," Jethro added from the wagon as he tipped his hat.

"We just need to figure out if there's anything left to save—anything Roy didn't already burn," Jacob said with furious eyes facing the flames in the horizon.

"Roy is focused on Fred," Louise said as she looked up at her husband. "Maybe he didn't bother with the rest of the ranch."

Worry and hope mixed in Louise's heart and mind. She was worried about what would happen next but so grateful that they were all together and safe.

"Let's spread out around the ranch," her husband said. "Jethro, if you'll take George's family, and Sheriff, if you'll allow my wife and child to ride in the wagon with you, I'll ride alongside y'all, and we can head up to the horse barn."

"Works for me!" Jethro nodded with another tip of his Stetson.

"I'll do you one better," the old sheriff said as he stepped down off the rig. "Why don't you ride with your family? Just let me unhitch my horse from the wagon and we can hitch your horse up here in his place. You take the wagon and I'll lead a few men to the other side of the ranch to see what else happened."

"Thank you, Sheriff," Jacob said as the two men shook hands. Louise's heart surged with gratefulness. At last, they were mending ways.

"It's the least I can do," the sheriff answered with what looked like regret in his eyes. Louise wasn't sure. "I should've believed you when you told me how serious it was with Roy."

"You're here now," Jacob said with a sincere smile. "And that's what matters."

Louise's heart was warmed by the touching scene, and she sent up a short prayer of thankfulness to the Lord as Jacob hoisted her up into the wagon. As Jacob hooked Gus up to the wagon, Louise settled onto the bench.

Minnie woke up and licked her hand reassuringly. She scratched her friend behind the ears, relieved for this simple comfort. As the cat settled back down into Louise's arms and closed her eyes, ready for another nap, a great *boom* sounded in the distance.

"What was that?" Louise asked, sitting up in shock.

"Hard to say," the sheriff answered, with concern layered in his face. "Sounds like dynamite... and I hope I'm wrong."

"Dynamite?" George's wife, Martha, exclaimed from the back of Jethro's wagon. "What do you think happened, Sheriff?"

"That's what I aim to find out. It looks like there's a change of plans, Jacob," the sheriff said as his bushy eyebrows pushed together in frustration. "I need to take the posse over that hill and see what explosion Roy's cooking up."

"Understood," Jacob somberly replied.

Louise looked up to see that all the men who had been dousing the house with water had now returned to the sheriff's side after the explosion, awaiting their new orders. Nearest the sheriff sat four large wagons driven by townsfolk.

"All five of these here wagons are loaded up with buckets of water," the sheriff told Jacob. "I'll leave these to you and your ranch hands to put out the fire and save what you can. After I take the posse to size up what happened with the explosion, we'll come back to join you. Don't make any move to take on Roy until we return."

The sheriff and his posse mounted up and took off over the hill. As Louise followed them with her eyes, her gaze drifted up above the hill, where the beginnings of an afternoon sunset mixed with the fire's gray smoke. The haze mixed angrily with the beautiful sunset colors of orange and pink, darkening it and threatening to stomp out its beauty.

Louise thought that it looked like a painting of good and evil in a fight for the horizon. She prayed desperately that good would prevail.

Chapter Thirty-One

What they found when they first reached the large red barn was worse than they thought. Roy and his men had been clever, and Louise kicked herself for not giving him enough credit. Not only had they set fire to most of the buildings on the ranch, but they had also managed to place giant wicks of rope soaked in kerosene to connect to several of the buildings. It made the flames move faster and more efficiently and was much harder to stop.

"Send that wagon around back!" Louise heard Jacob calling to her as she pulled the reins to the right and the horses surged toward the back of the barn.

Her heart raced and pounded in her chest, threatening to leap out, as she pushed the rig forward. She never thought she'd be racing a wagon of horses against flames that roared into the sky. The fierce smoke did its work, and she covered her mouth with the hem of her dress to keep from coughing as she urged the team of horses forward.

When they had first pulled up to the fiery scene, Jacob had the idea to divide the wagons around the giant barn. While Louise thought this was a good idea, she was surprised that he had asked *her* to drive one.

She was by no means a master horseman, but she was grateful that she had something to do to be helpful. This place where she had lived for nearly a year felt like home. She wanted to do whatever she could to save it. So, she had followed Jacob's directions eagerly.

As hard as it was to let go of Fred, she had placed him in the trusted arms of her best friend on a small patch of grass a safe distance from the flames before leaping into action.

Now, as she drove the wagon of water buckets around the back of the barn, she just hoped that there was something left to save.

She parked her wagon about thirty feet from the back of the old red barn, as Jacob's ranch hands ran toward her to grab the buckets of water.

"This way, men!" Jacob yelled as he grabbed a bucket and lined up the ranch hands.

She was amazed at Jacob's leadership as he commanded the men. His shaggy hair flew in his face along with the smoke as the wind whipped around him, giving directions to his crew. Once each man had their orders, they went to their posts, dousing the building as quickly as they could.

She saw Jacob dash toward the flames, arranging everyone into a line to make quick work of the water buckets. He spread out the ranch hands several feet apart leading from the wagon to the barn. The first man would take up a bucket from the wagon and hand it to the person next to him. The next would do the same, until each bucket finally reached the barn.

Louise tried to make their work go faster as she handed buckets to the men posted by the wagon.

They worked as fast as they could, each man moving in perfect unison with the team like a well-oiled machine, but as the minutes ticked by, the flames only grew higher.

What would happen if they lost the barn? The ranch would be doomed. Not to mention, where would they stay? Where would they *sleep?*

She pushed the thoughts out of her head and then turned her attention back to the task at hand as she continued to pass full buckets of water to the hands at the front of the line.

Suddenly, the men grew still as Jacob shouted something in the distance. What was he saying? She could not quite make it out, but it sounded like he told them that they were moving to a new building.

Her heart sank. She knew what that meant. If they lost the main barn, there would be nowhere to shelter the horses, not to mention having a place to store the feed, the hay, and all the supplies for the ranch. If they lost this building, they lost the ranch... or at least its effectiveness.

Surely something can be done!

Louise hopped down out of the wagon and ran to Jacob as fast as her legs could take her. When Jacob saw her rushing toward him, he came to her out of the smoke and covered his mouth in a hoarse cough. One hand shielded his face from the charred haze, and he held up his other hand, as if to urge her back from the smok.

When she reached him at last, she threw her arms around his neck.

"What are we gonna do?" she asked with a desperate cough.

"It'll be all right," her husband reassured her. "We can't save the barn, but there are other buildings we need to try and salvage."

"I understand," Louise answered as she pulled herself together. "Where will we go next?"

"Right now, we just gotta make it over this hill."

As if answering her husband's call, a rider tore over the mountain toward them as fast as the horse could run. Louise squinted into the setting sun, trying to make out the rider. As the figure on the horse came closer, she was able to make out a tanned, wrinkled face with a smile strewn across it.

"It's Jethro!" she declared triumphantly. She squeezed her husband's hand, hoping that their old friend had good news for them.

"What's left on the other side of the hill?" Jacob asked raggedly.

Louise could make out the hint of a crack in her husband's voice and her heart went out to him. She was so proud of the brave cowboy that he was, and she wanted to ease his pain. But there wasn't time for that now.

"Not much," Jethro conceded. "The fire has ravaged almost everything. But George sent me to tell ya that there's a smaller barn near the pasture, where y'all usually keep the supplies, and it's not succumbed to the flames yet. It must've been the last thing to light up before the gang ran off. If we can use the rest of your buckets of water, George thinks it can be saved."

"Well, what are we waiting for? Let's go!" Jacob said as he hopped onto his horse, whistling for his men to follow. He started to ride off before pausing to look back at Louise.

"You all right, love?" her husband asked with a tender look of concern.

Did he just call me "love"? A pleasant chill floated over her arms in approval.

"I'm fine," Louise said as she stood up straighter and smiled at her brave husband. "I will be right behind you. Just lead the way."

As Louise drove the team of horses and the wagon up the hill, she paused to look back at the burning barn behind her. It was a good thing that no horses were left inside it, as it was mostly ash now, along with all the saddles and feed that remained. She turned her attention forward and looked down the other side of the hill, at a small red barn where they kept the leftover supplies. It was holding a few flames and their last chance of shelter.

***

Once they arrived at the small red barn, it didn't take much time to put out the remaining flames. With all the men and women helping to heave the remaining buckets, they were able to make quick work of dousing the fire, and soon, there was nothing but smoke and what looked like a solid structure they could spend the night in. The outer walls were a bit singed, and a collection of ash lay in the grass, but the inside of the structure was sound.

It is a good thing too, Louise thought, since the sun had set. The only beacon that remained to light up the night were the stars in the sky and a small fire that George's wife had made outside for everyone to gather around.

While the other buildings were destroyed, at least the fires were put out. The men had done a good job of not letting the fire tear across the land. Thankfully, the flames had stayed mostly to the buildings that they had already decimated.

At least it's done, Louise thought to herself as she watched Minnie and Fred play near her feet in front of the fire. She was exhausted and her bones ached as the day took its toll. Still, she took comfort in her son and best friend playing so happily—so unaware of the tragedy that had just taken place.

She lifted her face and looked around the fire to see her friends that surrounded it. Next to her, sat Alice, sewing a sweater as she hummed. Across from her sat Martha, with all four of her little ones in her arms. Behind them stood Jacob and George, talking quietly, no doubt making plans for their next move. In front of them was Sarah. She stoked the fire and smiled across the flames at Louise.

Louise smiled back at Sarah, grateful for her friends and all their help. She put her chin in her hands and let out a giant sigh—content to watch the happy scene and forget about her problems—if only for a minute.

"You all good, darlin'?" asked Alice, sitting quietly beside her.

"You know, I think I am. It could've gone so much worse today, Alice... so very much worse."

Louise sank into her friend as Alice put an arm around her shoulder, feeling grateful that everybody was safe. She allowed herself to enjoy this peaceful moment, with her friends and family around the fire, although she knew in her heart that the day was far from over. The night was upon them, and she knew far too well that somewhere in the night was a band of outlaws waiting for their moment to strike again.

***

As night fell, Jacob's men joined them around the fire and were cheering victoriously as they entered the barn. They were talking as though they had won the day, sharing beef jerky that Martha had found in the storage shed. They laughed and cheered their valiant effort, while one of them played a harmonica by the fire. Fred sat with Martha's youngest son and the pair bounced and bobbed to the sound of the harmonica.

Louise smiled and looked around, wondering where her husband could be, as he no longer stood near the gathering of friends. Getting up, she walked around to the back of the small barn where she found him with George. The two men stood with hands on their hips as they spoke in a low tone.

She waved as she walked up to them. Although they acknowledged her, they continued their conversation, showing no intention to quiet themselves further, and she heard what they were saying as she walked up.

"We can't take off before the sheriff gets back," George said. "Our numbers of ranch hands are only about half of the gang's, and we would fare much better with a full posse."

"Agreed," Jacob said seriously. "It's Fred they want, so the gang will probably come to us anyway. There's no need for us to wander off and get picked off one by one. We need to make sure that the men stay near the fire, and we should have them carry torches, so we'll see what's coming."

"Who's coming?" Louise asked cautiously as she slipped one of her hands into Jacob's.

"Nothing for you to worry about, love," her husband said gently as he squeezed her hand in his, putting his other arm around her shoulder. "Just know that whenever they come, we'll be ready."

She wasn't sure why, but she believed him entirely. She'd never seen him so focused, so determined, so *manly.* If he said they'd be ready, then she knew they'd be ready. She knew that his men would follow him anywhere, and so would she. She'd follow him anywhere, even into death itself, if the need arose.

Chapter Thirty-Two

Jacob wiped the soot-ladened sweat from his brow as he drank a well-earned sip of water. He let out a sigh of relief and looked around at his family, and crew of men, gathered around the campfire.

So much had happened that day—so much that had been unexpected—and he was kicking himself for not being better prepared.

Escape from almost certain death made this moment feel victorious for his men, as was evidenced by their jubilant celebration, but Jacob knew that their fight was far from over.

He looked off toward the horizon, where the light from the stars touched the darkness of the hills, and he wondered where his enemy laid in wait. He may not know where Roy headed, but at least he knew that there was one building standing in which he could protect his family.

He heard the sound of his men talking happily and it drew his attention toward the fire. His wife sat next to Sarah and Alice, while Fred and Minnie played at their feet. Golden locks played about Louise's face as the light from the fire cast a rosy glow on her cheeks.

Jacob wished he could wrap her in his arms and kiss her deeply. He wanted to hold her through the night—to keep her safe and let her know that nothing would happen to her. But that would have to wait until another night when they weren't surrounded by his men and outlaws lurking in the shadows.

"Want us to ride out, Boss?" Waking Jacob from his daydream, the Wellesley brothers smiled bravely at Jacob with hands on their hips. "We can take some of the men and go look over the hill to see if we can find out where those snakes are laying low."

"Thank you, boys," Jacob replied, "but we can't afford to split up."

The brothers looked at each other and Jacob could tell that they were stifling a look of frustration.

"But if we stay here, we're sitting ducks. They have the high ground, and they can ride in on us at any time. We gotta go get 'em!"

"That's just what they're hoping for," George said as he came to stand next to Jacob. "They want to split us up, so that they can pick us off one by one."

"George is right," Jacob said. "They nearly did it this morning and I'm not gonna let it happen again."

The Wellesley brothers nodded in concession as they walked back toward the fire. Jacob turned to face his best friend, grateful for their camaraderie and the fact that they saw eye to eye on this matter.

"Do you get the feeling that the boys think this is over?"

"I think they're hoping that the sheriff and the posse finish the job that we started when we chased them over the hills. And who knows? Maybe they're right. Maybe the sheriff will get lucky and cut them off at the pass before they get out of town."

"Are we talking about the same sheriff?" Jacob asked with a laugh. "The only thing that I've seen him cut in the last ten years is beef jerky."

"You might be right about that, friend," George answered with a chuckle in kind. "But can you blame them for hoping? It's been a heckuva day... a day that we all want to be over."

"Not me," Jacob answered with a firm resolve. "I don't think I'll be sleeping until this business is finished, one way or another."

As Jacob looked at George, he could see the exhausted look in his eyes. His face, which was normally joyful, was downcast and looked like it carried the weight of the world. Jacob felt a twinge of pain and shame.

He had forgotten that he wasn't the only one who lost something that day. George's home was gone as well, along with the Wellesley brothers' home and many other homes of the people in town.

"George," Jacob began. "I'll understand if you want to take your family into town. It's been a hard night and you don't have to fight this war just because I'm fighting it."

"Are you kiddin'?" George retorted quickly as his cheeks lifted the wrinkles on his face into a tired smile. "Ya think that a few buildings burnin' down is enough to make me head for the hills? I'm not that easy to get rid of!"

Jacob let out a sigh of relief and slapped his friend on the back with a smile.

"Thank you, friend," he said sincerely, his heart warming. "Really—thank you for being someone I can depend on."

"At least we have the little equipment barn," his friend said. "It'll offer some protection."

"Agreed," Jacob answered, as he rested a hand on George's shoulder. "The rest of us need to stay alert, but that doesn't mean we all have to be alert at once. Why don't we take shifts sleeping by the fire and standing watch?"

"Now you're talking," said George as he slapped his friend on the back. "Let's go get the families settled in and let our wives get some rest."

"Have you met my wife?" Jacob asked with a hearty chuckle. "That beautiful woman has a mind of her own. I've got to get her to stay inside first."

**

Jacob lifted a box of feed out of the way while the women made pallets out of hay and horse blankets on the floor. The neglected old equipment barn wouldn't exactly be home, but with the friends working together, this might just be a safe place for his family to spend the night.

Jacob set the bag of feed in the windowsill, to block the view of any nefarious outlaws that might want to look inside. If Roy wanted to come for his family, he'd have to go through him first, and he wasn't gonna make it easy.

After Jacob was done blocking off the two small windows in the tiny barn, he climbed up to the loft to gather extra blankets. He lifted the heavy blanket under his shoulder and was about to climb down when he caught a glimpse of Louise's smile as she looked up from the baby.

"My, but this will do nicely," she said as she folded another blanket on top of the hay for Fred.

"Louise," he called down to his wife, "I found some more blankets up here that you can use."

"That'll be perfect!" she said with a twinkle in her eye.

He shook his head and smiled to himself. How that woman managed to make do with so little, but smile constantly, amazed him.

When they were out of meat, she could turn old vegetables into a delicious stew. When it was unusually cold last winter, she just sat closer to the fire and talked about how much she enjoyed the hearth. She was smarter than a fox, braver than a bear, and she'd tamed his heart entirely.

He realized that she was so much stronger than he had thought when he first met her, and he felt unworthy of her still. But one thing was certain… he would do whatever was necessary to keep her safe.

***

"Wake me if you need me," George said as he settled under the stars, the fire's flame heating his face.

"I'll be all right, George," Jacob said as he leaned against the barn and stared off into the distance. "The sheriff should be back anytime now with plenty of reinforcements."

"Just the same," George insisted. "Don't let me sleep more than an hour. I don't need it anyhow."

"All right, friend." Jacob smiled at him before refocusing on the horizon, where the stars met the top of the hills.

He knew that horse hooves could ride down into the valley at any moment. He hoped that it would be the sheriff coming, but he couldn't be sure, and he needed to be ready.

"I think Fred's finally asleep," Louise said, as she poked her head out the front door to talk to him. "I can come outside with you now," she said as she tried to tiptoe out into the night.

"Oh no, you don't," Jacob said with a smile, as he gently pushed back on the door.

"What do you mean?" Louise said, puffing out her chest in protest. "Why, I want to be out there with my husband."

"You just can't, that's all. Besides, if Fred wakes up, he'll need you."

"But he's asleep!" his determined wife challenged. "Why can't I sit out there with you? And don't give me some poppycock about how women can't put up a good fight. I think I've shown today that I can hold my own in a pinch."

"Okay fine," he said. "How about because I wouldn't be able to focus if I thought you were in danger?"

Jacob thought at first that Louise might make fun of him for the admission—for showing his soft underbelly. As her freckled face warmed into a soft smile, he realized he was wrong.

"All right then, Jacob Montgomery," she said with one corner of her mouth turned up. "If you insist. But it sure would be a lot easier to sleep if you were in here with me. I made a pallet big enough for the two of us."

Jacob looked down at the blue eyes that looked warm somehow, with the stars and the fire shining straight into them. He could tell by the quiver in her chin that she was trying to be strong for him. He knew he shouldn't waste a moment of distraction when he needed to be keeping watch, but when she placed a gentle hand on his chest and looked at him urgently, it was more than he could bear.

He lifted the chin that was pointed up at him and slipped his other arm around her waist, as he pulled her into him and kissed her hard. He felt her lean into him and knew that if he didn't pull away soon, he wouldn't be able to at all.

He leaned back and whispered to her, making sure the men at the fire couldn't hear, "Oh, I'll be sharing that pallet with you, love, but I've got to settle a few things out here first."

Chapter Thirty-Three

The crackling of the small campfire mixed with the sounds of crickets in the brush as Jacob stared determinedly at the horizon.

Half of his men were sleeping. Jethro and George were passed out on opposite sides of the fire with their rifles by their sides. Jacob smiled, grateful for such good friends. He would take a bullet for either of them. And he knew they'd do the same for him.

The other half stood guard around the perimeter of the small building. A few of them looked bored and tired as they stared down at their shoes or fiddled with sticks and leaves. But Jacob was anything but that.

He couldn't stop thinking about what might happen if the sheriff didn't return. If the posse came back quickly, then they'd have nearly double the men of Roy and his gang. Then again, if they were watching George and his men from somewhere even now, or if they came down upon them before the sheriff returned... it could end up much differently.

Jacob pushed that thought from his mind and hoped that the sheriff would return with the posse at any moment. Why, he might come bounding over the horizon ready with fresh reinforcements, or better yet, with news that Roy and his men had already been taken down.

The only thing that served to distract Jacob from his concerns about clashing with Roy was the memory of kissing Louise earlier that day.

Not just once but twice, no less, he thought with a smile before he stood up and looked off into the distance.

For the first time since his father died, he finally had something worth fighting for, and he would do whatever it took to keep his family safe.

Jacob heard a twig break on the ground behind him. He whirled around with his pistol drawn, fully expecting to see Roy.

"It's just me," Jimmy Baker called out in a whisper from the shadows. "Don't shoot!"

Jacob let out a sigh as he holstered his pistol. Jimmy was a new ranch hand. *"Fresh out of his mother's arms,"* as the other men often teased him. He couldn't have been more than seventeen and he was always messing things up.

Although he wasn't a huge help on the ranch, Jacob felt sorry for the boy and wanted to help point him in the right direction. But it was moments like this that made him wonder if it was a mistake.

"It's a good thing you said something, Jimmy," Jacob said with a mix of exhaustion and frustration. "You were about two seconds away from being full of bullet holes."

"I'm sorry, Boss... I'm so sorry," came the familiar voice on the edge of the shadows. Jacob couldn't be sure, but he thought he heard a crack in the young ranch hand's voice.

I should have sent the boy home to his mother, especially for tonight. The kid isn't cut out for this.

"No need to be sorry, but why are you whispering?" Jacob asked. "Step on out of the shadows and say what you got to say."

"I think you better come over here, sir," Jimmy whispered, more urgently this time.

"Now, Jimmy," Jacob said, getting more irritated as he walked over to the boy, still hidden in shadow. "This is ridiculous. We don't have time for whatever this is. We need to be on the lookout for..."

His voice trailed off when he saw what lay before him, and he wished that he'd kept his distance by the light of the fire. Standing there in front of him were two of the most desperate outlaws he'd ever seen, and one of them had a pistol pressed against Jimmy's temple.

"Like I said, Boss, I'm awful sorry." A single tear ran down the boy's cheek and Jacob couldn't help but notice his chin pucker as he tried not to cry.

Shock flooded Jacob's body. He could feel the blood leave his face as his heart raced a million miles a second.

"It's all right, Jimmy," Jacob said, trying to sound calmer than he was. "I understand. It's not you they want anyhow... is it, boys?"

"I reckon not," said a tall, lanky man with dirt on his face and a toothpick in his mouth. He stood next to the man that held the gun to Jimmy's head and he leaned his arm onto the boy's shoulder. He shuddered.

"Then again," the surly outlaw continued, "we can't go back empty-handed, now can we, Jenkins?"

"Afraid not," the man who must have been Jenkins replied, as he pushed his pistol harder against the left temple of the boy's head.

Jimmy let out a cry and threw up his hands, causing the taller man to flip out a knife and push it up against his throat.

Jacob's first inclination was to draw his pistol and shoot the man right between the eyes. The problem was, if he did that, the boy would fall dead right alongside him. Worse yet, if his men heard gunshots, they'd start firing, too, and Jacob didn't want to risk a stray bullet hitting the small barn where Louise and Fred slept. He had to draw the men away from his family, and fast.

"Don't worry, Jimmy," Jacob said as he raised his hands slowly into the air, an act of surrender. "They're gonna let you go in exchange for me going without a fight, and they're gonna do it real nice and quiet-like, so none of my men get spooked and start shootin'. Isn't that right, fellas?"

"Works for me," said Jenkins as he stuffed a bandana in the boy's mouth to keep him quiet. The taller man with the toothpick produced some rope and bound up his arms and feet.

"You're gonna stay real quiet, aren't you Jimmy?" the taller man said, as he cinched the rope around his feet, causing the boy to squirm. "Because if you make any noise at all, kid, and I mean even a lil' peep, we're gonna blow a hole in your boss here the size of Texas. Ya got it?"

Jacob watched as the boy nodded tearfully and hung his head in shame.

"Don't be afraid, Jimmy," Jacob said as he got a surge of adrenaline, followed by an idea. "In the morning when the sun rises, the men will find you and you'll head down to town to tell Louise and Fred that I'm all right. You'll find them at the sheriff's office and tell them that for me, won't you, son?"

Jacob wasn't sure if Jimmy understood or not as the boy lifted his head with a puzzled look on his face. Then a look of recognition shone in his eyes as he smiled at Jacob knowingly. He nodded his head and put it back down.

At least Louise and Fred are safe, Jacob thought, right before something hard and heavy hit him squarely on the head.

***

As Jacob slowly came to, he saw a blur of flames dancing before him. His head ached and throbbed from being hit. It made everything look and sound like a world of fog.

He could tell that he was laying on hard mountain dirt. The dust filled his nostrils and stung his lungs. Jacob coughed as he propped himself up with his left arm. He squinted through the smoke and flames to try and see just where he was.

"Well, it looks like someone's waking up at last," Jacob heard a stranger's voice call out from the other side of the fire. "What do you want us to do with him, Roy?"

At the sound of Roy's name, Jacob sprang upright as his instinct set in, and he readied himself for a fight. He had to protect his family, but where were they? He reached for the gun on his belt, but it wasn't there. Where was his gun? And where was *he?*

Jacob realized too late that his body had not been ready to stand as his head began to spin and sent him right back down into the dirt. The sound of angry laughter filled up the air around him as he remembered what had taken place.

His family must be safe. That much must be true or else he wouldn't still be breathing. The only reason he was here, the only reason Roy would've kept him alive, was if he hadn't found Fred yet. It was time to stop Roy once and for all.

Protective instinct and hope filled Jacob's bones and gave him strength as he dusted himself off and slowly stood back up once more.

"I'd like to talk to Roy," he said with the determination of all the wild horses that ever refused to break.

"And here I am, don't ya know," a cavalier voice called out from a tall, thin frame that walked toward him out of the shadows. The rowdy crowd of outlaws hooted and hollered as their leader spoke again.

"No one told me that we were having company, gentlemen. He looks a bit singed, doesn't he? Now, just who might this fine guest be?"

Jacob knew he was playing a dangerous game, but he also knew that if he played his cards just right, it might all work out. He wasn't bound, probably because he was surrounded by so many men, or perhaps it was Roy's pride that wanted an honest fight.

It was clear that he had Roy beat in terms of size and brute strength. Then again, Roy was surrounded by dozens of murderous thieves. Perhaps If he could draw him in close enough, he could grab his pistol and Roy would become his prisoner. Even outlaws wouldn't risk getting their boss shot. That could be one way to escape. He could just shoot him right between the eyes and end it once and for all—consequences be darned.

"You've got me here, Roy, just like you wanted," Jacob said, undeterred. "Now why don't you just cut to the chase and ask me what you brought me here to ask, or aren't you man enough to ask it to my face?"

"Fine by me," Roy said as he walked up to Jacob and bent down. The two men stood face-to-face at last. "Where is my son?"

"You mean *my* son?" Jacob asked as he stared squarely into the outlaw's cold, green eyes. "You seem to keep gettin' confused about that part."

Jacob straightened his spine as he stared into the outlaw's beady green eyes. Courage surged through him, and all fear dissipated as he had but one goal in mind: protecting his family.

Chapter Thirty-Four

"He's gone!"

Louise woke to the cries of the men as they scurried around the fire outside the small red barn. She could hear the flames crackle quietly as they hit the air and the sound of men's boots hitting the ground as they ran around in a hurry.

She sat up groggily and wondered what all the clamor was about. She could see light coming through the cracks of the tiny old barn and got up to see if the campfire had gotten out of control.

"He's been taken!" she heard a voice say.

Who's been taken?

She jumped up from her pallet at once and ran over to the small trough that had served as a makeshift cradle for Fred's bed. Her breath caught in her throat as she ran. But as she reached the edge of the trough and looked inside, she could see that Fred was sleeping safe and sound.

Louise sighed in relief and turned to see an orange blur running toward her. She scooped Minnie up in her arms, grateful for her furry friend.

"What do you think's going on outside, girl?" she asked as she pressed her ear against the wall of the barn, trying to hear what the men were going on about.

The shouting of the men grew louder until Louise couldn't make out any words and it finally woke Alice, along with Martha and Sarah. The three women stumbled to their feet to see what the matter was.

"Can you tell what they're saying?" Sarah asked as she lifted her ear to the window.

"Sarah, get down!" Martha cried out as she pulled her down to her pallet. "The way those men are hollerin' and carryin' on out there, it could mean that Roy's gang is here, and you are not going to get in the middle of it!"

"I'm okay, Mama," Louise heard Sarah answer behind her as she walked to the door.

She knew that Jacob would be mad if she went outside in the middle of a fight, but Martha was busy with Sarah, and Louise had to see what was going on.

She tiptoed to the door and creaked it open ever so slightly. As she peeked through the tiny opening, she saw two of Jacob's men barreling toward her at full speed. They nearly knocked her over as they ran to knock on the door, until Alice pulled her out of the way and the two men raced into the barn.

"What on earth is going on?" Louise asked.

"Is Roy's gang here?" Alice added from behind her.

"No, ma'am," said a large burly man standing next to the youngest ranch hand she'd ever seen. "Well, not anymore."

"So, they were here?" Louise poked her head out the door and looked around in a panic. "Did I hear that someone is *missing?*"

"Yes, ma'am," said a tearful young man who was ringing his hat in his hands.

"Did Roy's gang take someone?" she asked nervously.

"Why, yes ma'am, there was… You see…" The boy's words trailed off as he hung his head.

"It'll be all right," Louise jumped in, wanting to comfort the young ranch hand. He looked like he was hardly more than a boy. "My husband will find them."

But the boy simply shivered at that, refusing to look at her. Frowning, she called out into the wind, "Jacob!" But Louise got no reply.

As she spoke those words, Jimmy began to cry—really cry. She turned to look at him as if for the first time and noticed he had a black eye and a cut on his cheek. He looked like he'd just fought a war. Fear and panic struck her heart suddenly as she realized the worst.

"Where is my husband?" she asked, turning to the burly man still standing at her door.

"Well, that's just it, ma'am," Jimmy answered her as he continued to wring out his hat. "They took *Jacob.*"

A terror that Louise had not felt since her time at her adopted parents' house rushed back to her. White hot heat started in her face and drifted to her stomach as her heart sped up and threatened to beat out of her chest.

"What do you mean they took my husband?"

"They had the boy at gunpoint," the burly man said. "They were gonna kill him. Jacob traded himself to save the boy and they spared his life."

Jimmy hung his head in shame and the burly man placed a hand on the boy's shoulder. Louise's heart went out to him.

"Don't worry, ma'am," the large bear of a man continued. "The boy said that Jacob told the outlaws that you and Fred were down at the sheriff's office in town. They seemed to believe him, and they took Jacob up the mountain. You're safe here. The sheriff should be back soon. Just please stay inside."

Safe? As if she could feel safe when Jacob was in danger. He may have misled the gang for a while, but one thing she had learned about Roy was that he was not a patient man, and he would not spare her husband forever. No, Jacob was in far too much danger for her to sit around and do nothing.

"What's being done to find my husband?" she asked as she steeled her resolve with her hands on her hips and her hard eyes on the burly ranch hand.

"Well, George and Jethro have already taken about half the men up the mountain to search for Jacob. He told the rest of us to wait here with you until the sheriff arrives."

So, George and Jethro had ridden off to save the day with less than half of the amount of men Roy had? They were bound to get themselves all killed! And Louise knew it. But when she looked into the terrified stare of the overgrown ranch hand, she could tell that he was just as scared as she was. There was no use talking to him.

Suddenly, Louise felt someone barrel into her from behind as Martha pushed through the door.

"Did you say something about my husband?" Martha asked in a rush.

"It's okay, Martha," Alice began, "This gentleman was just saying that our husbands are off looking for Jacob."

Louise stumbled out of the house in a stupor, as Alice and Martha talked to the ranch hands surrounding them. She was uninterested in hearing the same story all over again. She had to figure out how to get to Jacob. That was all that mattered now.

She saw her husband's men running in every direction, some trying to find a horse to saddle, while others scurried around, looking for their guns.

Louise walked through the smoke of the campfire, unfazed by the flames dancing just to her left. She had seen enough fire to last a lifetime and it no longer startled her. She had grown accustomed to the smell of the smoke biting through the wood, although her nose twinged as it met her nostrils. The smoke stung her eyes and she winced as she wiped away a tear with her hand.

She had lost enough for one day—for a lifetime—and she would not lose Jacob today. Not when she finally realized just how much she loved him.

As Louise passed the fire and the smoke, along with the sounds of the clamoring men, she found the cool crisp mountain air at last. And as she took a deep, hungry breath, she looked up to the sky where it touched the top of the hills and wondered over which ridge her husband had gone.

Then, looking into the void, the whole day came back to her in a rush. Her home burning down, their first kiss, driving the wagon as she followed her husband, sweet promises whispered in her ear right before he was taken. It all overwhelmed her.

"Please, Lord," she begged out loud from the bottom of her heart. "I can't lose him now, not when I've finally found him."

"Mrs. Montgomery!" exclaimed a surprised voice behind her. "You must get back inside, ma'am!"

Louise turned to see the large burly ranch hand walking toward her with a look of concern in his large but gentle eyes. To the right of him, just behind the tiny barn, sat the wagon she had driven earlier that evening, with the same team of horses still attached, and Gus at the front of it.

"I'm going," she said as she ran back to the barn. Suddenly, the way in front of her was clear and nothing was going to get in her way.

***

"This is crazy!" Sarah said as she paced back and forth with Fred on her hip.

"It'll be just fine, Sarah," Louise said as she peeked out the door to see if the men had gone yet. "When the men aren't looking, I can move the sack of feed, climb out the window, and take Gus up the mountain."

"It's too dangerous!" Sarah insisted as she walked up to Louise.

"Sarah, get away from the door with Fred!" her mother said urgently. "If Roy's men are out there watching, we don't want him to know that Fred is *here!*"

"That's exactly why *you* shouldn't go!" insisted Sarah as she turned back to Louise. "Don't you see? Jacob left to keep you safe and if you run off and get yourself killed, then his sacrifice would've been for nothing."

"I tend to agree with Sarah here," Alice said from behind her, and she felt her friend's gentle hand rest on her shoulder. "There's no sense in Jacob's sacrifice being in vain."

"But that's exactly why I *do* have to go!" Louise said with a heart of determination. She scooped Fred out of Sarah's arms. "This little one needs a father, and right now, he's out there with no help."

Fred giggled and smiled as Louise planted two kisses on each cheek before handing him to Alice.

"Well, if you're going, I'm going with you," Martha said with a brave smile.

"You don't have to do that, Martha," Louise said. "Really, you don't."

"Nonsense," Martha replied. "My husband's out there too, and I'm sure the men could use another gun. I've got one of those kept in my saddle and I know how to use it, too."

"Well, if you're determined to go, Louise, you're gonna need a gun, too." She pulled a rifle and some bullets from behind a bale of hay.

"Alice! Where'd you get that?" Sarah screeched. "You've all gone crazy!"

"It's not crazy to be prepared. We brought this in our wagon and hoped we wouldn't have to use it." Alice sighed as she turned to Louise. "Put it in your saddle bag and if you must use it, shoot it like ya mean it, ya hear?"

"Mama, please don't do this!" Sarah protested tearfully to her mother. "Daddy told us to stay here. It's not safe out there. Mama, please!"

"We'll be fine, darlin," Martha said as she touched her daughter's cheek tenderly. "Besides, knowing your daddy, they'll probably have the whole thing wrapped up before we even get there."

Louise smiled at the sight of mother and daughter and hoped that she would get to see Fred all grown up, too. That would be a lot harder to do if her husband was dead—something she wasn't sure her heart could take. They had to go out there soon or it could mean the worst for Jacob.

"We gotta go," Louise said in a hurry. "Time's a wastin', and I don't know how much time Jacob has left."

As they headed for the door, Louise couldn't help but notice that her son had started crying. Always the faithful friend, Minnie was circling and mewing in suit.

"Shh! Hush now, my son! You too, Minnie!" Louise said, with a mixture of courage and remorse. She kissed Fred on the top of the head as he sat in Alice's secure arms, scratched her furry friend behind the ears, and turned to climb out the window.

"Ma," came a half-word from Fred's mouth.

Louise looked back, startled.

Did he just say mama for the first time?

Martha, Sarah, and Alice all looked at Louise with wide eyes, and she could tell they understood the importance of this moment. She rushed back to kiss Fred on his cheeks once more, tears falling down hers.

"I'll see you soon, my little love." Louise comforted him gently before she hugged Alice and then turned to Sarah.

"Please don't go!" Sarah whispered in her ear as Louise hugged her tight.

"Take care of the little ones and keep heart! We'll be back soon," Louise said before climbing out the window.

As Louise hopped down from the small window and then helped Martha through, she was reminded of another time, not quite so long ago, when she snuck out of a window for a much different reason. Then, she had snuck out to escape the cruel life at the Cankers, where she had been leaving to find the possibility of love with a man she didn't yet know.

This was altogether different. Now, she was leaving a perfectly safe home with people she loved to find the man that she knew she loved even more.

The irony was not lost on her as she tiptoed away from her son and furry friend, both still crying behind her. As she untied the horses and helped Martha onto one of them, she felt torn between the crying babe that needed her and the brave husband, whose life hung in the balance.

"Are you sure about this?" Martha asked as she smiled sadly down at Louise.

"I'm sure," Louise said as she saddled up Jacob's horse, Gus. As she stood on the wagon to help her mount the old stallion's saddle, she was glad it was Jacob's horse that would help track him down.

"Come on, Martha. Let's go get our husbands!"

Chapter Thirty-Five

Louise was grateful for the cool autumn air at her back. It urged her forward, as if in agreement with her mission. The bright autumn moon scattered patches of light on the ground, illuminating the fresh horse tracks from Roy's men. Louise was surprised at how easy it was to follow the path of tracks as they moved on up the mountain.

They traveled over the ridge and out of sight of the ranch hands when the fresh tracks started to fade.

"What happened to the tracks?" Louise asked in frustration.

"No idea. Looks like the outlaws got smart after they escaped over the ridge. They must have stopped to cover them up."

"Well, they've gotta be here somewhere," Louise said in a hurry as she got down slowly off Gus. She led him by the reins as she walked around, staring at the dirt, praying a footprint would show up somewhere.

As she walked toward a clump of cacti, a cool breeze blew her hair over her eyes. Suddenly, Gus reared back, pulling the reins out of Louise's hand.

"Whoa, boy! What is it?"

"Do you hear something?" Martha asked as her horse pulled up and stopped next to Louise.

"I don't," Louise answered. "But I think Gus here might."

"My horse, too," Martha agreed. "As soon as the wind picked up, his ears perked."

Louise stood in silence for a moment with Martha waiting patiently next to her. She listened intently to the breeze for whatever it was that the horses were sensing.

After a minute that felt like hours, Louise climbed onto her horse and urged the stallion to continue. They walked slowly up the hill past a briar patch and some tumbleweeds. She wasn't sure if she was relieved or disappointed that it had been nothing at all.

"Must've just been the breeze blowin' everything around," Louise said as she let out a sigh. "Let's keep looking for the outlaws' footprints."

Just as she finished speaking, she heard something new rustle behind a bunch of sagebrush.

"Did you hear that?" Louise asked as her horse huffed and whinnied. Gus kicked at the dirt, Louise bouncing around and nearly falling off before she grasped the front of the saddle and pulled herself upright.

As she finally got settled atop the old horse, she noticed Martha draw her pistol. Louise watched in terror as her friend cocked the gun and pointed it shakily toward the sagebrush.

"Come out or I'll shoot!" Martha shouted, a crack in her voice.

She knew they were in way over their heads, and part of Louise wished she had stayed with Fred in the safety of the small equipment barn. She held her breath and waited to see what would pop out from behind the sagebrush.

"I wouldn't move if I were you," a menacing voice called out behind her.

She heard a gun cock behind her and suddenly couldn't move. She was frozen in fear.

"Both o' y'all need to get your hands up real slow-like. And you with the gun—why don't you go ahead and get down off your horse and set the gun down real easy."

Louise slowly lifted her hands as her shoulders trembled. She remembered that she had Alice's rifle inside her saddle bag, but she knew there was no way she could get to it. She turned her head ever so slightly to see that Martha had already dismounted her horse and laid the gun down on the ground in front of her.

"I tell you what, ladies, this must be my day!" said the confident outlaw as he laughed and tapped his knee with his hat. "Here I was trying to set a trap for your husband's men when they came to fetch him, but instead, I hit the jackpot! The boss man's gonna be real happy when I bring you two back to camp."

Louise shuddered when she realized how foolish she'd been. With her and Jacob both captured, it would be far too easy for Roy to find Fred. She should've stayed back at the barn to protect her son. She thought she was helping Jacob, but now, she had put them all in much more danger.

"All right, you," the lanky outlaw called to Martha. "Go ahead and kick that gun over here, and don't try anything funny. My trigger finger has been real itchy today. I'd hate for my weapon to go off accidentally."

Louise couldn't bring her arms or legs to move. She managed to crane her neck around and look on helplessly as Martha walked toward the tall man who remained cloaked in the shadow.

She realized too late that, as she turned to watch her friend, her horse decided to move with her. Gus followed Louise's lead and turned to face Martha and the outlaw, but he went and lifted his front legs off the ground when he saw the man holding the gun. Louise held on for dear life and leaned into Gus as the old horse reared back and kicked his front legs into the air.

"Whoa!" yelled the startled outlaw. "I thought I told you to get off your horse! Don't make me say it again or that pretty little face won't be so pretty anymore."

"Sir, pl-please calm down," Martha said.

"What'd you say to me?" The outlaw raised his voice another octave and reached out to grab Martha by the hair. Then, he pressed his gun into her cheek.

"It's just that, you're startlin' the horse there."

"You mean to make me scared of a horse, lady? Now, that's funny! Why, I robbed every train between here and the Mississippi, and now I've found the woman that the boss wants to put down, and you think I'm gonna be scared of an old horse?"

The outlaw reared his head back and cackled into the cool night air. As if on cue, Gus bucked and kicked his feet at the overconfident man.

Louise closed her eyes when she heard the gun go off in the air. She held on tight to the reins and saddle as the horse bucked, spinning in a circle. She knew he was kicking up dust because she was breathing it in, practically suffocating her. But Louise could not bring herself to open her eyes for fear of what she might see.

Suddenly, she felt the front end of Gus come down hard as his feet hit the ground and stayed there. She stayed low, clinging to the horse's neck, and opened her eyes to see that the outlaw had taken control of the reins and brought the stallion to bear.

"See there now? I told you that I could take care of this here horse."

The outlaw laughed, but Louise could tell from the exhausted look on his face that he'd had just about enough. As he pulled the horse to him, Louise could see his face for the first time. It was long and narrow like a crevice in a rock, and his eyes looked equally as empty. His chin held a jagged scar that had never properly healed, and his cheeks were covered in dirt. The weathered wrinkles on his face proved that he'd lived his fair share of hard years. She wondered how many of the lines were from laughing and how many were from fits of rage. As if to settle the matter for her, the outlaw spoke up again.

"I thought I told you to get down, darlin'!" he hollered at Louise with a grunt and a mean gleam in his eye.

Louise wasn't sure exactly why, but when he yelled at her, it triggered something deep inside. Perhaps it was the fact that he called her *darlin'* like the old hog used to do, or perhaps it was the way that he looked at her with the same sadistic glare that Paw used when he was about to rage.

Whatever the reason, an indignant anger filled her bones, and she was determined to take no more abuse from cruel men. She also couldn't help but notice that when the outlaw reached out to grab the horse, he had taken his finger off the trigger, and it now dangled aimlessly from his pointer finger.

"I'm not your darlin!" Louise answered, with courage she didn't know she had. "I'm married to the best rancher on this side of the mountain. I'm also awful good friends with the sheriff, who just so happens to be huntin' down the likes of *you*. And like my good friend here said—ya best watch out for my horse!"

Louise clung to the saddle with both hands and kicked Gus's sides as she leaned into his mane and braced for his response. Without missing a beat, Gus reared back, breaking the grasp that the outlaw had on his reins and throwing the man to the ground.

The old stallion jumped and spun, kicking up dust along with anything else in his way. As Louise held on for dear life, she squinted through the dust and rejoiced to see Martha escaping down the hill. She thought her eyes might be tricking her, but it also looked like a group of men on horseback rode toward them from the other direction.

At last, the spinning stopped, and the dust settled when the outlaw grabbed the horse's reins hard and brought the beast to a stop. Louise leaned back into the saddle as she saw him lift the gun and point it squarely at her head.

This might be it! But at least Martha escaped. She'll be able to get more men to help and she'll make sure that Fred's safe.

"You're really testing my patience, lady!" the outlaw yelled. Gus whinnied as he yanked down on the reins again.

"Is that so?" Louise asked with her chin held high, trying to keep her voice from trembling.

She might not make it out of here, but she wasn't going to give him the satisfaction of her being afraid, either. She stared him straight in the eyes, determined not to give into the terror that he so clearly wanted to instill in her.

"Yeah, that's so!" he replied as he cocked the gun. "The boss wants you brought in alive, and I tend to follow his orders, but I might make an exception for you."

Louise felt a shiver run down her spine as a lump caught in her throat. She steadied herself and sat up taller, determined not to give into the fear that knocked in her chest.

"The thing is, *darlin'*," the cruel man continued his declaration. "I've got a bit of a temper."

"So do I!" called a familiar voice from the shadows. "The only difference is, I got a few more guns on me than you do."

Louise stared in shock as George and ten other ranch hands crept with their horses out of the shadows.

"It's about time you put your gun down so that we can have a little talk, don't you think? Or I suppose we could always let our guns do the talking. But ours might be a bit louder. Your call."

Louise watched as the outlaw lifted his hands in the air, his gun pointed to the stars. He looked like he was about to give in until his eyes locked with hers and a wicked smile crossed his face.

Quicker than a whippoorwill flying from its nest, he pointed his gun at Louise, and she heard a gunshot ring through the air.

It happened so fast that Louise thought for a moment that time was going by in slow motion. As the high-pitched noise rang in her ears, Louise put her hands to her stomach, wondering where the bullet hole had gone through. As she reached down, Gus kicked his legs into the air once more and took off like a buck shot out of a gun.

Her hands were able to find the reins, but she knew she had little control over the horse as he ran up the mountain. She had never moved this fast in her life and thought this must be what it felt like to be a train racing across the Rockies.

Her heart beat wildly in her chest and she was surprised to find that she felt less scared than she was excited. She felt her stomach for a bullet wound but the outlaw's shot had missed and her heart soared in courage. Her fear was gone and had been replaced by a focused determination. Louise was free to carry out her plan.

She managed to hold onto the saddle with one hand and the reins with the other. As she loosened the grip that her legs had on the horse, she felt the rhythm of his hooves slow, until he was walking once more. At last, the beast whinnied and slowed to a stop.

"Good boy," Louise said as she stroked his mane gently. "You're a lot friendlier when no one's shooting at ya, aren't you, Gus?"

The horse lifted his head as if to agree and then lowered it to nibble on a dry patch of grass. Now that her horse was calm, she could guide him up the hill and keep looking for Jacob, but she had to know where she was first.

She looked at the stars, but who was she kidding? She had no idea how to determine their location. She looked up and down the mountain, but nothing looked familiar. Dirt, cacti, and sagebrush covered the ground as far as the eye could see. The only noise to guide her was the sound of crickets and a coyote howling in the distance.

What do I do now, Lord?

She sat there for a moment, waiting, although she wasn't sure for what—until a fresh wind blew in and the stallion's ears pricked up once more.

"What do you hear, Gus? What is it?"

It didn't take long for the noise that her horse picked up on to reach her ears. It was the low rumble of men cheering and hollering. She lifted the reins and leaned forward. Remembering how much her legs affected the horse's movements, she tapped him gently with the heel of her boot.

"Come on, Gus," she whispered as the stallion walked carefully forward. "It's time to find Jacob."

Her heartbeat had steadied now, and she was surprised to find that her fear was gone. It had been replaced with an ever-growing peace, courage, and a steely determination to find her husband—no matter the cost.

Chapter Thirty-Five

Louise followed the muffled sound of angry voices, though she couldn't quite make out what they were saying. She was cloaked in the darkness of the night, but as she and Gus rode closer to the sounds, she knew she would be found out if she continued on horseback.

"I guess this is where you and I part, my friend," she whispered gratefully to Jacob's horse, who had saved her life that night. She felt deeply connected to the animal and regretted having to leave him behind.

She climbed down carefully and was relieved that she was able to make it to the ground without falling. As she patted him gently on the nose, he snickered quietly and pushed his nose under her hand. Smiling, she tied him up to a large bush and carefully pulled the rifle from the saddle bag.

"Here's hoping I can aim worth a darn."

With one last pat on the nose, she tucked the rifle under her arm and tiptoed away from the horse to find the men.

As she crept over a ledge, the midnight moon revealed the band of outlaws at last.

Positioned at the top of the mountain near the mouth of a cave was the wild band of outlaws and their prisoner—her husband. She could barely make out their faces, much less what they were saying. She could hear the mumbled chorus of angry voices talking, but she couldn't make out the words. She had to get closer.

Louise crawled on her belly through the dirt, hoping and praying that they didn't look in her direction. She reasoned that she was far enough away to be covered by the darkness, but her heart raced nonetheless as she inched toward their camp.

Finally, she came upon a large group of cacti and sat up behind it, grateful for the covering it provided. Their spikes and spines pointed out like knives toward her, but it was the safest thing she had to hide behind. She took a deep breath and peeked out to the side, checking to see that her husband was safe.

She could see them so much clearer now. Next to a campfire, surrounded by dirt and the angry faces of men with torches, stood her brave husband, standing up to Roy. Her heart surged with a mixture of pride for Jacob's bravery and fear for his safety. He stood with his chest puffed out and his chin held high. He had a look of confidence in his eyes—a certainty that gave her courage.

She was amazed by his rugged confidence and bravery in the face of certain death. How did she not see this in him before? Louise hoped that she had a chance to tell him later.

She shifted her focus and closed her eyes for a moment, straining to hear what the men were saying. She thought they must not have suspected that she was coming or else they wouldn't have been so loud.

Then again, it was Jacob she heard talking the loudest.

"You mean *my* son?" Her husband's voice rang out over the mountain top. "You seem to keep getting confused about that part."

Louise smiled with pride when she heard her husband say those words. She'd longed to hear them for such a very long time. Though she knew that Jacob cared for Fred and was willing to keep him and defend him, his determination to call Fred his son in the face of danger wiped away any trace of concern. But when she heard Roy's reply, her concern for Jacob came rushing right back.

"You either tell me where he is or I'm gonna shoot you where you stand!"

"I already told your man that he's down with the sheriff back in town," Jacob replied with his head held high. "If you want him, why don't you march on down to the sheriff's office and get him?"

Roy let out a vicious cackle that sent a chill down Louise's spine.

"Nice try," the ruthless outlaw said as he circled Jacob with the gun pointed square at him. "I already sent two men to town, and they said that the sheriff's nowhere around. Nothing's in his office—much less a babe."

"Well then," Jacob replied, "if you know the sheriff's not there, then you can put two and two together and expect that he's headed your way. Are you sure you want to waste time camping out on my mountain when you could be hightailing it out of town?"

"You wish!" Roy laughed again. "But there's no way that they know where we are. All our tracks have been covered and we can see whoever's coming."

"That may be," said Jacob with a sly smile. "But you can't hide from the eyes of God or from justice. This isn't gonna work out for you, Roy. If I were you, I'd turn tail and run—while you still can."

"The eyes of *God?*" Roy mocked as he looked up into the sky, as if searching for something. "I don't see your God anywhere around here, Jacob, nor do I see these supposed *long arms of justice.*"

As if it had been planned on cue, a rumble of horse hooves sounded out in the distance. Louise realized in horror that the sound was coming from behind her, and all the outlaws looked in her direction, expecting to see a team of horses.

She ducked quickly behind the cactus and held her breath, wondering if she'd been found out.

"Billy! Johnny! Get on your horses and go see what's coming up our hill," she heard Roy say.

Louise couldn't help but notice a trace of fear in his voice. She smiled to herself as new hope surged through her heart.

Perhaps she wouldn't have to try her hand at shooting a rifle today after all. Maybe George or the sheriff would be coming over the mountain any moment now.

She was distracted from her hopeful thoughts by the sound of horse hooves pounding toward her. She tucked her head down and laid low behind the cactus as two scrappy men hurdled past her on horses. Louise tried to stifle a cough as the kicked-up dust filled her lungs, and she watched as they galloped down the hill at the sound of more horses.

When they were out of sight, she sat up tall and peeked out again to see how her husband was fairing.

Roy and all his men had guns drawn, pointing them down the hill. She searched for Jacob but couldn't find him in the place he had stood before. She realized in horror that he'd been moved farther away from her, and a squirrely looking outlaw of Roy's was holding a gun to her husband's head.

"No!" she whispered, before forcing herself to stay quiet. If they intended to use her husband as a hostage, then it might be too late.

Please God, Louise prayed earnestly. *Please save my husband. Show me what to do! Just please, don't let me lose him now.*

"*Have I not commanded you? Be bold and courageous. Do not be afraid or terrified. For the Lord your God is with you wherever you go.*"

That verse might've been written for Joshua, but maybe it applied to her, too.

Suddenly, she heard two shots go off in the distance, followed by about a dozen more, and then total silence. Whatever those outlaws found on the hill must not have agreed with them.

On the other side of her, she heard Roy and his men clamoring about, readying themselves for battle. It was now or never. If she was going to act, it had to be soon.

She mustered all her strength as she picked up the rifle that she was unsure how to use. She leaned over the top of the cactus and set the barrel of her rifle between two of its sharp spines.

Louise looked down the barrel of the gun and noticed her husband in the distance, his face pointed toward her. Roy's back was to her as he mumbled something, before roaring a little louder. She strained her ears to hear what the outlaw's plans were.

"Looks like the long arm of justice isn't so far away after all," her husband's voice rang out proudly.

She winced as Roy lifted his gun and shot it right past Jacob's face. Louise looked on in shock as the man behind Jacob holding a gun to his head didn't move a muscle.

"You're really starting to test my patience," Roy yelled without any trace of laughter now. "Looks like your friends might be coming to pay us a visit. Problem is, ya got two guns pointed at you, Jacob, so I don't know if you'll be in the mood to accept comp'ny when they arrive. What do you think?"

"I think that you're running out of time to scurry off like the snake that you are," Jacob said coolly.

"Last chance!" Roy roared in Jacob's face as the crowd of outlaws behind him cried out for blood. "Tell me where my son is, and I'll leave here to go and find him. You can live and go home to that awful woman if you'll just tell me where to find my son."

"I'd thank you to not talk about my wife like that," Jacob replied. "As for the boy, I wouldn't tell you where he is for anything. But what I *will* tell you is that he's no longer your son. If dyin' is what it takes to keep my family safe from the likes of you, then so be it."

"You're a fool!" Roy raged, as he cocked his gun and his bloodthirsty men roared in approval.

"I'm surprised, Roy," Louise heard her husband say. "I thought you'd be the type of man that wanted an honorable fight. Why don't we settle this man to man?"

"Fine by me!" said Roy, and the crowd cheered as he tossed his gun to the ground and the other outlaw released Jacob. The two men started to circle each other with fists up.

Louise needed to get a clear shot at Roy, but the back of his head was blocked by the crowd of men. All of them had turned to face Jacob and Roy, and were cheering him on, ready for bloodshed. She knew if she shot bullets into the crowd, they would think that it was the sheriff coming in and then shoot Jacob where he stood. She was running out of options and had to think fast.

If she played her cards just right, she just might be able to get around the crowd in the shadows. Maybe she could pick off Roy that way. If she could take out just one of them, any of them, it would give her husband a fighting chance. Better yet, maybe she'd get lucky and find herself in a standoff to keep them busy—just long enough for the sheriff's men to reach the hilltop.

The crowd booed angrily, and Louise smiled, knowing that Jacob must have landed a punch.

Louise stood up, figured out how to cock the rifle, and held it out in front of her. She took a deep breath of the cool night air, hoping it wasn't her last, and then ran toward the men as fast as her feet would carry her. Her arms sagged beneath the heavy weapon and her muscles shook as struggled to hold it in front of her.

Still, she ran stealthily around the group of men who were hollering something she couldn't decipher. As she neared the front edge of the fire, she was relieved to find that the men didn't notice her and that she remained shrouded in darkness.

The rumble of horse hooves in the distance grew louder and the two men stopped their scuffle as each looked toward the noise.

"Enough of this!" Roy said as he stood up and wiped off a bloody lip. "I could beat you 'til the cows come home to pasture, but I hear your men headed up the hill and I reckon' we outta finish this."

Her breath caught in her throat as she lifted the gun and pointed it square at Roy's shoulders, hoping it wasn't too late.

"Looks like you're outta luck, Jacob." Roy's cruel words hit Louise's heart like a knife. "Time to go meet your maker."

Much to her terror, Louise saw Roy cock his gun with a wicked grin and closed one eye as he aimed at Jacob for the last time.

"No!" she screamed as the rifle fell to her feet. She ran out of the shadows toward Jacob as fast as she could. She thought of nothing but stopping the bullet meant for her husband.

She got a glimpse of Jacob's eyes, that were first filled with surprise and then with horror as she heard the gunshot break the air.

Louise fell into Jacob's arms as she reached them at last and a strange fire filled her belly. She sank to the ground with Jacob beneath her as he held her in his arms.

Something was wrong. Had he been hit?

She looked up at his soft brown eyes that were filled with tears and fury. The man who had once been holding a gun to his head had fallen to the ground and was unconscious behind them.

"Louise," Jacob cried out as he held her. "What's happened to you, my love?"

She followed Jacob's worried look to her side and saw her dress filling up with blood. She saw the fear in his eyes as he ripped off his jacket and tied it around her waist, trying to stop the flow. Her eyelids grew weak and fluttered to a close as her head spun.

"Louise!" he pleaded! "Open your eyes! You gotta stay with me!"

She stared up at Jacob's face and struggled to keep her eyes open. She tried to reach a hand up, wanting to comfort him, but it fell back into her lap. She tried to offer words of comfort, but nothing came out. She was too weak.

"Now look what you've done," she heard Roy's caustic voice call out from behind her. "You've gone and gotten that little gal o' yours killed! Don't worry. I'll send you to meet her."

Louise turned her head slightly to see Roy laughing cruelly as he pointed the gun at Jacob again. Unable to watch the bullet come, she turned her head upward to look at her husband's face. If they were about to meet God, at least they'd do it together.

To her surprise, she saw Jacob pull a pistol off the man on the ground next to him. Without missing a beat, he lifted the gun and shot it as the roaring sound of the bullet's release pierced the air.

Louise heard a loud thud shake the ground behind her. Roy lay flat on his back, surrounded by a cloud of dirt kicked up in his wake.

Suddenly, there were more gunshots everywhere, and the dust was stirred up by horses and men running in every direction. Louise tucked her head into Jacob's chest and waited for it to stop as he held her close. Her side had grown suddenly warm, and she winced from the pain as she leaned into him.

"Hang on, love!" Jacob pleaded into her ear, but it sounded faint. She could hardly focus, but she willed all her strength to pay attention on her husband's voice. "Help is here and everything's gonna be all right. Just please, hang on a little while longer!"

As the fighting carried on around her, she knew somehow that she was safe in Jacob's arms. She heard the gunshots and the whine of the bullets whizzing past, but she knew somehow that all would be okay.

"Watch yer back, sheriff!" a familiar voice shouted. "This one's lively!"

"I got them, George," the sheriff's voice replied. "Just make sure Martha stays out of the line of fire until we rope the rest of 'em up!"

"Right behind you, George!" she heard Jethro's voice call out in the distance right as another bullet whizzed by her and Jacob.

"They're going over the ridge to town!" The sheriff's voice was clear as day. "Head down the hill and we can cut 'em off at the pass!"

Slowly but surely, the gunshots became fewer as the fighting sounded like it was getting farther away. Louise could feel the ground beneath her rumble as the thundering of horse hooves grew quieter and quieter until they were gone at last. She held a hand to her side, sticky from the blood, and noticed that a chill covered her now. She shivered in response.

"Let me help her, Jacob," she could hear Martha say over her shoulder.

She felt Jacob's grip on her loosen and she cried out in pain as she felt the wound in her side afresh.

"The good news is that the bullet's just grazed her side. It's bleeding plenty, but the bullet won't have hit anything vital," Martha said. "And you've done a mighty fine job of stopping the bleeding, Jacob! But the wound needs to be cauterized before we can move her."

Louise tried to open her eyes. As she squinted, the light hit them like a blinding flare. She winced when she saw the torch that Martha held over her.

"This is gonna hurt a little bit," her friend said. "But then you're gonna start feeling better real soon."

She wasn't sure what she was talking about, but before Louise could ask, she felt a fiery pain slap at the side of her stomach.

She cried out in pain as hot metal singed her side, forcing the wound closed, and she squeezed Jacob's hands as he helped her sit up and gave her a drink of water.

She felt weak but the dizziness started to leave Louise's body, and she looked down at her wound to see that it was closed up. She took a deep breath and then she heard a baby crying from not so far away.

"Is that... Fred?" Louise asked in shock. "Please tell me nobody brought my baby to a gunfight!"

"Sorry," Martha replied. "But after Jacob was taken and you disappeared, we had to gather back at the barn. Luckily, the sheriff showed up and he had us bring everyone together. They couldn't leave us there alone, not knowing where the outlaws were. So, we're a bit of a travelin' crew at the moment. And after everything the gang's pulled tonight—from burning houses all over town to setting off dynamite just to distract us—well, we couldn't risk separating."

"To be fair," George said as he came to stand by his wife. "Jethro did a good job of keeping the wagon with the women and kids guarded and out of sight until the outlaws took off. We just needed to stick together, ya understand."

"Don't worry," came a chipper voice from the wagon. "He's in good hands!"

Louise smiled at the sound of Sarah's voice; she'd never been so happy to hear it.

"In that case, please bring me my baby," Louise said as her voice cracked in anticipation.

Louise's heart filled with joy as Sarah placed Fred in her arms.

"Ma!" Fred cried happily as he touched his soft, chubby hands to her face and kissed her on the cheek.

"Hello, little one," Louise said weakly as she buried her face in his hair and took a deep breath. "Never thought I'd see you again."

She held her precious son tightly, as if she'd never let go.

"Please," a desperate voice coughed out from the other side of the fire. "Please, can I see him just once more before I die."

Louise gazed at the once-terrifying man who laid on the ground just a few feet away. Somehow, against all odds, Roy was still alive. But from the looks of things—he wouldn't be for long.

To Louise's surprise, her heart went out to him, and she was filled with sorrow on his behalf. She remembered the pain that had gripped her heart when she'd feared Fred being taken from her, and she knew his pain must be much more amplified as he'd failed in his mission once and for all. Outlaw or not, he had lost his son and was now about to lose his life.

Jacob lifted his gun and pointed it again at the wounded man. "You're crazy if you think that we'd let you near that baby after all the pain you've caused. You're lucky I don't finish you off right now."

"Jacob," Louise said as she lifted a weak hand and placed it tenderly on her husband's cheek. "I think we should give him this mercy. We have each other, but he has nothing... and by the looks of things, he's not long for this world."

She watched as her husband's countenance softened, and he bent down to kiss her on the forehead.

"Okay," Jacob said gruffly. "But the babe never leaves my arms. He can have a proper goodbye, but Fred stays where I can protect him," he warned the dying man, as he held Fred close to him, but out for the outlaw to see.

"Thank you," Roy said hoarsely, as he looked upon his son for the last time.

"Don't thank me. Thank her. I would've just put another bullet in you."

Louise heard Roy try to laugh before he started coughing again and cleared his throat. She watched as the man who had terrorized her family for almost a year finally got the one thing he wanted, if only for a moment.

"You're so big!" Roy said as he started to tear up. Louise sat up protectively as Roy reached out to hold Fred's tiny fingers. She saw her husband brace in response as he held their son's hand, and she was grateful that her husband was there to keep him safe.

"I'm sorry that I couldn't bring you up, son," Roy continued as he coughed a little more. "I should've done it when I had the chance with your Ma. I'm sorry I didn't give you the chance to look up to your Pa."

And just like that, Roy was gone. His head fell back as if he was looking up at the sky, and the hands that had inflicted so much pain fell limp at his sides.

"Hey Fred! Look at me, son," Jacob said, as he distracted the toddler away to a happier place. Louise gazed at the truer father, as he lifted their son away from the outlaw and brought him back to Louise.

"It's over," he told her as he wrapped them both up in his arms.

The gratitude in Louise's heart drowned out the pain in her stomach as she held Fred, and Jacob hugged them both.

"You sacrificed yourself for us," Louise said. As she leaned into Jacob's chest she gazed up into his warm brown eyes. "For a second, I thought I'd lost you."

"You're the one who just took a bullet for me, love." Jacob stroked her hair tenderly and kissed her cheek. "I don't know what I would have done if I'd lost *you.*"

"I'm not going anywhere," she said as she leaned into his chest. She tried to say more but her body and mind were too weak to form words.

"Please rest now, my love," Jacob said tenderly.

Louise held Fred close as Jacob held them both, and she felt the strength of his love like she never had before. As she drifted off to sleep, she thanked God that they were all somehow still there—still a family.

Chapter Thirty-Six

The morning sun shone through the window of the Main Street Hotel as Jacob pulled the curtains back gently. Louise loved to have fresh sunlight fill the room and wake her up naturally in the mornings, and Jacob was determined to do whatever it took to help her recovery go as smoothly as possible.

Jacob walked over to the bed to check on his sleeping wife, who was curled up with Minnie in her arms. Her golden locks covered her eyes and played around the edges of her mouth like curtains that were blocking a window with a beautiful view. He brushed her hair gently out of her face and leaned down to feel her forehead.

Cool as a cucumber, at last.

The fever that she'd had for a few days after the incident was no joking matter, and he was grateful that the infection from the cauterized gunshot wound had subsided. The fever had been gone for a couple of days, but he wasn't going to take any chances.

The doctor had been kind enough to visit every day and told Jacob to watch out for the return of a fever, as that would be the sign of a worsening infection. Jacob smiled contentedly to himself that the fever hadn't returned, and he thought of how stubborn a patient Louise had been over the last few weeks.

She had insisted that she was "just fine", convalescing in the equipment barn as she healed from her bullet wound, but Jacob knew better. No wife of his was going to be laid up in a barn on the hard ground without a decent bed and a doctor nearby.

Still, he loved how determined and unselfish she was. He knew that many a woman or man would have left him on that mountain to die or would've thrown a fit about living in a barn—but not Louise. He was in awe of how strong she had turned out to be, both in mind and body.

But now wasn't the time for her to prove she was worth her medal. Now was the time for her to rest and let him care for her.

After a little bit of convincing, she had finally agreed to his plan of resting and healing in town at the new Main Street Hotel. It was within walking distance of the doctor's office, should she need it.

Jacob had also loved their stay at the hotel for other reasons. Martha and Sarah had been determined to keep Fred with them, just while Louise was healing, and he was grateful for the alone time it had afforded them.

With only her recovery to keep him busy, they'd had plenty of time to talk, and Jacob had been surprised at how easy the talking became. Each day, he checked her bandages and made sure that she rested, and each night, he was able to hold her gently in his arms.

Three quick knocks at the door shook Jacob from his thoughts, and he walked quickly to see who had intruded on their peace.

He cracked open the door, revealing Sarah and Martha standing in the hallway. Sarah held a smiling Fred on her hip, while her mother held a tray of fresh bread and fruit.

"Ma!" Fred declared merrily as he reached for the door.

"Shhh!" Jacob replied, as he held his hand to his lips. "Mama is sleeping right now, son. Let's give her a couple minutes to wake up."

Son.

It was the first time he'd called Fred that. It felt right and it was true at last. He lifted Fred in his arms as he stepped into the hallway.

He was about to shut the door to keep them from waking his wife when he heard an excited declaration come from the other end of the room.

"No, please... Mama is awake!" He heard his wife insist. "Please bring Fred in!"

Jacob opened the door, revealing the visitors to Louise. She was already sitting up in bed with a smile on her face and her arms outstretched, ready to hold the child she had fought so hard to keep.

"I hope you don't mind a little extra company!" Sarah said as she skipped through the room to hug Louise carefully around the neck.

"I never mind when it's my dearest friend," Louise said as they gently embraced.

"I just hope you're hungry," Martha said as she sat the abundant tray of food at Louise's feet. "Remember, you've got to eat if you want your body to heal. Not even the determination of a rancher's wife can heal a bullet hole without proper nutrition."

"Thank you, Martha," Louise said as she took her friend's hand in hers. "But the food will have to wait just a few minutes. Holding my little one is the best medicine there is."

"Well, he's not so little anymore," Jacob said with a chuckle. "But he's all ours nonetheless."

Even though they were laughing, Jacob knew that there was some truth in what Louise had said about her son being the best medicine. The first few days after the shooting had been touch and go. He'd been afraid he was going to lose her. She had asked for Fred constantly, and when they had brought him in for a visit, she started to feel better the next day. Each day after that, Martha and Sarah would bring Fred by for a short while. And afterwards, his wife always seemed better. Even though he couldn't prove it, Jacob was sure that it was a medicine better than anything the doctor could give.

As Jacob handed him off to Louise, Fred kicked out his feet and waved his arms wildly, as if to prove just how big he had gotten.

"There you are, little one," Louise crooned as Fred touched her cheeks. "Now, tell me and Minnie all about your adventures in the barn."

"Ma!" Fred said again as he laughed and danced around the bed beside Louise.

Jacob looked on as Louise tickled Fred and gave him kisses. Minnie the cat danced in a circle around them, periodically stopping to throw her paws in the air and bat at the pair. He couldn't help but think that it renewed her energy, and his heart was warmed by the scene.

As he was about to sit on the bed next to his family, he realized he had not offered his friends a place to stay.

"Martha, Sarah, please have a seat," Jacob said as he pulled up a chair for each of the women.

He looked on in confusion as the two women glanced at each other with smiles on their faces.

"We'd love to stay," Sarah said, "but we should leave you to eat breakfast together, alone—as a family."

"Don't be silly!" said Louise with a look of consternation on her face. "Why, you've only just gotten here! What could be more important than catching up with your best friend?"

"Well, we wanted it to be a surprise," Sarah said with a sigh, "but you haven't bothered to touch the food yet."

Jacob followed Sarah's line of sight to the tray of food at the foot of the bed. He walked over to look closer and realized that there were several pieces of paper underneath the fresh bread. He knew that Louise saw it as well, because suddenly she was leaning forward and digging under the bread to see what their friends had in store.

Jacob watched his wife's face as she read the paper intently for what seemed like several minutes. At last, she held it tightly to her chest as tears fell down her cheeks.

"What is it?" Jacob asked, terrified that something was wrong. They had just survived the worst he could imagine. What on earth could this be?

"Oh, Jacob!" his wife said as she looked up at him with watery blue eyes.

He stared into the captivating eyes that had captured his heart, a lump in his throat. He couldn't bear seeing her in more pain. But then, as his gaze drifted down to her quivering chin, he realized that her tears were in response to a smiling face.

"Read this," she said, smiling more clearly now, and she placed the paper on his chest with a gentle hand.

Confusion gave way to excitement as Jacob took the paper from his shocked wife's hand and read it intently.

Dear Mr. and Mrs. Jacob Montgomery,

We are pleased to inform you that your request for legal guardianship of Fred Montgomery has been approved on this 31st day of August 1888.

If there is any dispute in this matter, feel free to contact the office.

Jacob dropped the letter and looked up at his wife. She smiled at him with a joy that could outshine the sun. He took her in his arms and kissed her before remembering that they had guests.

"Like I said," Sarah laughed. "Mama and I must be heading out. You three need some family time. But we'll be back later this afternoon to fetch Fred, so that you can have, well, your *own time.*"

"Hush girl!" Martha reprimanded, an embarrassed look on her face as she ushered Sara into the hall and turned back to Jacob and Louise. "You must forgive my daughter. She seems to have forgotten her manners. Congratulations, you two."

At last, they were alone. Although visitors were nice, Jacob was ready to be solely with his wife and child.

"It's done, Jacob!" Louise cried happily as she gathered Fred into her arms. "Can you believe it?"

"Yes, actually," he said as he gazed at his happy wife. "I can."

He embraced his family, his wife's head on his shoulder as Fred poked his head up in between them. They sat there that way, with the sunlight streaming through the window, until Fred started reaching for the bread. They laughed at their son as Jacob savored the moment, grateful for the hope that flooded his heart.

***

The sweet scent of sunflowers drifted up to Jacob's nose and he took an eager whiff of the cool autumn air. He knew this would be some of the last sunflowers to bloom for the season as he had to look longer than usual to find them.

He'd almost given up hope of finding fresh sunflowers for Louise, until a small patch of grass behind the church caught his eye. He had gathered up as many as he could and was finally on his way back to his wife.

As he walked by the church where they had gotten married nearly a year ago, he couldn't help but think of how much had happened—how much had changed. It was way more than he could handle, but somehow, he wouldn't switch out any of it for the world.

Jacob let out a contented sigh and smiled to himself as he stepped onto the road headed back to the hotel. Then, a familiar voice broke his train of thought.

"Well, if that isn't the rancher that put down Roy Taylor. What are you doing over here?"

Jacob turned in surprise to see his friend walking up behind him as he came out of the church.

"George! Ya nearly made me jump a mile high," Jacob exclaimed as he caught his breath and then let out a relieved chuckle. "I thought you were back in the hotel with the women. What are you doing in church on a Tuesday?"

"Why, a Tuesday is as good a time as any to catch up with the preacher. Besides, I thought I'd give the women a little while to themselves. What about you? What are you doing back here behind the church? You looking for outlaws? Cause I'm pretty sure they're all put away now."

"Naw, I think I can hang up my pistol and holster for a bit," Jacob said as he lifted the flowers. "I was just picking some sunflowers for Louise. Do you think it's too much?"

"Too much?" George scoffed as he nudged his elbow into Jacob's side with a chuckle. "I think it's just about right for a happily married man, and I think it would make your Pop proud, too."

"You think so?" Jacob asked as he allowed his gaze to drift up to the horizon.

"Oh, I know so," George replied as Jacob felt his friend's hand clap down on his shoulder. "This is exactly what he wanted for you: a family to share your life with. You fulfilled your promise to your Pop, Jacob. He'd be right proud of you, and for what it's worth, I am, too."

"That means a lot," Jacob said honestly as he considered what his friend had said.

They were silent as they walked back to the hotel, Jacob considering the enormity of his friend's words.

Pop would be proud.

Although his father wasn't there to confirm it, Jacob knew deep in his heart that it was true.

***

"Jacob, I can't sleep. Are you awake?" Jacob felt his wife's hand on his shoulder as she woke him up.

"Well, I am now," he answered with a sleepy laugh as he rolled over to face her. "What's the matter?"

"Jacob," Louise began, and he could tell from the sound in her voice that she felt unsettled. "I need to talk to you about something."

He felt his stomach drop as Louise spoke the same thing another woman had said right before she broke his heart. Was this it? Had his wife finally had enough of him?

Don't be ridiculous, he told himself. *Louise isn't Jessie—not by a long shot.*

He shook off the old insecurities and sat up to see what his wife needed. She was probably fine, but he wasn't going to assume it. If there was one thing that he'd learned in a year of marriage, it was to not assume anything.

Assuming had ended up with him outside in the cold while an embarrassed Louise dressed furiously behind closed doors. Assuming had ended up with him sleeping on the floor for the better part of a year, when it turned out that his wife would've preferred him in the bed. He was all done with assuming.

"What's wrong, love?" he asked with genuine curiosity.

He could tell that she liked it when he called her that. He enjoyed seeing the way her nose wrinkled up and her lips puckered into a smile when he said it, just as she was doing right then.

"There it is again," she said with the puckered grin that he had grown so attached to. "You keep calling me love, but, well..."

"Don't you like it?" Jacob asked, confused once more.

"Oh, I do!" Louise replied as she fidgeted with her hands and twisted her nightgown. "It's just that, well, do you?"

"Do I what?" he asked, perplexed as the first day he met her.

"Do you... Do you *love* me?" Louise asked with her eyebrows raised high and her shoulders clinched around her ears. "It's just that you call me your love all the time, but you've never said it, not once. It's the sort of thing a girl likes to hear… if a fella means it, that is. And I got to thinking, well … do you mean it?"

"And that's why you can't sleep?" Jacob fumbled groggily as he put two and two together.

"Forget I said anything," Louise said shortly as she stood up and walked to the window.

Jacob was grateful that her wound had all but healed as he watched her gaze out of the hotel window. But his heart broke at her pain.

"Oh, Louise," he said sorrowfully.

How could she not know how much he loved her? Couldn't she tell by the way he ran into the burning building for her cat? Couldn't she tell by his kiss? Couldn't she tell by the way he held her in his arms?

He had so much to say, but he wasn't sure just exactly how to say it. He dreaded putting words together when her heart was on the line, but for her sake, he needed to figure it out… and quick.

"Seriously, Jacob. You're a good husband," she hurried on. "I'm just being silly, I suppose. I've got a good man and a beautiful baby. What more could I want?"

Jacob could tell by the tone of her voice that she was thoroughly humiliated. It was all his fault, and it was his job to make it right.

He bolstered himself as he walked toward the window, determined to fix what only his words could. He laid a gentle hand on the small of Louise's back and swallowed a lump in his throat as he felt her body tense and then relax with his touch.

She turned toward him with eyes wider than the western sky. He could feel her heart beating. He longed to respond with a kiss but knew she needed something else first.

"Louise," he said softly as he caressed his wife's cheek. "I have loved you from the moment I saw you sitting by the fire with Fred. I just didn't know quite what to call it then, and I didn't have the guts to tell you, because I couldn't risk losing you. When I almost lost you for good, I realized how foolish that was. I may not be good with words but believe me when I say that I love you—more than my simple words can explain. I will spend the rest of my life making sure you believe that. I just hope that one day, I'll be worthy of you."

He watched as her face warmed from his words, a smile crawling up her cheeks. Then, it fell away, her chin lifting sharply toward him. "Wait, how could you say that?"

"What do you mean?" Jacob asked, wondering what he had said wrong.

"You aren't *worthy* of me?" Louise declared as she placed both hands on his chest. "You took in a child that wasn't your own, along with a woman who had nowhere else to go. You're the first man I've ever met who treated me like I was more than a burden... or a *prize*. You've sacrificed yourself for me every step of the way. You slept on the floor for almost a year, for cryin' out loud, and I'm honestly starting to lose track of how many times you've risked your life for me. Jacob, you're so much more than worthy! You're the best man I've ever met."

Jacob's heart swam with pride tempered in humility as he gazed into his wife's eyes.

"How did I get so lucky?" he asked tenderly as he brushed a stray piece of hair out of Louise's face.

"I don't know," she said as she bit her bottom lip and looked up at him longingly. "Why don't you kiss me and find out?"

And he did.

***

Jacob could hear a dove cooing in the distance and the wind sweeping past his ears as they traveled up the mountain. He regretted agreeing to wear a blindfold for the surprise and considered taking a peek to see exactly where George was taking them. He lifted his hand to the bandana, as his curiosity finally got the best of him.

"No peeking you two!" He smiled at the determination in Martha's voice and laughed quietly, knowing he was caught.

"You didn't have to do this for us," Louise spoke warmly. "It's not like we're the only ones who lost something to the fire and Roy's gang."

"That may be true," George said from the front of the wagon. "But your husband is the one that brought down Roy once and for all. That's not the type of thing a town forgets. Now all you two gotta do is keep your blindfold on, like my wife said. Besides, we're almost there."

As the wagon rattled to a stop, Jacob caressed the inside of Louise's palm with his thumb and squeezed it gently. He knew she was excited, as this was a big day for them both.

They had been in the hotel for over a month now, and while Jacob was grateful for the time alone with his wife and for her healing, he was ready to get back to the land. He'd expected that when his wife was healed, they'd move into the equipment barn temporarily while he worked on building a new cabin, but his friends had other plans.

The day before, George, the preacher, and Jethro, had all stopped by the hotel and told Jacob that they had a surprise waiting on his land. George had demanded that they wear blindfolds on their way there. Jacob's mind had raced with anticipation for the past day, and he admitted to himself that he felt like a child about to open presents on Christmas morning.

"We're here!" George said with a satisfied chuckle. "Told you it wouldn't be long."

Jacob stood up with his blindfold on before realizing it was a mistake, as he got dizzy and swayed before falling quickly backward onto his seat. He could hear laughter and cheers from the townsfolk along with roaring applause.

"What are you waiting for?" George asked. "Take off your blindfolds!"

When Jacob removed the blindfold, he was shocked to see dozens of people hurrying around with planks of wood and ropes to lift them with. Teams of townsfolk worked together as they heaved and shoved the beams into place.

On the far side of the hill, a couple dozen women laid out blankets with picnic baskets and a feast of food.

"Oh my!" Louise gasped as she squeezed Jacob's hand in delight. "This is too much!"

"Nonsense!" a familiar voice called out behind them. "It's high time that you have a new barn, especially now that we're partners starting a venture together. The town is grateful for what you've done, Jacob, and they were more than happy to join in the barn raising."

Jacob turned with his wife on his arm to see their friends Alice and Jethro waiting by the wagon.

"Alice!" Louise exclaimed as she jumped down and threw her arms around her friend's neck.

"Mind if I steal your wife away for a little bit?" Alice asked Jacob with a warm smile.

"Not at all," Jacob said as he tipped his hat at the couple and stepped down out from the wagon.

"Oh Martha," Louise said as she looked back. "Would you mind handing me Fred, now that I don't have my blindfold on and all?"

"That won't be necessary," Martha replied. "I'll take care of the little one. You go enjoy yourself."

As the two women walked away arm in arm, Jacob turned and looked all around to see where they had landed.

He turned around, admiring the hill they stood upon. He could see most of his land from that spot. Off in the distance, sat the acres that had been burned by fire, and ashes of old building still lay in piles there. His heart felt a twinge of pain as he remembered that horrible day. But as he looked at this fresh patch of land on which he now stood, his heart was filled instead with hope.

He saw some lovely cactus flowers at the ridge of the hill and suddenly realized exactly where they were. His heart leapt in astonishment as he realized that the new barn was right next to his parents' gravestones.

He swallowed a lump in his throat as George laid a hand on his shoulder.

"George," Jacob said as he swallowed the lump. "You didn't have to do this."

"O' course I did," George said with a smile in his voice. "If we're going to go into business as partners, it only makes sense that the man who taught us how to be ranchers be a part of it, too."

"I suppose you're right," Jacob said as he cleared his throat and put a hand on his friend's shoulder. "But I don't know how I'm going to repay you."

"I do," George said without missing a beat. "Let's make the biggest dairy ranch on this side of the mountains. I reckon that'll pay for itself."

"I reckon you're right," Jacob replied as the two men shook hands with a laugh.

"Jacob! Come quick." He turned when he heard his wife's voice and saw her running toward him as fast as she could.

Without any other thought in his mind, he ran to Louise as fast as he could to make sure she was all right.

"What's wrong, love?" he asked when he reached her at last.

He looked from her toes to her head to see if she'd been injured, but she looked like she was in one piece. When his eyes reached her face, he could see that she was all smiles and he let out a sigh of relief.

"Come with me," his wife said with a sweet smile as she grabbed his hands, and he followed her downhill toward the sound of a trickling brook.

They ran until they reached the top of the hill. Jacob looked down over the ridge into a small valley. While mostly dry, like the rest of Nevada, there were patches of grass and a tiny trickling brook that wound its way down the hill.

"Look over there," Louise said.

Jacob strained, looking toward the bottom of the hill. There, next to the brook, a dozen or so men were working at a large house.

"Is that...?" Jacob's voice trailed off in disbelief. He knew that George and the preacher had mentioned a few ranch hands cobbling together a new cabin in the future, but this was something altogether different.

"It's our new house!" Louise declared as she flung her arms around Jacob's neck and kissed him on the cheek. "Can you believe it?"

"George," Jacob said as he turned to the friend standing behind him. "We can't accept this. It's too much."

"You're repeating yourself too much today, partner," George said with a grin. "Besides, if we're gonna have the best dairy ranch in Nevada, you've gotta have a proper ranch house."

Jacob was at a loss for words. He looked at the community that had come out to support him, the friends that surrounded him, and the toddler who had walked up to hang on his leg. Finally, he glanced at the woman in his arms.

It was too much blessing for one man to bear, and he couldn't believe that it was all his.

Thank you, Lord, he prayed. *Thank you for doing what only you can do.*

Just then, an orange ball of fur tore past them and ran down the hill.

"Mi-mi!" Fred yelled as he took off after his cat.

"Well," Jacob said as he took the hand of his smiling wife. "I think the young'ins wanna go see the new house. We'd best not keep them waiting."

"I suppose you're right," Louise answered with a smile that could light up the night.

As they took off down the hill, all of Jacob's cares flew away, save for the thought of the beautiful blonde running down the hill before him.

Epilogue

August 1st, 1889

Dear Diary,

It's incredible to think how much can change in a year, much less two. Mississippi feels like another lifetime, and indeed it was.

It's strange to remember the fearful child I was at the Cankers', compared to the happy woman I am today. I was so used to being mistreated that anxiety was my close companion. I don't know how I had the courage to run away, but by the grace of God, I escaped.

The first few months in Nevada came as a shock for sure and brought with it a lot of growing up that Heaven knows I needed.

I expected Jacob to be my knight in shining armor, and he did become that in a way, but not how I anticipated. I was sure that he would be a perfect prince, full of charm and all the right words. When I first met him, I couldn't get past my own expectations to see the good man that he was.

Now, I can say in truth that I love him with all my heart. While he's plenty handsome with or without his beard, it's his strength of character that I've come to love the most. His strength is tempered with gentleness, bravery, and humility, and he's altogether mine.

Louise set her pen in the inkwell that Jacob had bought her. She considered writing more, though she was distracted by Fred and Minnie.

"Frederick Montgomery!" Louise said as she turned to see Fred holding Minnie upside down. "What did I tell you about playing too rough with Minnie?"

"Her *wants* to play with me!" he answered with determined eyes.

"I know, Fred," she said as she ruffled his hair, "but cats aren't as strong as big boys. You've got to be gentler."

"Okay, Mama!" Fred answered with a toothy grin. "I play more gentle."

Smiling, Louise went into the kitchen to make supper but stopped to sit in the rocking chair next to the window. She let out a deep sigh as the heavy oak chair started to sway.

Why was she so tired lately?

Whatever the reason, Louise embraced the moment to rest and admire her new kitchen. She looked at her countertops made of fresh pine, the beautiful cast-iron stove, and her new Dutch oven. While she was grateful for her big kitchen, she wasn't sure she'd ever have enough mouths to feed to make its size worthwhile.

Food, she thought to herself.

It was time to get cooking. She grabbed her favorite cast-iron skillet and checked on the stew that had begun to bubble before she began to grill some chopped onions. Suddenly, an unwelcome burp rose up her throat and she covered her mouth as she ran outside.

Not again.

Out in the garden, she took in a deep breath and smelled fresh peppermint floating on the breeze. She bent down and buried her nose in the peppermint plant until her stomach calmed down.

"Louise?" Alice's voice called from behind her. "What's wrong?"

"Oh! Hello, Alice," she replied as she rose to her feet. "I'm fine. I've just been gettin' a bit nauseous lately when I cook. Is Jethro with you?"

"Jethro is still workin' on the new fence," Alice said with a warm smile. "Why don't we go sit a spell? You'll feel better after you rest."

Louise was grateful for the opportunity to lean on her friend's arm. But as they walked to the house, she saw Alice sneak a smile to herself as if she had a secret.

"Alice, what are you smiling about?"

"It sounds like you might be with child," her friend said with a wide smile.

"A baby?" Louise asked incredulously, pointing to her flat stomach. "Are you sure?"

"You wouldn't be showing yet," Alice answered with a chuckle. "But you've got all the early signs. You're nauseous, you're tired, and I hope you don't mind me saying so, but you're a bit moody to boot. When was the last time you had your monthly?"

Louise blushed at the thought. She didn't feel comfortable talking about such intimate things, but she knew that it needed to come once a month. That's when it hit her like a big bale of hay.

"Oh no!" Louise said urgently. "I think it's been at least *a couple* months! How could I not have realized?"

"Louise," Alice comforted. "You just moved into a new home, and you've got a toddler to chase after. You've got more than a little on your plate!"

As if on cue, Minnie raced out the door with Fred on her heels. Minnie leapt onto the white picket fence at the edge of the garden, but Fred wasn't able to stop. He barreled face-first into the fence and fell down in tears.

"Oh, Fred!" Louise consoled as she ran to her son. "That fence snuck up on ya, didn't it?"

She lifted him into her arms and noticed a large red bump on his forehead. She knew it would swell if she didn't ice it soon.

"Mama's gonna get somethin' for that bump on your head. Oh, Alice, would you mind?"

"Not at all," her friend offered with a reassuring smile.

As Louise hurried to the icebox, she couldn't help but wonder if Alice was right. She put both hands to her stomach and pondered the new life inside her. Her heart warmed instantly at the thought and joy flooded through her.

But how would Jacob react? Despite their house that the townsfolk had built, money was tight. It could take years for the new dairy ranch to become profitable. Although she knew he loved her, she couldn't help but wonder what he'd think about another mouth to feed.

Louise grabbed frozen venison from the icebox and turned to see Alice carry Fred through the front door.

"Come here, my love," Louise said, lifting Fred to her hip.

As she put the frozen venison on his forehead, Louise couldn't help but notice how much Fred had grown. But was he ready for a little brother? Louise sighed, wondering how Fred would handle it.

"It'll all be worth it," Alice said, as if reading her thoughts.

"How do you know?" Louise asked sincerely.

"When I had my first child, I was fearful for his safety. It stole the joy out of everything."

"What changed?" Louise asked.

"I almost lost him," Alice said with eyebrows furrowed over teary eyes. "He got a fever that he couldn't shake, and it was out of my hands. I knew only God could save him. All my worryin' didn't help a thing. I determined that, if he made it, I'd surrender whatever was out of my hands and just appreciate the blessings the Lord had given me."

"How'd you do that?" Louise asked as she gazed seriously into her friend's eyes.

"Well," Alice explained as she lifted her palms toward the ceiling. "Each time I request something of the Lord, I give it to him like this and I say, 'Lord, you know what I need, so I give it to you and ask that Your will be done.'"

Louise glanced out the window at the sunset as she pondered the importance of her friend's words.

Before she could reply, Jacob burst into the room with a hungry smile on his face.

"Supper ready yet?" he asked as he pulled Louise into his arms.

"Just about," she answered and gazed into his deep, brown eyes.

She could see how much he loved her every time he looked at her. It warmed her heart and made her feel silly for ever doubting him. He'd be a wonderful father to the baby, just as he was to Fred.

"I hope you don't mind a few more because I brought some great company," Jethro said as he entered the kitchen with George and his whole family in tow.

"We always have enough for our friends," Louise answered happily. "Now, let's sit down for supper."

**

Louise was happy to see her table filled with her most treasured family and friends. She sat next to Jacob, who was at the head of the table, and Louise couldn't help but think he looked every part the leader of the group. Fred bounced contentedly in her lap as Minnie lay curled up at her feet.

To her left sat Alice and Jethro. Across the table sat her best friend with her parents on either side. At the far end of the table sat Sarah's younger siblings, all chatting excitedly amongst themselves. There was nowhere else in the world she would rather be; there was nothing that could ruin this moment.

"I have an announcement," George declared as he stood with his glass raised. "It's with great joy that our Sarah will be gettin' married next spring."

"Married?" Louise asked in shock. "I didn't even know that you were courting!"

"The preacher's family came over for dinner last month and his son Adam is, well, just too wonderful," Sarah explained with an excited smile as she fiddled with her napkin. "He's called on me every day since, and last night, he asked me to marry him. O' course he had to ask Papa's approval first but…"

"Congratulations!" Louise said as she jumped up from the table and embraced her best friend.

"I'm sorry that I didn't get the chance to tell you," Sarah apologized. "It just all happened so quickly!"

"It's all right," Louise encouraged. "You deserve every bit of happiness that comes your way, whether you tell me or not."

"Why do they have to wait six months?" Jethro interrupted. "That's an awful long engagement."

"He wanted to marry her right away," George admitted with a chuckle. "But he's attending seminary in California, and I told him he had to graduate and have a job before they could wed. He'll graduate this spring and he's got a local church that's agreed to take him on. That's when he'll come to marry Sarah, and they'll move into his parsonage in California."

California? Louise was in shock.

"It'll be so hard for me to leave all of you," Sarah admitted. "But I can't wait to start a family of my own with Adam!"

"Take your time havin' babies," Jacob cautioned. "You're young yet. Enjoy being married before you have children keepin' ya busy."

"The more the merrier, I say," Louise added defensively.

"Sure," Jacob agreed. "As long as you can feed and clothe 'em all. Just give it some time."

Louise's heart sank. Why would Jacob say that? He wouldn't be upset when she told him about *their* baby... Would he?

***

The stars in the sky shone dimmer than usual when Louise followed her friends outside to say goodbye. A cool breeze blew through her hair, sending a chill down her spine.

"Don't waste your time with worries," Alice whispered in her ear as they hugged goodbye. "All will be well. Just give it to the Lord."

Louise smiled weakly and waved as Alice and Sarah climbed into their wagons and rode off to their respective homes. She waved until both wagons disappeared over the hills.

"Why don't we put Fred to bed," Jacob said warmly, "so that we can have some time alone?"

"O' course," Louise said as she pulled away from Jacob's arms. "Best get Fred to sleep first."

She picked up the toddler clinging to her skirts and walked into the house without another word.

**

Louise stared out the window as she held her sleeping son on her shoulder.

Please God, let all be well, just like Alice said. And please help me to give my worries to You, somehow.

She laid her son in his bed when she heard the creak of the nursery door open behind her, Jacob's footsteps approaching. She felt his strong arms surround her and naturally leaned back into him. Her body warmed at his touch but then she tensed, remembering the conversation they still needed to have. She turned to him anxiously.

"I best go clean up from supper," she said as she walked out of the nursery.

"Louise, what's wrong?" she heard him ask as she hurried to the kitchen.

"Nothin," she insisted as she turned to face him. "I've just got such a mess to clean up and you've had a long day. Why don't you get some shut eye and I'll join you in a bit."

She could tell by Jacob's furrowed brow that he was crestfallen. She longed to tell him everything, but she didn't know what to say, and she couldn't bear it if he was disappointed about the baby. She couldn't stand to see the pain in his eyes, so she turned away from his gaze and continued to the table.

"Please tell me what's wrong." Jacob's voice was warm in her ear. She felt his hand rest on her hip as she picked up the bowls from supper.

"I know you, love," he continued. "And I can tell you're upset now. If I've done something wrong, just tell me what it is and I..."

"Why don't you want a baby?" she asked as she turned to him, unable to keep it from him any longer.

"Who said I don't want a baby?" he answered with confusion in his eyes.

"*You* did!"

"When?"

"At *dinner!*"

"Did we sit at the same table? What are you talkin' about?"

"You told Sarah to wait before having babies!"

As she ran out of air and paused to take a breath, she couldn't help but notice that Jacob had started to grin. She followed his gaze down to her belly and realized too late that she'd been holding her stomach, giving the news away.

"Louise," Jacob said tenderly as he reached out a hand to hold hers. "Are you with child?"

"I am, but I'm not sure I can bear you bein' unhappy about it."

"Unhappy?" Jacob asked as a look of bewilderment filled his face. "You carryin' my babe is the best news I've had since you let me kiss ya."

"But," Louise stammered. "You *discouraged* Sarah! You went on and on about it being a good idea to wait!"

"For *Sarah* to wait. She's marryin' a penniless man and she's barely more than a child herself." Jacob's smile widened as he took her in his arms.

"It would be good for Sarah to wait, but not for *us,* love. *Never* for us."

Louise felt Jacob's hand touch her belly gently as a warmth filled his eyes, telling her that all would be well. Then, he turned his head to the side and kissed her deeply, ensuring the matter.

March 3rd, 1890

The early morning sun kissed Louise's face as she stepped onto the porch. She smiled as its rays covered her in warmth. She lifted her arms to rest on her now swollen belly, holding all her hopes and dreams.

She felt a kick, which startled her, and made her laugh as she looked down.

"Good morning, little one," Louise said as she rubbed her stomach gently. "Just another few weeks and then I'll get to hold you at last. You're gonna love the springtime."

She heard a noise behind her and turned to see Fred tumble into the garden. To her relief, he jumped up with a big smile.

"And what are you up to, son?" she asked happily.

"I chasing kitty, Mama!"

"O' course you are! I'll help you find her. Minnie! Where are you?"

A moment later, her furry friend came bounding out of the house and jumped onto her shoulder.

"Here she is, Fred! Why'd you think she was in the garden?"

"No!" Fred insisted. "I not chase Minnie. I chase *kitty*. Over there!"

Fred pointed to the sunflower field behind the house and then took off.

"Fred!" she called as she dashed in between large green stalks with Minnie in her arms. "Where are you going?"

"Here I am, Mama!" She heard him say as a tiny hand appeared and waved to her from beneath a sunflower leaf.

When she caught up to him, Louise was surprised to find a fluffy white kitten in his arms.

"See," Fred said, smiling proudly. "I has new kitty."

"Oh, Fred honey," Louise replied softly. "I don't know if that's a good idea. Cats don't always like it when there are other animals in the house."

"But he *for* Minnie," Fred said in a hopeful tone as he held up the kitten to Minnie's face.

Louise watched as Minnie wiggled her nose and sniffed the strange new kitten as it pawed and licked her playfully. Minnie tolerated the kitten until she'd apparently had enough, and then she crawled back onto the safety of Louise's shoulder.

"See, Mama?" Fred said with a huge smile on his face. "Minnie adopt kitty like you adopt me."

Before Louise could utter another word, Fred was off for the house with a skip in his step and a kitten in his clutches.

"I guess there's gonna be another change around here, Minnie," Louise said as she scratched her oldest friend behind the ears. Minnie purred and nuzzled her head under Louise's chin.

"Papa's home!" Fred called out from the porch.

Sure enough, she heard the wagon rumble up to the house.

"Louise," Jacob called to her as he waved a piece of paper above his head, "I've got a letter with me you're gonna wanna see."

***

Dear Louise,

I hope that our letter finds you well. If it does, we admit that it's not because of us.

You must be wondering how we found you. We've been begging the ticket man at the station for months to tell us where you went. Paw finally convinced him. You know how he can be.

I don't know exactly why you ran away but I can imagine we gave you good reason. I was a hard woman to live with, which I see clearly now, albeit much too late.

You should know that we lost Ella to the consumption last winter. Paw has been inconsolable, and I haven't been much better.

It's been unbearable but this terrible loneliness has allowed me to consider how you must have felt growing up. I've had a lot of time to think on my many regrets. They haunt me now like a ghost I can't shake.

One of my biggest regrets is that I treated you as the help instead of a daughter. If I had done so many things differently, I would have one daughter now instead of none at all.

I want you to know how sorry I am for the pain I caused you, and for the pain you must still carry. It's far too late for me to make up for your childhood, but I want to make things right however I can—that is, if you'll let me.

If you would be open to visiting us or to letting us come and visit you, please let me know. Whatever you decide, I'll understand.

With Hope,

Maw

Louise felt as though her heart were caught in her throat as she lowered her head to her hands. It was too much to take in at once.

They had bothered to look for her. Ella was dead. They were sorry and wanted to see her.

She lifted her hand to her mouth. It covered so many thoughts that she didn't know how to speak. She shook her head as tears rolled down her cheeks and wounds she thought long healed began to break open and fester anew.

It was then that she understood what Alice meant by surrendering to God what was already out of her hands. She lifted her palms up in surrender as she gave the Cankers to the Lord and asked for His will as she wept.

March 5th, 1890

"How's the matron of honor this mornin'?"

Louise smiled at the sound of her husband's voice as he opened the door. She enjoyed the view as he leaned against the oak frame.

"Good morning," she said with a sleepy yawn. "Sorry I slept in."

"It's all right," Jacob said as he came to sit next to her on the bed. "There's a babe growin' in your belly. But I'm more concerned with how the mama's feelin."

"I'm fine," she insisted. "Now tell me, how's everything on the ranch this mornin'?"

"Honestly, it's going better than I imagined," he said with a smile that could light up Nevada. "The fence is up, and the new cows are producing. If we keep on at this rate, we'll be able to afford to fill this whole house with babies."

"Well, let's see how this first delivery goes," Louise said with a nervous chuckle.

"You're gonna be just fine," Jacob said in a low, warm voice.

She was comforted by Jacob's presence as her mountain man leaned in and kissed her softly. She could feel the smile that played on his lips, and it made her smile in turn. She ran her fingers through his hair and then rested them on his shoulders as she took a deep sigh.

"Have you thought anymore about seeing the Cankers?" Jacob asked, pulling her out of her thoughts.

"We'll never be close by any means," she said, "but I must forgive them. I just don't know if I can *face* them."

"You can forgive them without meeting them, you know," Jacob said as he squeezed her hand.

"I know," she agreed with a nod. "I just need to think on it."

"Just know I'm on your side whatever you decide," Jacob said as he put his arm around her.

She knew that he meant it as he held her, and she much preferred her husband's arms to worrying about the Cankers. Louise reached up to kiss his pillowy soft lips and lingered there awhile. She sighed as she rested her head on his chest.

"How's the little one?" she asked.

"Which one are you referring to?" he replied with a chuckle. "The toddler or the kitten?"

Louise felt a laugh well up inside that started as a giggle, then turned into a hearty chuckle as Jacob joined her.

At last, she swung her legs over the bed and started to stand up, when she felt a sharp pain in her side. Louise put a hand to her belly, wincing as she sat right back down.

"What is it, love? Is it the baby?"

She'd had a few birth-related pangs lately, but Doctor Johnson had assured her that she was having false labor, which was normal toward the end of pregnancy. He'd said that as long as the pains didn't continue for long periods of time, there was nothing to worry about.

"I'm okay," she said. "It was just a kick, I'm sure."

But the truth was that she wasn't sure at all. Nevertheless, it was Sarah's big day, and she had a wedding to get ready for.

***

The wagon rumbled beneath Louise as she held onto Jacob's arm, and they rolled down the mountain toward town. With her other arm, she held tightly to Fred, who bounced alongside her.

The clear blue sky opened before her with nothing but a few cotton-like clouds dotting the horizon. It was the perfect day for a wedding.

Louise rested her head on Jacob's shoulder, grateful that although she would miss Sarah, she was left with a husband and a son whom she loved. She couldn't help but be reminded of Maw and Paw Canker, alone in an empty house—surrounded by ghosts of a dead girl and the would-be daughter that'd fled from them.

Every thought of them reminded her of the night she'd almost lost Jacob and Fred. She didn't know where she'd be without her family, and it gave her a newfound empathy for the Cankers' pain.

"I'm gonna write to the Cankers tonight," she told Jacob.

She felt his body stiffen, and his chest puffed up protectively.

"You don't have to do it, Louise," he said with concern laced through his voice. "They don't get to guilt you into it."

"It's not guilt," she said sincerely. "I've learned that life is far too short and beautiful to let old wounds fester and spoil it. So, if forgiving them face-to-face offers them comfort and closes an old wound, I gotta try."

"That's good enough for me," Jacob sighed as he kissed her hand and then lifted the reins to urge the horses onward.

She heard the church bells ring as they rode into town. The townsfolk crowded the street and sounds of jubilation filled the air.

"Louise!" she heard Sarah call to her.

Standing in front of the church and waving like a child at the state fair stood her best friend. Louise nearly leapt over Jacob as she climbed down from the wagon and ran toward Sarah.

The bride wore a simple white dress that her mother had made. It had a touch of lace around the neckline and slight puffs at the top of her sleeves. It was full of joy and hope—just like the girl who wore it.

"I'm so glad you're here!" Sarah exclaimed. "I was starting to think you might not show."

"I'd never miss your wedding," Louise declared as she squeezed Sarah's hands.

"So, you're not mad at me for going to California?" Sarah asked as her eyes widened and she bit her lip.

"I'm gonna miss you like crazy," Louise said earnestly. "But I can't be mad at your happiness. Besides, who am I to stand in the way of your great adventure when I've had such a grand adventure of my own?"

The two women embraced once more as they turned toward the church and the crowd that waited for the bride.

***

The grand wooden arches of the church loomed over Louise as she gazed up at them and stood behind the bride at the altar. She looked around the room, full of townspeople eager to see the preacher's son marry the rancher's daughter.

Louise's eyes found Jacob's, and she remembered their own wedding not so long ago. She could tell by the love in his eyes that he held the same memory. She appreciated the beauty of the moment until pain hit her like a punch in the gut.

No, not yet... It's too early for the baby to come.

She felt her left leg buckle under her as another jolting ache of pain hit. Louise felt sweat emanate from her brow. She wouldn't allow herself to look in Jacob's direction. She knew if she did, he'd be by her side in a moment, and she was determined not to ruin the wedding.

At last, the preacher said, "man and wife." The crowd cheered as the new couple turned to face them.

Louise walked to the first pew wearily. She leaned on it with one hand and took a deep breath, trying to steady herself. She looked up to see Jacob and Fred walking toward her, so she plastered on a smile and took another deep breath.

Then another contraction hit her, much harder this time, and she started to fall.

"Jacob!" she cried out in desperation as she collapsed.

She felt strong arms catch her suddenly. She looked up to see that her husband was there, looking down at her with worried eyes.

"It's the baby," she said in between short breaths. "But it's too soon, Jacob!"

"Has anyone seen the doctor?" Jacob hollered to the wedding guests.

The crowd split in two and Doctor Johnson hurried up to them.

"I think I'm gettin' those false labor pangs you told me about, Doc," Louise said.

The doctor put a hand on either side of her belly and examined it carefully, just as another contraction hit and Louise writhed in pain.

"Like it or not, this baby's on its way," he said. "We need to get you to a bed, and quick. The hotel will have to do. Hurry!"

***

The labor wasn't easy, but it wasn't as hard as Louise had imagined. Although she'd been scared, all was well. She'd pushed barely half an hour when the baby was born.

"Where's my baby?" Louise called out through tears of joy, eager to hold her new child.

"It's a girl," Jacob said as he laid their daughter on Louise's chest. "And she has her mama's eyes."

Louise exhaled a grateful sigh of relief as she stared at her newborn daughter. Tiny blue eyes squinted, intermittently opening and closing as they got used to the brightness of their new world.

"What do you think we should call her?" Jacob asked as he came to sit by Louise, and they gazed at their daughter together.

"What about Selah?" Louise asked. "It's from the book of Psalms. In between different passages, sometimes it just says the word 'Selah.' It means to pause and consider. I want her to be someone who pauses and considers the Word of God and the beauty of life that He's given her. Do you think that's silly?"

"I think it's perfect," Jacob said as he kissed her cheek softly, and she felt his arms surround her.

The evening sun filtered through the window and released fragmented rays that shone around the room. Louise could smell the scent of fresh pine and leather as she leaned against her husband's chest on the hotel bed—their only option as the baby had come so quick.

To her right sat her precious Fred, the unexpected son that they'd fought so hard to keep. He was worth it all. Fred leaned against her arm as he cuddled her.

A knock at the door shook her from her reverie and she looked up to see Martha poke her head in the room.

"Everyone's here," she said. "Is it all right if I send 'em in?"

"That'd be lovely," Louise answered, and her heart filled with joy as her friends entered the room.

First came in George, with his four small children in tow.

Next, Alice and Jethro came arm in arm.

"How are you feeling?" Alice asked, leaning in for a hug.

"All is well," Louise said with a smile. "Just like a wise friend of mine said it would be."

Much to her surprise, the door opened again as Sarah walked in, her new husband at her side.

"Sarah," Louise mumbled as her heart filled with joy. "What are you doing here? Shouldn't you be off with your husband?"

"I could hardly leave town without seeing my niece, now could I?" Sarah said as she hugged Louise. "I wouldn't miss this for the world."

"I'm so glad you're here," Louise said sincerely. "I'm so glad you're *all* here. I don't know where I'd be without everyone in this room."

As the group of friends talked happily, Louise's heart filled with gratitude as she paused and considered all the blessings that surrounded her. The beauty of it all hit her like a hug from Heaven and she savored the moment completely.

She sent up a prayer of thanks as Jacob leaned down to kiss her on her cheek. She turned to look up into his warm brown eyes that made her stomach dance with butterflies.

"How did I get so lucky?" she whispered to him.

"Don't you know yet, love?" Jacob said as he whispered in her ear. "One thing I've learned from your faithfulness is that luck has nothing to do with it. We are blessed, my love. So very blessed."

As she gazed into the face of the man she loved, the one she'd been through so much with, she knew that the best was still in front of them.

THE END

Also by Nora J. Callaway

Thank you for reading "**A Mountain Man for the Sweet Bride**"!

I hope you enjoyed it! If you did, here are some of my other books!

Also, if you liked this book, you can also check out **my full Amazon Book Catalogue at:**
https://go.norajcallaway.com/bc-authorpage

Thank you for allowing me to keep doing what I love! ❤

Printed in Great Britain
by Amazon